Dear Reader,

Lots of sisters grow apart as they grow up but we believe you can always find a way back to one another, which is just what you'll find in this story. There is something so special about the bond between sisters, especially twin sisters, and we have been lucky enough to share this ourselves!

Nancy and Nina may share the same looks but their personalities are completely different, and this only makes them stronger.

We are so proud of this story. To us, the characters have always been real but with the amazing Katy Birchall we have been able to bring these sisters to life!

We can't wait for you to enter the exciting world of Nancy and Nina, and we know that as you read, you too will be able to see yourselves in one of these girls!

Happy Reading!

Love,

Lucyandlydia ♥

LUCY AND LYDIA CONNELL

Written with Katy Birchall

PENGUIN BOOKS

PENGUIN BOOKS

UK | USA | Canada | Ireland | Australia
India | New Zealand | South Africa

Penguin Books is part of the Penguin Random House group of companies
whose addresses can be found at global.penguinrandomhouse.com.

www.penguin.co.uk
www.puffin.co.uk
www.ladybird.co.uk

First published 2018

001

Text copyright © Lucy and Lydia Connell, 2018

The moral right of the authors has been asserted

Set in 12.2/18 pt Sabon LT Std
Typeset by Jouve (UK), Milton Keynes
Printed in Great Britain by Clays Ltd, St Ives plc

A CIP catalogue record for this book is available from the British Library

HARDBACK
ISBN: 978–0–241–34023–3

INTERNATIONAL PAPERBACK
ISBN: 978–0–241–34027–1

All correspondence to:
Penguin Books
Penguin Random House Children's
80 Strand, London WC2R ORL

CHAPTER ONE

NANCY

For as long as I can remember I have been in love with Chase Hunter.

I love everything about him. The way his thick, dark-brown messy hair sticks up when he runs his fingers through it (which he does whenever he's nervous) and how he gets the cutest dimples whenever he smiles, showing off his pearly white teeth. He has the most beautifully sculpted cheekbones and chiselled jaw, but my favourite thing is his vintage indie style of dressing; he looks hot in whatever he's wearing, but I love him best in his simple, favourite combo of black skinny jeans, a white T-shirt and leather jacket, and that fedora hat he hardly ever goes without. And who could miss those piercing bright blue eyes framed by long dark eyelashes, which make your knees turn to jelly and cause your brain to go blank and forget all the words in the English language as you look into them.

Chase is also the most talented human being on the planet. He plays a whole host of instruments, but he's the best at piano. He's been playing since he was four years old, when his dad first plonked him on a piano stool. And Chase has a seriously beautiful singing voice that makes a shiver go down my spine and the breath catch in my throat.

Chase and I are made for one another. We like all the same things, including, but not limited to, the following:

1. Music (mostly pop, but we also both occasionally dip into soundtracks from the West End)
2. Fashion (we can both pull off hats, and that is something you just can't teach)
3. Dogs AND cats (but neither of us are fans of pigeons – they are pure evil)
4. Art (for me, that includes nails and make-up; for Chase, it's songwriting and, also, photography is one of his favourite hobbies)
5. Yoga (we are both totally spiritual)

Basically, we're soulmates.

'Nancy? Hello, Earth to Nancy!'

I snap my head up as my friend Layla's voice cuts through my daydreaming.

'Sorry!' I smile as she rolls her eyes, sitting down next to me and pulling her phone out of her bag. 'I was in my own world.'

I'd just been remembering Chase's birthday last year, when he went to his party wearing an open red-and-black check flannel shirt over a vest. I had inhaled so sharply when I saw him in such a great layer combination that I had accidentally swallowed my gum, making me cough and splutter all over the place.

Which is proof of how good-looking Chase Hunter really is.

He, literally, almost made me die.

'Whatever.' Layla sighs impatiently, busy texting. 'So, what's this big news you wanted to tell me?'

'You have got to see this app I downloaded.' I grin, sliding my phone across the table towards her.

Her eyes flicker towards it reluctantly.

'What is it?' she says in a bored voice. 'And who opened the window? Seriously, it's freezing in here.'

I shrug and reach up to close the classroom window, deciding not to mention that it was actually me who had opened it earlier, just before she came in. I had been spritzing my new perfume and gone a bit overboard, spraying so much that I sneezed about a hundred times and could still taste it in my mouth.

I can confirm that perfume does not taste as nice as it smells.

'Morning!' our friend Sophie says brightly, sauntering across the classroom and sitting at the table in front of us.

We don't have seats officially assigned to us in morning registration, but Layla made sure at the beginning of the year that everyone knew these three places were ours, because, being right at the back and next to the window, they are the best seats in the room.

A few weeks ago, Timothy Davies tragically forgot about this unwritten rule and we came in one morning to find him sitting at mine and Layla's desk, doodling cartoons in his notebook. Layla was furious and I had to step in quickly before she went full-on Disney villain at him. I know what she can be like. Don't even get me started on the time I took a sneaky bite out of her red velvet cupcake.

I will never commit such a crime EVER again. The punishment was so not worth the bite.

'Hey, Sophie.' I grin as she sits down, swivelling to lean on the back of her chair and face us. 'I have to tell you about this app. Basically –'

'Did you get my message?' Layla asks her, cutting across me.

'Yeah.' Sophie nods, rummaging about in her bag before passing Layla a lip gloss. 'Sorry, I completely forgot I'd borrowed it. I'm glad you reminded me. My brain has been all over the place this morning, stressing about the English test today.' She lets out a long sigh. 'Who knew Jane Austen could be so complicated!'

'*Jane Eyre*,' I correct.

'Oh.' Sophie stares at me blankly. 'Are those two different things?'

I smile. Sophie always has her head in the clouds; sometimes I think she's on a completely different planet.

She lives next door to Layla, so they've been best friends for years and I often wonder whether Sophie is ever annoyed that Layla chooses to sit next to me at school now, rather than her. However, whereas I'd be upset if my best friend since forever did that to me, I genuinely don't think it crosses Sophie's mind.

'Jane Austen was an author, and Jane Eyre is the main character of Charlotte Brontë's book. Totally unrelated except for the first name.'

'Wait, what?' Her dark eyes widen with panic.

Sophie always goes on about how lucky I am to have blue eyes and poker-straight blonde hair, but I think the exact opposite. I would do anything to have her intense dark-brown eyes and beautiful brunette curls. I get really mad at her when she straightens her hair. She has no idea how long it takes me – and how many times I burn myself with curling tongs – to achieve anything near the kind of volume her hair has. Layla has lovely natural waves too, and whenever she stays over at mine she complains about how much hair spray I use in the morning, accusing me of poisoning her lungs.

The straight-hair struggle is real.

'I was just telling my parents this morning that I've been studying Jane Austen,' Sophie continues. 'No wonder Mum looked confused at breakfast when I mentioned all the moors.'

'The moors?'

'Yeah,' she says. 'You know, all the moors in the book. I read that this morning online. It's an important theme,' she adds proudly.

'Ah,' I begin carefully, 'I think you're getting confused with *Wuthering Heights*. That's a different book, by Emily Brontë.'

Sophie stares at me blankly. 'I'm lost.'

'Charlotte Brontë is the author who wrote *Jane Eyre*, the book we're studying,' I explain slowly. 'Emily Brontë was her sister, who wrote another classic book, *Wuthering Heights*, which we're *not* studying. That book has the important moors theme in it. And neither of those books are anything to do with Jane Austen.'

Sophie slumps her shoulders forward. 'I'm never going to pass my English GCSE. I can't even get the book right!'

'Don't be silly – you'll be fine,' I say, trying to be as convincing as possible. 'It's only September, so this test doesn't mean anything. You've got the entire year to read the right book before the actual exam.'

'I suppose.' She sighs. 'What am I going to do about the *Jane Eyre* test?'

'I can give you an overview of all the important points, if you like,' I suggest.

'You seem to know a lot about *Jane Eyre* and classic literature all of a sudden,' Layla notes, watching me. 'I didn't know boring old books were your thing.'

'They're not,' I insist hurriedly. 'It's because of the

test. And I just ... I know a lot about them because of Nina. She often talks about books at dinner.'

Layla rolls her eyes. 'That figures.'

Technically, that wasn't a lie. Nina does sometimes talk about books at dinner. But what I don't mention is that I've also read all those books myself. Twice. I just can't admit that to Layla and Sophie.

They would think I'm as big a loser as my sister.

'Did you see Chase is working in Manchester today?' I say to Sophie, keen to change the subject. 'He was meant to be taking time off this week, but he is so dedicated.'

I swirl the tip of my finger gently over my current phone background: a black-and-white picture of him laughing, with his dimples very pronounced and all these cute crinkles round his eyes.

I sigh dreamily. 'He's just perfect.'

'He really is,' Sophie says enthusiastically, as Layla nods in agreement. 'If only we knew him! Can you imagine meeting Chase? Like, face-to-face?'

She squeals loudly at the thought of it, causing Mrs Smithson, our form teacher, who has just sauntered into the room, to jump and splash her coffee all over the floor. 'I think I would pass out on the spot!'

Which brings me to the teeny, tiny snag in my otherwise perfect relationship with Chase Hunter ...

I've never actually met him.

And the reason I've never met him is because he just so

happens to be the lead singer in the globally famous band Chasing Chords.

But that doesn't mean we're not soulmates.

I know it sounds mad but I've been loyally supporting Chase since his band first uploaded one of their songs on to YouTube, which went viral in a matter of days and landed them a big record deal. I was the first one in our entire school to stumble across the video online of the band playing a song that Chase had written, in what I now know to be his mum's dusty old garage. I lay on my bed and played it over and over on repeat, until Nina knocked on my door and went, 'Can't you put some headphones on?' in an unnecessarily narky tone.

I didn't care though because I knew then that I had stumbled upon something really special. I showed the video to everyone the next day at school, and by then the band's YouTube hits had skyrocketed. I followed them on every possible social media platform and registered for their newsletters, so that I could stay on top of all their updates, like when they signed the record deal. I couldn't stop listening to their latest song until they uploaded the next one, and then I couldn't stop listening to that one either. I have always been into music – Nina and I used to pretend we were pop stars all the time when we were little – but no songs have ever had the effect on me that Chase's songs do.

Layla and Sophie love Chasing Chords, but they don't

compete with my appreciation of Chase. They don't really get him. Which is why I write the posts for the blog we created together, the one dedicated to our amazing fan fiction about the band. When I first suggested we set it up, Layla was really keen, but she never actually contributes anything. She just lies on her bed Snapchatting, while I sit at my laptop and work hard writing the stories, with occasional helpful comments from Sophie (although I have to put my foot down when Sophie suggests stupid plotlines like Chase and Miles, the band's drummer, going on a space adventure with NASA).

It's not like I always get As on my English papers or anything, and even if I did I wouldn't tell anyone in case they thought I was a big nerd, but writing fan fiction about Chasing Chords is one of my favourite things to do. Through my stories, I get totally lost in the band's world and I feel as if I know them better than they know themselves. I get loads of comments on my stories from fellow Chasing Chords fans begging me for the next instalment and I always secretly hope that the band might actually log on every now and then and read the stories, or even comment under another name.

Once the band replied to a tweet I sent them about how much I loved their latest single:

Chasing Chords @realchasingchords
@npalmer Thnx! Without fans like you, we'd be lost xox

I took a screenshot of it, which I printed out in a blown-up size, and then I bought a really expensive frame, and set the picture up on my dressing table next to my framed picture of Chase and my mirror, so I can read it every morning while I get ready.

I just have to meet Chase, and then everything else will fall into place. And ever since this morning, when the band announced they would be playing a surprise gig in London on Saturday, with tickets going on sale this week, I'd been coming up with a brilliant plan to make that happen.

'I have to tell you both about this new app,' I say, slightly distracted by Mrs Smithson, who was attempting – and failing – to mop up the spilt coffee with a piece of paper in absence of a tissue.

'What is it?'

'It gives me priority when buying any gig tickets in London,' I explain eagerly, clicking on the app to show them. 'We'll get first dibs as soon as the tickets for the secret Chasing Chords concert go on sale!'

'Amazing!' Sophie squeals, just as Mrs Smithson raises her mug to her lips, making her jump again and spill what's left in the mug down her shirt. 'Is it expensive? Getting this priority thing?'

'Who cares?' I shrug. 'It's Chasing Chords. We HAVE to get tickets and this is our best chance.'

'Will your mum mind?'

'Sophie, you've met my mum.' I sigh, sharing a knowing

look with Layla. 'It's not like she'd understand anything about apps. She can barely work her mobile and it's ancient. It doesn't even have a camera.'

'What?' Sophie replies, stunned. 'Do phones like that actually exist?'

'Trust me, they do.'

I had tried to update my mum's phone and I'd even got so far as to take her into a mobile phone shop in town, but that ended up being a total disaster. She completely embarrassed me in front of the really cute shop assistant by asking the WORST questions, like, 'Why are young people so obsessed with your own faces? I'll never understand this selfie malarkey you go on about, Nancy. Although, I do have to say, Nancy, *you* have a very beautiful face. Like mother, like daughter, eh?'

That wasn't even her worst joke, and every time she made one she cackled really loudly afterwards when it was clear that I wasn't finding any of them very funny at all. Then she insisted on making the cute shop assistant guide her round all the phones on display so that she could 'gather all the facts', before declaring to the entire store that she couldn't POSSIBLY discard the phone that has loyally stuck with her through thick and thin for the past four years, and she wouldn't be purchasing anything today, but did the cute shop assistant want to note down his number for her beautiful daughter, standing right there next to her.

It was MORTIFYING. I literally had to crawl out of the shop and couldn't speak to her for the rest of the afternoon, making a promise to myself that I would never again attempt to lure my mum into any kind of modern technology.

Just thinking about the phone-shop incident was actually making my cheeks burn hot with embarrassment, even though it was months ago.

'What is your sister doing?' Layla suddenly says, looking towards the front of the classroom curiously.

I hadn't even noticed Nina come in the room, but she must have been in there for some time because her notepads and pencil case were open on her desk, as though she'd been working.

I watch as Nina, with her clunky purple headphones round her neck like always, gets up from her desk and holds out a pack of tissues to Mrs Smithson, who is now standing looking in despair at the coffee stain on her shirt. She takes one gratefully before Nina quickly returns to the safety of her desk. But, of course, one of Nina's shoelaces has come undone and she trips, stumbling forward and quickly steadying herself on Timothy's shoulder as she passes his desk.

'Sorry!' she mumbles, as he jolts his head up in surprise.

Layla sniggers next to me.

Oh, Nina, I think, staring at her, *you can't even walk from the front of the class to your seat without somehow messing it up. Why do you have to be so embarrassing?*

I don't think anyone noticed except me and Layla, and Nina was only at the front of the class for a matter of seconds, but still I notice the familiar crimson blush appearing on my sister's cheeks as she ducks her head down to her notebook, pulling her headphones back into place over her ears.

'What is with her?' Layla asks, shaking her head. 'She is so clumsy. I swear I saw her trip in the canteen yesterday. It's like she can't handle her own feet!'

'You two are so different, Nancy,' Sophie chimes in.

'Thank goodness,' I quip, laughing nervously.

'It's really weird. Apart from your looks –' Layla begins, leaning back in her chair, as the bell for morning registration trills loudly through the room – 'I'd never guess you were twins.'

CHAPTER TWO

NINA

I pull my headphones on, burying my face in my book as my cheeks grow hot with embarrassment.

The music fills my ears, blocking out Layla's cackle from the back of the classroom. WHY did I have to trip over in front of EVERYONE? I should have just left Mrs Smithson using that stupid piece of paper to mop up her coffee, rather than bother to offer her a tissue. I wish Layla hadn't seen. I've overheard her and Nancy talking about how clumsy I am before and now I've just given them even more ammo against me.

I glance up at the clock on the wall. Morning registration is about to start and then it's only a couple of hours until I can escape to the music rooms for my piano lesson, the only highlight of the school day.

Please, time, move faster.

Mrs Smithson raps her knuckles on the desk to get everyone's attention and I reluctantly lower my headphones, letting them sit round my neck like a safety blanket. I can hear Nancy giggling with her friends and I wonder whether they're still laughing at me or whether they've moved on to someone else.

I glance round and catch Nancy's eye as she looks my way.

Yep. Guess they're still laughing at me, then.

I hurriedly face the front, slouching even further into my chair, wishing it would swallow me up. Mum is always on at me about my posture – 'You'll end up hunched right over like your Great-uncle Walt if you don't roll those shoulders back, and, let me tell you, your Great-uncle Walt was constantly walking into things because his eyes faced the floor.'

I don't want to burst Mum's bubble, but I checked out our family tree and Great-uncle Walt doesn't exist.

Still, I do try my best not to slouch all the time, but it's difficult because when I sit up straight and roll my shoulders back with my chin up, I immediately feel too open, so I hunch forward again. Just like a hedgehog becomes a spiky ball, safely curled up into itself.

Nancy, on the other hand, has perfect posture. But then she would. She wants to be the centre of attention and have everyone looking at her all the time. Nancy doesn't fall over her own feet walking across the classroom and she always looks amazing. School for her is a daily fashion show – she gets up super early in the mornings to get ready, selfishly waking up the whole street as she wails along to loud pop music, pretending her hairdryer is a microphone.

You'd think that being identical twins we'd have a similar appearance, but, honestly, there's no chance of getting us mixed up. I don't know how she gets her hair so shiny and glossy. It must be something to do with the hundreds of bottles lined up around the shower. And her make-up takes her hours and is flawless, as though she's about to step on to the red carpet for a premiere, not get in the car to go to school.

I have no idea how to use cosmetics. I tried once and I just ended up looking like a child playing with her mum's make-up. I quickly scrubbed it off before Nancy could get a glimpse and tell the entire school how stupid I looked.

I would ask her for some tips but that would require talking to her.

'Nina Palmer, I know is here,' Mrs Smithson says, smiling at me and ticking the registration list. 'Thank you for the tissue.'

'No problem,' I say quickly, feeling my face on fire again. I know she's being nice but I wish she wouldn't draw any more attention to me.

Someone sniggers at the back. I don't have to turn round to know it's Nancy.

I keep my head down for the rest of the morning and by the time the lunch bell goes, signalling it is time for my piano lesson, I am ready for the day to be over. I get up so fast, scrabbling my books together to rush out of the room, that I don't look as I slide out of my chair, knocking straight into Layla.

'Hey!' she growls, looking offended that someone like me had touched her.

'Sorry,' I squeak, clutching my books. 'I didn't see you.'

She glares at me in disgust and then swans out of the classroom, Nancy following her closely, without giving me a second glance.

'Perfect!' My piano teacher, Mr Rogers, grins as I come to the end of Bach's *Prelude in C*. 'I knew I didn't call you my star student for nothing.'

I blush. 'I fumbled some of the beginning section. I have been practising all week, but I guess it took me a while to get into it today.'

He nods thoughtfully. 'Was it because I was in the room?'

'What do you mean?'

He hesitates. 'Nina, you've got a real talent. But, if you really want to get a place on the Guildhall music course next summer, you're going to have to practise performing in front of an audience.'

My stomach tightens at the mention of the summer music course. I have dreamt my whole life of going to Guildhall School of Music and Drama after I finish school, and next July they are running a special summer course for younger students who one day might attend the school for real. I HAVE to get a place on that course.

But there's also no way that I can play the piano in front of people. I feel sick to my stomach just at the thought of performing in front of an audience or on a stage.

'This year, it's the most important thing I want you to work on,' Mr Rogers continues as I swallow the lump in my throat. 'Playing in front of an audience. I know how nervous you get just playing in front of me, so I think it would be very good practice to get used to controlling those nerves. It's a very natural thing to be scared about, but, unfortunately, if you want to be a musician, you have to get over your stage fright. Maybe you could start with your family? This week you could play them this piece. You play it beautifully; I'm sure they would love to hear it.'

My family? No chance. Nancy is hardly going to want to spend an evening watching me play the piano.

'I don't think I'll ever be able to play in front of an audience,' I admit.

Mr Rogers regards me carefully. 'Just start getting used to the idea. We can take it slow. We have a whole year to work on it. Now –' he smiles, reaching for another piece of sheet music – 'let's move on to some Beethoven, shall we?'

When our lesson ends, I stay in the music room to practise for the rest of lunch break, thinking about what Mr Rogers said.

How am I ever going to be able to play in front of the Guildhall tutors if just the thought of playing in front of anyone but Mr Rogers makes me break out into a sweat?!

'I can't do this,' I announce to an empty room, slumping forward and resting my forehead on the piano keys.

'Do what?'

I almost fall off the back of the piano stool, but breathe a sigh of relief when I see it's only Jimmy leaning on the door frame, watching me with a bemused expression.

He grins and comes to lean on the piano instead. 'I thought I'd find you here.'

Jimmy and I have been friends ever since we were paired together one PE lesson when we were ten and forced to come up with a gymnastics routine to show the rest of the class. Both of us are useless at any kind of sport, plus I get stage fright so badly that I physically freeze. Needless to say, our routine ended up being a complete disaster.

But it succeeded in making us best friends for life.

'What is it you can't do?' he asks, pressing down on random piano keys.

'Just something Mr Rogers has asked me to do. It's nothing. How was your morning?'

'Long. I wish we were in the same classes,' he says with a sigh. 'Mr Barber gave me another warning.'

I can't help but laugh. Jimmy has never been one to hold back his opinions; one of the many qualities I love about him.

'What did you do this time?' I ask gleefully. 'Accuse him of being a repressor of basic human rights?'

'Oh please, that was so last week.' He frowns. 'It wasn't my fault; I was provoked. Jessica Hawks decided to give her opinion on *Jane Eyre.*'

'Oh?'

He rolls his eyes. 'Jessica Hawks thinks that Jane is, and I quote, "too gobby," and she doesn't understand why someone "as hot as Mr Rochester" would want to be with someone "who won't stop whining".'

'Wow. That's . . . interesting.'

'That's not the word I used. I asked her whether she'd have the same opinion if Jane was a man. I said, if Jane was a man, standing up for himself, not letting anyone boss him around or make him feel inferior, would Jessica Hawks still consider him "too gobby"? I accused her of promoting the idea of gender constructions by expecting female characters to stay in their place, under the power of men, and not protest. Then I said she was an embodiment of everything that's wrong with our society.' He pauses for breath.

'And? What did she say?' I ask admiringly.

'I believe her exact words were, "Oh, sod off."'

I giggle at the idea of Jimmy facing up to Jessica Hawks, one of the popular girls. I doubt she even knows who Jimmy is.

'Mr Barber gave you a warning for that? Seems a bit harsh. Isn't it just a healthy debate?'

Jimmy puts his hand on his heart. 'And *that* is why you are my best friend in this mad, mad world. That's exactly what I think, and yet, according to Mr Barber, I was being unnecessarily aggressive in my opinions. How am I ever going to get into Oxford if I'm not aggressive – no, not aggressive – *assertive* in my opinions? That's what I'd like to know.' He absent-mindedly repeatedly taps the A key. 'Yet again, proof of the Man trying to neatly mould us into deluded social norms.'

I smile, nudging him gently. 'Keep fighting the good fight. Oxford won't know what's hit it.'

'Neither will Guildhall. Do you want me to leave so you can practise?'

'Actually, Mr Rogers wants me to try and do the absolute opposite. He wants me to start practising in front of people.'

'As in, performing?' Jimmy raises his eyebrows. 'Has Mr Rogers met you?'

'I know. But he's right.' I sigh. 'I won't get into the Guildhall summer school if I can't play in front of anyone, will I?'

Jimmy nods, running a hand through his unruly curls. 'Why don't you ask your hero about this on Saturday? I'm sure he might have some tips on getting over stage fright.'

Immediately a rush of excitement washes over me. 'Can you believe he's in London? He's there –'

'– for one night only and he's coming all the way from Manchester.' Jimmy laughs. 'You've told me maybe five hundred times since last night!'

'I'm sorry, I know I must be boring you, but I can't help it. Shall we go together?'

Jimmy looks at me guiltily. 'I'm so sorry, Nina, I can't come. I wish I could!'

'That's OK,' I say hurriedly, trying to hide my disappointment. 'Mum will take me.'

'You'll have to tell me all about it. Imagine,' he says, smiling wistfully, 'seeing Austin Golding in the flesh! I'm not sure you'll be able to handle it.'

I'm not entirely sure I'll be able to handle it either. Austin Golding is one of the most talented living composers and pianists in the world, and ever since Mr Rogers introduced me to his work I've been completely obsessed with him. Whenever I want to hide away from the world – which happens on a daily basis – I put my headphones on, I listen to one of his albums and I escape from everything into his music. No one can play the piano like he can. As Mr Rogers says, he is truly a genius.

I saw the advert in the newspaper for his upcoming signing in London and immediately rang the music shop supplying the event to secure his latest book (according to the lady on the phone, they only had one left). It is ready and waiting for me to pick it up on Saturday and take it to Austin to autograph.

'Do you think I should tell Austin I'm a pianist too? Or is that really lame? It's really lame, isn't it. I'm sure he gets it all the time. Maybe I should just say I'm his biggest fan. But that kind of sounds silly, too. What do you think?'

Jimmy opens his mouth to speak but hesitates, distracted by something over my shoulder. I swivel round on the stool just in time to see Nancy's face disappear from the window of the door before she flounces off; I could tell she was pretending that she wasn't looking in. I turn back to face the piano, resting my hands on the keys comfortingly.

'The Queen Bee herself,' Jimmy remarks, before shooting me a look of sympathy. 'Have you two spoken recently?'

I shake my head.

Nancy and I never speak. Not properly. We say stuff in passing, because it's hard not to when there's only three of us in the house and Mum still insists that we have dinner at the table together every single night. But Mum will always be the one talking, desperate to get us more interested in each other. Nancy isn't interested in me. The only thing she's interested in is her phone and how many likes each of her posts receives. Her phone is, and I quote, 'everything' to her.

'She's been brainwashed,' Jimmy once said to me, trying to excuse her behaviour. 'Yet another victim of a society that promotes unattainable perfection. It's not really her fault. One day, she'll see the light and maybe you two will be friends again.'

Jimmy is an only child and insists that I'm lucky to have a sibling, especially a twin.

Thing is, I used to think I was lucky. I used to think I was the luckiest person in the world to have a sister like Nancy. We were best friends and the fact that we were identical twins made it even better. We did everything together, so much so that people didn't even bother referring to us by name.

We were just The Twins.

I remember feeling really sad when Nancy wanted to do one thing and I wanted to do another, and we would make the decision to split up. I would feel odd without her next to me, as though I'd lost a limb. She was always the more confident twin – 'I'm older,' she used to say with her mischievous grin, 'so don't you worry, Nina – I'll be in charge' – but I didn't mind that; I liked that she took the reins on everything we did. She never made me feel like I was less important. She knew I was shy.

But then Dad left and everything changed.

We all coped with the family split in a different way. Nancy refused to talk about it, snapping at me any time I mentioned Dad and telling me off for making Mum sad. She started hanging out with different people at school, who were loud, brash and confident, while I just wanted to block out everything and everyone with music or go somewhere quiet with my camera and take photos. When I tried to hang out with her and her popular friends, she ignored me or looked annoyed whenever I said the wrong thing.

It was as though everything she used to love about me embarrassed her.

As we grew up, we started having less and less in common, so then we had less and less to talk about, until one day I noticed that we barely talked at all. By that point, I was so used to it that it was just how it was.

'I don't know what happened to you two,' Mum always says, with sad eyes. 'I don't know why you resent each other so much.'

It's hard not to resent someone who makes you feel inferior to her phone.

'I wonder why she felt the need to peer into the music room,' Jimmy says. 'Maybe she wanted to hear you play. She knows you like coming here at break times.'

'Nancy has no idea what I do or where I go, and she couldn't care less.'

'How do you know?' He raises his eyebrows. 'How else do you explain her looking through the music-room window?'

'Simple,' I say, pulling the piano lid down over the keys. 'She must have mistaken it for a mirror.'

CHAPTER THREE

NANCY

Nancy created group 'Operation Chasing Chords'

Nancy

I just got a notification from my app!!!

Sophie

OMG WHAT DID IT SAY?

Nancy

Priority tickets go on sale in 20 MINUTES!!!!!!

Sophie

AHHHHHHHHHHHHHHHHHHHHHHHHHHHHHHH

Layla

SO exciting

Nancy

Don't worry, guys, I'm at the ready to refresh the page and get us tickets

Nancy

Layla

How many tickets are you getting? You're getting some for us, right?

Nancy

YESSSSS! Are you kidding? I'm not going to go on my own, am I?! I'll buy four this time rather than three, in case one of our parents insists on coming . . . like my mum did at the Little Mix concert!

Layla

Yeah, that was awkward with your mum standing outside the stadium the whole time

Nancy

Don't think she minded. She said she could just about hear the music and was dancing outside with the security guys

Layla

Doesn't she think you're old enough to go to a concert yet? It's not that big a deal

Nancy

You know how weird parents can be! Ha ha

Layla

Well, my parents are hosting a big dinner party that day. And Sophie's parents are invited. So unless she realizes that she can stop babying you, your mum will have to come because ours can't

Nancy

That's fine. Anyway, so excited to try and get tickets to see Chase!

Sophie

I'm so excited I just fell into a bench!!

Nancy

Wait, what?

Layla

How do you fall INTO a bench?

Sophie

I wasn't looking where I was going because I was looking at my phone typing all those Hs above and I didn't see the bench

Nancy

So, you walked into it?

Sophie

Yeah, and my foot kind of tripped on the leg and I fell right across it

Nancy

Are you OK???

Layla

Oh my god, you're so embarrassing. Sounds like something Nina would do!!

Sophie

I know, right? I have to go buy some soup now

Nancy

Why are you buying SOUP??

Nancy

Sophie

A man was sitting on the bench when I fell across it and I spilt his soup all over him

Layla

This story keeps getting worse

Sophie

I hope he likes minestrone because the shop has sold out of everything else. Do you think he'll like minestrone?

Nancy

Um . . . not sure because we don't actually know him

Sophie

Oh yeah. Everyone likes minestrone though, right? I've just bought it so I'll take it to him now and see what he thinks!

Layla

I am so pulling out of this conversation. I have actual things to do. Nancy, let us know about the tickets

Nancy

I will!! Don't worry, won't let you down!

Sophie

In case you're interested, he doesn't like minestrone

*

I don't know why Mum makes us have dinner together EVERY night. It's so stupid. We're not five years old any more; we're fifteen. We actually have lives of our own now.

Well, I do anyway.

But every weekday she insists on us spending time together 'as a family' at the dining table, pretending to be normal when it's obvious that none of us really want to be there. Nina couldn't be less interested in anything I have to say and she doesn't even bother hiding it, pulling faces and rolling her eyes whenever I talk about my friends. And she does this really annoying secretive smirk too, like she's making fun of me in her head. I see her doing it whenever I bring up Layla or Chase or something else important to me, and then when I call her out on it, she plays it so innocent. 'I didn't say anything!' she claims, always looking to Mum for help.

But she doesn't need to say anything, I know exactly what she thinks; it's written all over her face.

Nina and that weird friend of hers, Jimmy – who thinks just because he's the cleverest student in the school that makes him better than anyone else – love to look down their noses at everybody else. They walk around school, huddled together, judging everyone else, snidely remarking that we're all 'clones' – I heard Jimmy say that once under his breath when he walked past us in the canteen – and then they act all offended when no one includes them in anything.

Why would I want to invite someone to sit with me when they make me feel so inferior? I know Nina likes to play the 'but-I'm-shy-and-introverted' card that gets Mum on her side, but when she really wants something, she has the ability to go get it, whether she likes to admit that or not. I've seen her do it before. They CHOOSE to set themselves apart from everyone else. It's like they're proud of being different and clumsy or something. And I put up with it because, whatever, each to their own, she can do what she wants, but every now and then I like to remind them both that they're not as above everyone else as they think they are.

Mum gets home just as I'm sending a message to Sophie, emphasizing how excited/nervous I am about getting Chasing Chords tickets. Out of the corner of my eye I see Nina and Jimmy smirk at each other as I pull a face and take the selfie.

'Good evening, girls,' Mum chirps, swanning through the door in her bright turquoise sunflower-print dress with a big purple bow in her hair. I once asked Mum if she should be tested to see if she was colour-blind. She just laughed and told me I was adorable.

There's no helping some people.

'Hello, Jimmy! Are you joining us for dinner?'

'If that's all right,' he says.

Ugh. I roll my eyes. Another evening having to listen to him drone on about whatever society is doing wrong now.

'Of course, we love having you. Sorry, I'm a bit late tonight.' Mum smiles. 'I had this one customer who would not stop telling me all about the time he found a chicken-and-leek pie in his coat pocket. Who knew it would be such a long story? Anyway, it delayed the closing.'

Mum owns a shop that's about as quirky as she is, on the village's high street. It's one of those shops that's kind of difficult to describe; it sells everything, from tourist merchandise with the village name on it, like keyrings and mugs, to old-fashioned sweets in those big, clear jars, to strange jewellery and local artists' work. When we first moved to Norfolk after Dad left, Mum made it feel like a brand-new adventure, whisking us away to a beautiful village in the middle of nowhere near the coast and setting up her own shop, full of hidden gems. Nina and I used to love helping Mum at weekends, learning how to use the till and recommending interesting items that a customer might have missed.

We used to dress the same when we helped out at the shop, too, which people found adorable. Mum has what Layla describes as a 'very loud' sense of style – she loves polka dots and tying bandanas into a bow at the top of her head, like she's walked out of a vintage postcard from the 1950s, so the three of us must have looked quite the vision to the tourists ambling about our 'quaint little village'.

Now that I've grown up, the 'quaint' village is completely boring, and the shop has lost its magic.

'What are you cooking, Nina?' Mum asks, sniffing the air and making some over-the-top '*mmm*' sounds.

'Just a pasta bake,' Nina says, putting on the oven gloves and pulling it out of the oven.

'What a treat! Isn't that great, Nancy?'

I really hate the way Mum does this. She tries to put enthusiastic words in our mouths.

'Swell,' I reply drily, without looking up from my phone.

I refresh the tickets page, to make sure that I've got the time right. Only five minutes to go.

Mum frowns. 'I think it's really kind of Nina to cook this evening.'

'I cooked last weekend,' I remind her, scrolling down the screen.

'Yes, and that was lovely too. Honestly,' she sighs, undoing the buttons of her coat and going to hang it up in the hall, 'just because I compliment one of you doesn't make it a dig at the other.'

'It smells delicious,' Jimmy adds, getting out the cutlery.

Nina starts serving the pasta bake, spooning heaps on to a plate.

'I don't want that much pasta,' I say, as my phone vibrates. It's Layla, asking for an update. I tell her that it's almost lift-off and I'm ready and waiting.

'That's Mum's portion,' Nina says sharply.

'Whatever, don't make mine as big then.'

She doesn't think I'm paying her any attention because I'm looking at my phone but I catch her pursing her lips and sharing a look with Jimmy, as though my request is completely unreasonable.

Three minutes until the tickets are on sale.

Mum comes to give me a kiss on the cheek after she's planted one on Nina's and then sits down at the top of the table, leaving the place opposite me for Nina. That has always been the way we sit at the table. Before, Nina and I used to love being opposite each other, catching each other's eye and giggling at our own in-jokes that left Mum baffled.

Now, it just means it's a lot more effort not to make eye contact.

'So, how was everyone's day?' Mum says brightly, putting her napkin on her lap and shooting me a big smile. 'Nancy?' she prompts, but I just shrug, staring at my screen, so she gives up. 'Very informative, darling, but must you give so much detail?'

She bursts out laughing and Jimmy chuckles along with her. I scowl across the table at him as he slides into the chair next to Nina's.

'And how was your day, Jimmy?' Mum asks.

Here we go. When. Will. She. Learn.

'I got a warning from Mr Barber, even though I did nothing wrong.'

'You never do, darling.' Mum grins, winking at me. I pretend not to notice.

'And I'm still fighting the fight on the school uniform issue . . .'

I sigh loudly. He folds his arms and raises his eyebrows.

Two minutes to go. I hover my thumb over the screen nervously.

'I'm surprised, Nancy, that you're not more concerned about the topic of school uniform,' Jimmy continues. 'Yes, *I'm* opposing it because it is clearly a means of society suppressing our individuality and causing us to "fit in", but I would have thought from your point of view you'd enjoy the superior feeling of wearing "fashionable" clothes every day.'

'Because I'm just a stupid clone?' I retort. 'Actually, Jimmy, as fascinating as your argument is, I think that uniforms reduce fashion competitiveness and image-conscious bullying. Plus, we can still express our individuality through them. Look at me and Nina. We're identical twins in identical uniforms and no one ever gets us confused, thanks to my natural talent for accessorizing.'

You could have heard a pin drop. Jimmy looks as though someone's just slapped him round the face. Mum is staring at me in awe and Nina is frozen to the spot.

Ha. That showed them.

'Some very good points well made here.' Mum smiles, before Nina hurriedly brings the plates over and places them in front of us. 'Wonderful, Nina, you're so clever! Hopefully, I won't be late tomorrow and in return I can make you your favourite . . . cheese-and-potato pie!'

'That's Nancy's favourite,' Nina corrects her, sliding into her seat and picking up her fork.

'Oh! Whoops.' Mum giggles.

'It's not any more,' I inform them, anxiously watching the clock at the top of my phone screen. 'I'm not eating cheese.'

'Really? Why's that?' Mum asks, interested.

'Chase doesn't eat cheese.'

One minute. My heart slams against my chest and I feel very hot. *Please, please, please let me get these tickets. PLEASE.*

'All right, darling, no cheese. I'll make sure to remember it.' Mum takes a mouthful of pasta. 'This is exquisite!'

'Delicious!' Jimmy nods, still looking at me strangely.

'No, it's not,' Nina says hurriedly, her cheeks flushing red. 'It's only simple.'

'Understatement of the year!' Mum exclaims, pointing her fork at Nina. 'You are a culinary genius. I think I have some cookbooks in the shop somewhere; they might give you some inspiration.'

ZERO MINUTES! GO, GO, GO!!

The BOOK NOW button flashes on to the screen, sending me leaping to my feet and I hold my breath as I click it, filling in my details on the form and quickly pressing in the numbers of the credit card that Mum gave me for emergencies.

I'll tell her about that in a minute. She won't mind. This really IS an emergency.

Because this is going to change my life forever. I'm finally going to be in the same room as Chase and I have the PERFECT plan for how I can meet him.

Mum is watching me in confusion as I click ACCEPT on the terms and conditions and CONFIRM PAYMENT. Nina looks mildly confused and then loses interest after a few seconds. I can't even breathe.

The loading page changes into five of the most beautiful words in the English language:

YOUR BOOKING HAS BEEN CONFIRMED

'AHHHHHHHHHHHH!' I squeal, holding up my phone in victory and launching into a dance on the spot.

Mum bursts out laughing as I shake around the table and Nina does one of those strange little smiles of hers, but I don't care because I have tickets to the Chasing Chords secret gig in London and NOTHING can ruin this for me. Especially not my twin sister.

'What's going on?' Mum says. 'Your food's getting cold!'

'Who cares about food?' I wheeze, grinning at her. 'I've got tickets to Chasing Chords!'

'Is that some kind of music thing?' Mum asks, looking to Nina and Jimmy for help.

'I'd hardly describe what they produce as music,' Nina says under her breath, stabbing some pasta with her fork.

I glare at her. 'Have you ever even bothered listening to one of their songs?'

'Can you call them *their* songs if someone else writes them?' Jimmy adds.

'You literally have no clue! Chase is an extremely talented –'

'All right, Nancy,' Mum cuts in hurriedly, sensing the tension. 'Tell me more about this Facing Hordes thingy.'

'Chasing Chords! Only the best band in the world and they're playing in London and I've got tickets!' I hold up my hand as she opens her mouth to speak. 'Don't worry, Mum, I made sure I got four tickets, so you can come chaperone us, blah blah. Argh, I have to go call Layla!'

'I don't think so,' Mum says sternly, as I turn to go. 'Finish your meal first.'

'But, Mu–'

'I know it's all very exciting, darling, but your sister has worked hard making this delicious meal. The least you can do is sit down and eat it. You can call your friends afterwards.'

'She can go if she wants,' Nina says quietly, looking at her food. 'I don't mind.'

'Sit down, Nancy, and tell me all about the concert,' Mum instructs, ignoring Nina. 'Where is it, did you say?'

I reluctantly sit down and pick up my fork, even though I am *way* too excited to eat. I move the food around my plate impatiently.

'It's in London. This Saturday.'

Nina snaps her head up.

'Saturday?' she asks nervously.

'That's what I said.'

'That's when Austin Golding is here.'

'Who?'

Nina shifts in her seat. 'Austin Golding. The really famous composer. Mum has already promised me she'll take me to see him on Saturday in London. He's doing a signing and it is my dream to meet him.'

'Who cares about some composer that no one has heard of? This is *Chasing Chords*!'

'You can see them any time.'

'No, I can't!' I slam my fork on the table. 'This is a SECRET concert.'

Jimmy smirks. 'It's hardly secret if they announce it a week before and then anyone can just buy tickets to it.'

'Ugh, that's not what "secret concert" means. It means there're limited tickets because the space is smaller than a big arena, like they're used to playing. This show is seriously important, it's for their true fans.'

'Mum's taking *me*,' Nina says quietly but

39

'No, Mum's taking ME! I've bought the tickets!' I waggle my phone screen across the table in her face.

I can already tell that she's flustered by me raising my voice at her but, seriously, she can't avoid confrontation for the rest of her life, especially if she insists on being constantly annoying.

She can't even look me in the eye as she argues her point.

'That's enough!' Mum suddenly stands up, pushing her chair back and leaning on the table. 'Honestly, what is wrong with both of you?'

I glare at Nina but she's still staring at her feet.

'I'm afraid that I can't accompany either of you to London this weekend,' she announces, folding her arms.

'What?' Nina looks panicked.

For a moment I feel annoyed, but then I realize that this works quite nicely for me.

'No worries!' I shrug happily. 'I'll just go with Layla and Sophie. We can get taxis to and from the station and I'll sell the extra ticket on the door.'

'That's not happening,' Mum says, giving me that nice-try look that only parents are capable of.

'Mum,' Nina squeaks, 'you said you would come with me.'

'I know, darling, and I'm sorry,' she says, more gently now.

Honestly, how come Nina gets all the sympathy? Talk standards.

'I have to work. You know how busy Saturdays are in the shop. And I would have taken the day off just this once so I could take you to the composer signing, but there's a big arts festival this weekend in the village and it's going to be packed with tourists. I've already said to the council that I'll be open for business to support the event. It's a wonderful opportunity,' she says, before adding quietly, 'and we could do with the money.'

Nina nods in understanding.

'I have a solution, though,' Mum says, her eyes lighting up. 'I'll ask someone to look after the shop for me for an hour while I take you girls to Norwich station, and I'll allow you to go to London for your events –'

I smile triumphantly. *PHEW!*

'– if,' Mum continues, shooting me a warning glance, 'you go together.'

WHAT???

Jimmy drops his fork and it clatters loudly on his plate. Nina and I stare blankly at one another. The first time in the conversation that she's actually bothered to look at me.

'What do you mean?' I ask hurriedly.

'I will allow you to go to London on Saturday if you go together.'

'What do you mean, *together*?'

'Really, Nancy, do I have to explain myself?' She sighs, sitting back down again.

'Yes, you do have to explain yourself!'

Nina nods in agreement. We haven't agreed on anything in years, so it would have been quite the moment if it wasn't such a serious topic.

Mum rolls her eyes. 'I'll drive you both to the train station, you can get the train together; then, Nancy, you can accompany Nina to her signing; and Nina, you can accompany Nancy to her concert.'

'NO!' we both say in unison, although I kind of scream it and Nina says it more like a gasp.

Jimmy laughs. 'Whoa, would I like to see that happen.'

'Mum, I can't go to some stupid composer's signing!'

'And I . . . I don't want to go to a pop concert,' Nina stammers.

'See? It won't work!' I argue, but Mum refuses to budge.

'You'll just have to make it work! Either you go together, or you don't go at all. And maybe, just maybe, you'll have a nice time. Nancy,' she says as I open my mouth to protest, 'I won't hear another word. My offer is on the table and you can take it or leave it. If you're so adamant that Nina can't take that fourth ticket you've bought, then Layla and Sophie will be selling *two* tickets on the door come Saturday night. Do I make myself clear?'

Nina and I both stay silent. I slump back into my chair.

'Good,' Mum says, picking up her fork and digging into the last bit of her pasta. 'Now that is all sorted, we can move on. So, Nancy, when were you going to ask my permission to use your emergency credit card for the tickets, and how are you planning to pay it back?'

After a painful dinner during which I touched hardly any of my food and Nina said nothing except 'yes' and 'no' to Mum's over-enthusiastic barrage of questions, I sit in my room working out what I should do.

I message Layla and Sophie to let them know we have tickets and they go crazy on the group about how excited they are. I post 'CHASING CHORDS SATURDAY' and a load of hearts on to every social media platform I have, to make sure everyone knows. I decide not to tell Layla or Sophie about my awkward situation until I see them at school. By then I will have a solution to help them with the shock.

I try to come up with a way of getting round Mum's stupid rule. The idea of Nina coming along to the show AND having to waste my time at some old man's music-book signing sucks most of the excitement about the concert out of me, so I have to take a moment, lying on my bed, listening to Chase's aptly named song, 'Torn Up Inside'.

His music never fails to hold the answer.

CHASE, TELL ME THE ANSWER TO THIS DIRE PROBLEM WITH YOUR SWEET LYRICS!

Nothing.

Bummer.

I listen to the song three times, but it's no use. The only answer I can think of is the one Mum already offered, which means Nina and I will just have to play nice. I sit up and exhale, burying my head in my hands.

I know Mum thinks she's being clever and that this is some crazy way of bringing us together but I already know it won't work. For one thing, I'm not going to risk missing the beginning of a Chasing Chords show by going to this signing thing, and Nina may be shy but she's stubborn. She's not going to back down easily. If anything, Mum's scheme will just push us further apart. I decide to go talk to her now that Jimmy has gone home.

I take a deep breath and get to my feet, turning off my speakers and heading out of my room on to the landing. I lift my hand to knock on Nina's door but stop at the sound of her music. Because mine had been blaring so loudly, I hadn't realized that she was in her room listening to music, too.

It sounds familiar and I wait a moment outside her door, trying to work out what it is. Then it hits me: it's 'If the Rain's Got to Fall' from that musical we used to love, *Half a Sixpence*.

I haven't heard it in years and I've forgotten how much I like it. The happy tune immediately prompts my head to do a weird little bop to the beat. And then suddenly the introduction ends and the singing bit kicks in and I realize Nina isn't *listening* to music – she's *playing* it. She's so . . .

good. It's weird hearing her play. I tried to sneakily listen in when I saw her in the practice room at school, because Mum always says how good she is and I don't have a clue, but Jimmy spotted me, so I had to pretend I was just walking past.

I stand outside her bedroom door for the whole song, listening to her play and sing, swaying along as though in a weird kind of trance. Something about that song makes me feel really . . . happy.

Someone clears their throat and I gasp, caught off-guard.

'She's talented, isn't she?' Mum whispers, standing in the middle of the stairs, leaning on the bannister, watching me. I have no idea how long she's been there.

'Whatever,' I say, before knocking loudly and breezing in to her room.

Nina is sitting at her keyboard at the back of the room and, as I swing it open, the door bangs loudly against the wall, making her jump.

'Can I come in?' I ask.

'If you want,' she replies, watching me suspiciously.

I shut the door behind me and I'm about to launch into a speech about Saturday when something stops me. I haven't been in Nina's room since . . . well . . . forever. I know that seems strange because we're sisters and we live in the same house, which really isn't all that big, but I've never had a reason to go into her room before, just like she never comes into mine.

Because I post on social media so much from my room, I have to make sure that it always looks really neat and beautiful. Everything in my room matches, and it's all very white and clean, with pink fairy lights along the wall, and plenty of matching pastel-coloured cushions on the bed. I've got the posh scented candles that Mum got me last Christmas on my bedside table, next to my tall white lamp, and my dressing table is my pride and joy – make-up brushes sitting perfectly in pink and white floral pots; every nail varnish colour you can imagine in perfect rows (with more in my varnish bag I keep in the bathroom); drawers full of foundation, bronzers, blushes, contouring kits, eyeshadows, eyelashes, mascaras and perfumes; and a beautiful large gold-framed mirror hanging over the table that Mum found in a vintage shop and cleverly snapped up for me. And, of course, the framed picture of Chase and the tweet from Chasing Chords.

Walking into Nina's room is like stepping into another universe.

There are books everywhere, and I mean EVERY-WHERE. A whole bookcase bursting with rows and stacks of them, little piles of books in the corners of her room, and ones on her bedside table with bookmarks sticking out.

She can't possibly have read all those books, right? I mean, you'd have to be some kind of weird hermit with no social life!

Which, now that I think about it, actually explains a lot.

And, instead of a dressing table, she has a desk with all her homework spread out, and some folders and binders stacked neatly across the back. While I have photo frames of my friends propped up neatly around my room, Nina has big framed pictures of record covers hanging all over her wall, a couple of them signed in black marker pen. I'm not too surprised to also see bits of her wall dedicated to weird artistic photos. Nina has always had a thing for photography and Mum bought her a really expensive camera for her birthday a couple of years ago.

There is a cork board hanging up too, with loads of those photo-booth strips pinned over it. All of them are her and Jimmy pulling different silly faces, or her larking about with Mum.

I feel a pang of sadness as I look at those photos. I don't know why.

'Did you want something?' Nina asks from behind her keyboard, as I gawp at her room.

'Yes, right. Look –' I bring my focus back to the matter at hand and perch on the end of her bed – 'I think the best thing to do, for us to both get what we want, is to try and make this London day work.'

She nods. 'I agree.'

'Good. Strong start.' I take a deep breath. 'So, if you tell me all the details about where this Arthur composer person –'

'Austin.'

'Whatever. If you let me know the details about his signing thingy, then I will work out our route. Sort out what train we get and how we get from the signing to the concert. Stuff like that.'

'Are you sure you don't mind organizing it?'

'I'm sure.'

'Cool,' she says. 'Thanks.'

'Right, well, I'll leave you to it.' I stand up but then hesitate as I reach the door. 'That song you were playing . . .'

'The *Half a Sixpence* one? Did you like it?'

I pause and, maybe because she sounds so sincere, like she might actually care what I think for once, I decide I might as well be honest.

'Yeah, I liked it. I had no idea how talented you are.'

Then I walk out and shut the door behind me, leaving Nina looking stunned.

CHAPTER FOUR

NINA

'GET OUT OF THE WAY!'

As Nancy yells at the car in front of us, I slide further down into my seat, so that I'm almost horizontal. If I didn't have to wear a seatbelt, I would have been lying on the car floor by now.

'Nancy!' Mum snaps. 'What is wrong with you? We're coming up to a roundabout! He has to slow down. You almost burst my eardrums.'

'Mum, I don't think you understand,' Nancy whines from the front seat, checking her phone for the billionth time, 'if we miss the train, my life is OVER.'

'You can just get the next one.'

'No, we can't just get the next one! We are on a very strict schedule!'

To prove her point, she opens the notes on her phone and holds it up. She has typed out a minute-by-minute timeline of the day ahead of us.

'See?'

'I'm driving, I can't look,' Mum mutters. 'But I get the picture.'

'It's very simple,' she explains, pointing at each time slot. 'If we miss the train, then we'll be delayed getting on the Underground, which will delay our arrival at the Southbank Centre for the music-book signing, by which time the queue for this Aaron person will have built up –'

'Austin,' I correct quietly from the back seat, but she ignores me.

'– which means we'll be late getting back on the Tube to head to Brixton for the concert, and that means that we would miss the beginning of Chasing Chords and that absolutely can NOT happen.' She stops for breath. 'And that's why, if we miss the train I carefully selected to get us to London, my life will be officially over.'

'I will do my best to get you there, Nancy, but I can't control the traffic,' Mum grumbles.

Nancy shakes her head. 'I knew we should have left earlier.'

Mum doesn't say anything, but she and I share a look as we catch each other's eye in the rear-view mirror. The last thing I want is for Nancy to be in an even worse mood than normal because her plan has been messed up. I already feel nervous enough at the idea of getting on London Underground and going to see a band I don't know, not to mention spending the entire day with my twin sister, who I haven't had a proper conversation with in years.

I still feel a bit shaken up about what she said earlier this week: that she thought I was talented. I know it sounds strange, but the fact that the compliment came from her somehow makes it way more meaningful. Because there is no chance that she would ever pay me a compliment just for the sake of it. She doesn't even *like* me.

I gaze out of the window as we turn down a bumpy country lane. I love where we live, surrounded by fields, woodland and winding lanes lined with hedgerows. We're near to the coast too and, while it can get busy in the summer, the beaches are practically dead in the winter, except for dedicated dog owners. I know Nancy thinks our little village and unspoilt countryside is boring, but I think it's wonderful, especially for photography. I love capturing little moments and strange sights that other people miss.

When Mum bought me my special camera, she glanced at Nancy who was, as usual, on her phone picking a filter for her birthday selfie, and said, 'I have one daughter who loves being in front of the camera and another who loves being behind it. Strange, isn't it?'

If we weren't in such a rush to get to the station, I would love to have taken some pictures of the sloping landscape we were zipping through – a lot of people describe Norfolk as flat, but it's more gently rolling green countryside. And you should see the sunsets we get on the coastline.

I bite my lip as I steel myself for the opposite in London. I'll have to get used to the idea of living in a city if one day I want to go to Guildhall. But, as soon as I think about the Tube and the crowds and the noise, I immediately feel terrified.

'THIS CANNOT BE HAPPENING!' Nancy screams as a tractor pulls out in front of us and trundles along the road, slowing us to a crawl. 'TELL HIM TO LET US PASS!'

'What can I do, Nancy?' Mum replies, raising her voice. 'I can't overtake him on this road; it's too narrow!'

I pull my headphones up over my ears and switch on one of Austin Golding's most relaxing piano works. I tell myself that everything is going to be OK today, that I have nothing to worry about, that I just need to focus on breathing calmly.

I haven't said anything to Nancy about how the last time I was in a big crowd I felt completely out of control, like everyone was closing in on me. My throat closed up and my breathing turned to short, sharp rasps as I tried to catch my breath, while my heart pounded so loudly against my chest it hurt. Jimmy had to guide me out and get me some water away from everybody.

I skip to another of Austin's songs and focus on what I'm going to say to him when I meet him later today. We are still stuck behind the tractor and, although my noise-cancelling headphones are doing a great job of drowning out Nancy's wails, I can still see her wild gestures as she yells at Mum. I glance down at my watch.

We're not going to make it.

By the time we get to Norwich train station, Nancy is in such a strop that she barely says goodbye to Mum, getting out and slamming the car door behind her.

'You had better hurry after her,' Mum says, swivelling round in her seat to smile at me. 'Enjoy today and I'll see you this evening.'

I nod nervously and get out of the car, while Nancy looks over her shoulder to check I'm coming. She throws her hands up in annoyance as I hurry towards her, tripping over the curb.

'Are you and that tractor in this together? Take your time!' she huffs, before turning on her heel and marching into the station.

She stops and looks at the train boards displaying the departure times before letting out a loud groan that echoes through the station.

'This has got to be a joke!' she cries. 'The next train to London is delayed! What a nightmare! This cannot be happening.'

I blush furiously as people around us glance at Nancy in disapproval.

'Maybe you should keep your voice down,' I whisper, stepping closer to her. 'People are looking.'

'I don't care if people are looking, Nina,' she snaps, glaring at me. 'I care about our plans being ruined. It may not be important to you, but I spent ages working out our schedule. You haven't done anything, except follow behind – as usual.'

Her words sting and I look down at my shoes.

'Come on,' she continues coldly. 'We're platform one.'

We sit on a bench on the platform in silence. I bite my thumbnail nervously and catch Nancy looking at me in disgust. We both used to bite our nails but Nancy grew out of it much quicker. She would never dream of such a habit now; she takes a lot of pride in her nails. I can't do anything with mine because long nails are a nightmare on piano keys, and I don't have the patience to paint them all the time.

I love seeing Nancy's nails every morning, catching a glimpse of what crazy colours or design she's decided on for that day. She's really good at it. I have never told her that though. She'd think I was being sarcastic.

'Nancy,' I say quietly as she checks the time on her phone and huffs, 'what sort of space is this concert in?'

'What do you mean, Nina?' she grumbles impatiently.

'Is it like a big open space or . . . a compact, crowded space?' I gulp.

'I don't know. Who cares?' she replies dismissively. 'Guess we'll see when we get there.'

Our train finally arrives at the platform and Nancy immediately leaps up and walks over to a carriage, slamming on the button repeatedly until the train doors open. She picks a table seat by the window.

'You sit over there,' she instructs, nodding at the opposite seat.

I suppose she doesn't want me sitting next to her, within touching distance. I slide into my seat and people-watch as everyone starts boarding. The whistle blows and the train eventually pulls out of the station. I get my camera out of my bag, checking that it's ready to go.

Nancy watches me curiously. 'What are you going to do with that?'

'Take pictures.'

'Yeah, thanks, I got that,' she says, rolling her eyes. 'I meant, what are you going to do with it *now*?'

'Get some train shots,' I explain, nodding to the window. 'You can get some pretty weird and wonderful photos with this kind of movement and we'll be speeding through some beautiful countryside. I'm going to experiment.'

She nods thoughtfully. 'That's cool.'

'It is?' I say in surprise before I can stop myself.

'Yeah.' She hesitates and raises her eyebrows. 'Why are you looking at me like that?'

'I'm not looking at you like anything,' I reply hurriedly, even though I was definitely looking at her as though she'd gone mad. Because I'm almost certain that was another compliment.

'I'm glad I'm sitting this way,' I remark, just to change the conversation. 'I like facing the direction the train is going, otherwise I –'

'Feel sick. I know,' she says, finishing my sentence impatiently and leaning back in her seat. 'Why do you think I took this seat and said you should sit over there?'

Her phone rings and she picks it up, informing Layla that she'll forward their tickets to her so they don't have to wait around before the concert if they don't want to.

For a moment, I just stare at her, amazed by what just happened and then I return my focus back to the blurred landscapes whizzing past.

I feel a warm, comforting tingle in my stomach. It may only be the tiniest of gestures that she won't even think twice about, but to me it is just like when we were younger and Nancy would always boss me around, taking care of me. She used to make me feel safe.

We don't say much for the rest of the journey, apart from Nancy remarking every now and then that her plan has been completely ruined, and she thinks tractors and traffic lights should be completely banned.

'I think both of those things are actually quite important,' I mention, when she repeats her viewpoint for the third time.

'Whatever,' she huffs. 'If I miss a SECOND of Chasing Chords, I am personally going to hold all tractors responsible and will SUE.'

As the train drags itself slowly into London Liverpool Street, Nancy jumps up and goes to stand by the doors, encouraging me to do the same.

'I've got an app that tells me exactly which lines to take,' she announces confidently. 'So this should be a breeze.'

I gulp as we step out on to the busy platform, heading through the barriers and towards a large archway that says 'UNDERGROUND' across the top.

I follow Nancy so closely that I step on the back of her shoes twice – 'Ouch, Nina! What's with your clown feet?' – terrified of getting lost in the mass of people, all barging their way through unapologetically. I wish Jimmy was here to guide me and hold my hand. I'm too afraid of Nancy making fun of me, or saying I'm being stupid, to tell her that I'm starting to panic about getting on the Tube with all these people. I don't know if I can handle it.

'Right, Central line this way,' Nancy says, once we're through the next lot of barriers. 'It's really easy. We just go one stop across to Bank and then change and get the Waterloo & City line. That is one stop to Waterloo, which is the nearest Tube station to the Southbank Centre. We should have time to make both events.'

I get caught up in a group of tourists coming through the barriers behind me and, for a moment, I lose sight of Nancy. I spin round, searching for her frantically, until I spot her up ahead by the escalators, waving impatiently at me.

'Keep up,' she says, and frowns.

I don't say anything and just follow her on to the escalator, leaning on the handrail. I use this precious time of standing still to close my eyes and steady my breathing. I feel much too hot and waves of fear roll over me, one after the other, as others grumpily push me over to the side so they can race down on the left. My camera jostles in my bag as they pass, and I clutch it to my stomach, terrified someone will break it. My heart is racing and I feel lightheaded.

Suddenly a loud, booming rush of noise and screeching brakes echoes through the station. I grip the handrail tightly in fright.

'That's the train arriving! Come on!' Nancy cries, flying down the rest of the steps and disappearing round the corner.

I stumble off the end of the escalator, attempting to navigate my way through the bustling crowd. I seem to be in everyone's way as I look for Nancy among the sea of faces moving along the platform.

'Nina! Over here!'

She's standing on the train, leaning out of the open doors of the next carriage along. I desperately try to make my way to her and get barged in the shoulder so hard by a grumpy woman weighed down with shopping bags that I stumble backwards into a man right behind me.

'Careful,' he says kindly, as I steady myself.

I hear a beeping sound and the doors of the Tube begin to close.

'Nina!' Nancy yells in frustration, but it's too late.

The doors shut together firmly, and within seconds the train is off, speeding away into the pitch-black tunnel. I watch helplessly as Nancy is carried away from me.

I'm on my own.

I try to slow my breathing down as the fear overwhelms me, but it's hard to focus when there are so many people around me and my eyes prickle with hot tears. I stand frozen to the spot as people weave in and out of each other's way behind me. I consider asking someone for help, but everyone seems like they're in a rush and I feel too embarrassed and scared to talk to any strangers. *What am I going to do?* I know that if I start crying everyone will stare at me and that will make everything even worse. *What am I going to do?*

I close my eyes and try to concentrate on remembering what Nancy said when we went through the barriers.

'It's really easy. We just go one stop across to Bank and then change . . .'

Bank. One stop across to Bank. I open my eyes and look down the tunnel to see the bright headlights of the next train looming towards us. I step backwards as it roars past, coming to a halt at the platform and I stand to the side of one of the carriage doors, preparing myself for the mass of people about to get off the train. I wait until the last person strides past me and then I hurry on before anyone else, neatly tucking myself into the corner next to the door. The carriage begins to fill up and soon I'm pressed against the side of the train, barely able to breathe. It's stifling hot and I can feel the back of my neck growing damp with sweat as my cheeks and forehead burn.

I can do this. Just one stop.

The train jolts forward and I hold on tightly, as the cranking noise of the train drowns out the chatter of others around me. It's barely a minute or so to Bank, but it feels like forever and when the train comes to a halt, and the beeping sound of the doors opening pierces the air I practically fall out of the carriage.

'Nina!'

Nancy is standing by the wall of the platform and she rolls her eyes when she sees me, coming over to tell me off. I'm so relieved to see her that I feel faint.

'What is wrong with you, Nina? All you have to do is stay with me, OK? It's really not that hard and we're already so late. We can't afford for you to –'

I try to listen to what she's saying but my heart is pounding against my chest so hard that my ears start to ring. A rush of heat runs through my body and I feel dizzy, suddenly reaching out to lean on her before I lose my footing.

'Nina?' She looks at me strangely, as she steadies me. 'Are you OK? You're shaking!'

'I'm fine,' I whisper. 'I need to sit down.'

'Come on,' she says in a much softer tone than normal, guiding me over to a bench on the platform.

I slump on to the seat and Nancy sits next to me, leaning forward and taking my hand in hers.

'It's OK, Nina,' she says gently. 'Deep breaths.'

She starts to provide an example, inhaling and exhaling deeply and encouraging me to do the same along with her. I do my best to try to match my short breaths with her long, deep ones. Someone stops in front of us and leans over to Nancy.

'Is she OK?' the stranger asks before holding something out to her. 'Here, take my water.'

'Thanks so much,' Nancy replies, and the woman walks away, hopping on the next Tube that has pulled into the platform. 'See? People are nice; they're just in a rush here. You're OK now. Try drinking some water.'

I nod and take the bottle, sipping the water gratefully. I start to feel in control of my breathing again.

'Do you think you can stand?' Nancy asks hopefully. 'It's stuffy down here. Let's get you some air.'

She offers me her arm and I let her lead me towards an escalator. She doesn't let go of my hand, even though it's clammy, and continues to hold it until we emerge out of the station and into the cold, fresh air. I instantly feel a little better and a cool breeze washes over me. Nancy takes me over to some stone steps that lead up to a large, imposing building with beautiful old columns. If I wasn't feeling so nauseous, I would have been a lot more appreciative of the architecture and taken some photos.

'I'm so sorry,' I whimper, when I finally feel better enough to speak. 'I don't know what happened.'

'It's fine,' Nancy says, and she sounds like she means it. 'Don't worry.'

'I just get so anxious when I'm in a big crowd of people and I start to panic, and then I lost you and I didn't know what to do.'

I begin to cry, feeling overwhelmed by everything that just happened.

'Don't get upset, Nina – it happens to lots of people. Keep drinking that water, come on. You'll feel better soon, I promise.'

Her being so nice makes me want to cry even more. I drink the rest of the water under her close scrutiny and then wipe my tears with my sleeve.

'Hey, don't do that! You'll ruin your top.' She frowns, rustling around in her bag. 'Aha!' she says triumphantly, pulling out a pack of tissues.

I can't help but giggle through my tears. 'You're turning into Mum. She always carries tissues with her.'

'I am NOT turning into Mum,' she protests, horrified. 'I need them for any make-up mishaps on the go. And I might get emotional during Chase's songs. Some of them are real tear-jerkers.'

'Chase!' I say suddenly, scrunching up the tissue in my hand. 'We have to go! We're already behind schedule and I've just messed it up even more.' I check my watch. 'Let's head to the concert. We'll make it easily if we just go straight there.'

She gives me a funny look. 'What about Andrew?'

'Austin.'

'Whatever.'

'I can see him another time. Maybe Mum will take me to Manchester sometime instead. It's my fault we're late.'

As I speak, my heart sinks in disappointment. I have been so excited to finally get the chance to meet Austin Golding and now I've ruined it. But it is only fair – Nancy has put up with me dragging behind and causing a massive fuss. She could have shouted at me or been annoyed when I missed the Tube and then arrived on the platform a big mess, but instead she's been kind and patient and caring.

Nancy nods at what I'm saying, watching me closely, and then takes a deep breath before speaking.

'Nah.'

I blink at her. 'What?'

'We'll stick to our plan. We'll go to the signing and then on to the concert.'

'But there's no chance we'll make it to the show in time.'

'So, we'll miss the beginning,' she shrugs. 'It doesn't matter. There will be a support band and they might overrun. They usually do. We'll get all the good songs.'

'Nancy –'

'Nina, don't try and fight me on this one, OK? I've made up my mind and you know I'm as stubborn as you are, so I wouldn't bother. It will only make me cross.'

She stands up and holds out her hand to help me up on my feet.

'I think we should get a taxi the rest of the way, don't you?' she says, winking at me and patting her bag. 'Mum gave me some emergency cash to look after. Because I'm the responsible twin.'

I shake my head at her as she marches over to the side of the pavement to look for a free taxi.

'Nancy,' I say as I sidle up to her, 'you don't have to do this. I know the concert is important to you.'

'That's exactly my point,' she says, craning her neck to look over the traffic. 'If meeting this Anthony guy is half as important to you as the Chasing Chords show is to me, then I'm not going to let you miss it.'

'It's Austin.'

'I know,' she grins mischievously, before shooting her hand out to flag down a cab.

CHAPTER FIVE

NANCY

Nina keeps giving me strange looks in the taxi.

'OK,' I sigh after a few minutes, 'what is it? Is my make-up smeared or something?'

'No, it looks fine!' she says hurriedly, staring out of the window as we speed towards the book signing.

'If you're worried I'm going to change my mind, you can relax. You're not going to miss out on getting your book signed or whatever.'

'I'm not worried,' she says. 'It's just nice of you, that's all.'

Which is obviously true, but I don't want to rub in how selfless I'm being, so I just go, 'No worries,' and leave it at that.

Because, you know, I'm so nice.

We pull up at the building for the signing and, after I've paid the taxi and jumped out to follow Nina, I stop in my tracks. There are HUNDREDS of people there, all clutching the same book that Nina has reserved. The queue leading to his signing table goes all the way round the sides of the hall and practically out of the door.

'What the –' I stand frozen to the spot, taking it all in. 'What's going on?'

'What do you mean?' Nina says, looking confused. 'You *know* what's going on. It's Austin Golding's signing. That's why we're here, remember?'

'Hang on. These people are all here to see some conductor?'

'*Composer.*'

'Seriously, though, all of them are here just to get their books signed by this guy?'

'Yes!' Nina laughs, shaking her head at me. 'I told you, he's very famous!'

'Yeah, but I thought, you know, he was just famous to nerds and old people.'

A boy about our age, who looks like he's just walked off the set of *One Tree Hill*, saunters past us, talking into his phone to someone about how he has managed to get all his records signed and he can't wait to show them.

'Whoa.' I smile as he brushes past. 'Who knew this Aiden guy could draw such a good-looking crowd?'

'*Austin.*'

'Whatever. Where do I sign up to become a conductor?'

Nina rolls her eyes at that. She collects her reserved copy from the stand by the entrance and pulls me across the hall to join the end of the queue, where she proceeds to nervously hop up and down on the spot, tuck locks of her hair behind her ears, then in front of them and then behind them again, and bite her nails so frantically that they almost start bleeding. I stand there with her patiently, gradually shuffling forward as the queue moves, until I can't take her mad fidgeting any longer.

'What is with you?' I whisper in her ear, as the signing table gets closer and Austin's VERY bright yellow shirt looms into view. 'You look like you're desperate for the loo.'

'No, I don't!'

'Yes, you do. Just like that time on the way to the airport when Dad couldn't pull over and you wet yourself.'

'Nancy! Shush!' she hisses, blushing furiously. 'I was only five years old!'

'Whatever, I know that expression when I see it. You want me to hold your place in the queue while you go?'

'I do NOT need the loo. I'm just a little nervous, that's all.'

'About him signing your book? Just shove it in front of him – he'll know what to do.'

'It's more than that.' She sighs. 'Look, it sounds silly, but Austin Golding is my hero. And you know what I'm like: I never say the right thing.'

I hesitate.

'Actually, it doesn't sound silly,' I admit. 'I guess it will be like when I meet Chase. What do you say to the person you admire so much?'

'Exactly.' She nods, looking at me gratefully. 'Any ideas?'

I shrug. 'You're the musician. What sort of thing would you like to hear? Just say exactly what you feel.'

When we are finally ushered forward to the table, Austin beams up at Nina as she shyly places her book in front of him. His shirt is the brightest thing I have ever seen and I seriously consider asking him if he intends to burn every retina in London.

'What's your name?' he asks, holding his pen at the ready.

Nina mumbles her name incoherently and he looks up at his PR in the hope that she might have caught it. I step forward and clear my throat.

'Her name is Nina and she's a big fan of yours. She's a pianist herself.'

'Is that so?' he says, shooting me a grateful smile before turning his attention back to Nina. 'So, Nina, what do you like to play?'

I nod encouragingly to her and she answers sheepishly, but he seems impressed by what she says which leads to him asking her another one. Nina grows in confidence every time he asks her something else and he asks her a LOT of questions. Honestly, I try to pay attention but I zone out pretty sharpish when he starts going on about some dude from the eighteenth century who liked cellos or something.

It is also very difficult not to be distracted by Austin's loud shirt. I can't stop staring at it.

'Pleasure to meet you, Nina.' Austin smiles as he passes her the signed book. 'I look forward to seeing you perform some day.'

Nina says goodbye, gushing about how amazing it was to meet him and I practically have to drag her away from the table and out into the street to hail a taxi to Brixton. For someone who is supposed to be shy and introverted, she won't shut up all the way to the concert and, thanks to her giving a long monologue about how wonderful Austin Golding is and a broken-down timeline of his life, both myself and the taxi driver are now experts on the man.

'Here you are,' the taxi driver says, parking outside the concert.

Suddenly she goes deathly silent. Her eyes are wide with fear as she gazes out of the window at the clusters of people swarming in crowds through the doors into the lobby.

'Come on, Nina,' I say excitedly, leaning across her and opening the door. She hugs her Austin book to her chest tightly, like a safety blanket. 'Straight through and to the merchandise stand. The others will be in there already. Let's go.'

Nancy created group 'WHERE ARE YOU?!'
Nancy added Layla
Nancy added Sophie

Nancy
I'M HEREEEEEEE!!

Sorry I'm a bit late, stuff came up

Find The Girl

So happy I didn't miss the start of the concert though!!

Where are you two?? Have you gone in already?? I'm just at the merch stand

I'm definitely buying a T-shirt. Have you guys bought one? Which one did you get? I'm thinking the black one

I'm getting the hoodie too

And the phone cover

OMG they have CHASING CHORDS PILLOWS!!! It has Chase's face on it!! I CAN LITERALLY SLEEP ON CHASE'S FACE!!

OK, so I've bought four

Do you think that's enough?

Hellooooooooooooo, earth to Layla and Sophie!!

Maybe you've already gone in and you're watching the support band??? Is that why you're not looking at your phones??

You're not angry about the whole Nina thing, are you?? It will be like she's not even there, you know how quiet she is

I tried to get out of bringing her, TRUST me

It's not that big a deal though, right?

I think you must be in there already, you haven't read any of these messages. I'll come join you now!!

See you in there! I'M SO EXCITED!!!

Xxxxx

P.S. Great chat! Hahahaha

'Do you really need *four* tote bags?' Nina asks, giving me a strange look as I lean forward on the merchandise stand to scan what's on offer in case I've missed anything.

'Nina, no offence, but you asking that question clearly displays the fact that I'm the twin who got the common-sense genes.' I sigh sympathetically, unzipping my purse to get some money ready. 'How else am I going to carry my *four* pillows?'

'I suppose,' she agrees, finally realizing that I'm right. 'But I still don't see why you need four pillows in the first place. It seems a bit . . . weird.'

'Coming from the girl who just spent the afternoon begging a conductor no one has heard of to sign her forehead.'

'Composer, not conductor.' She blushes. 'I asked him to sign a *book*, not my head. And I didn't beg.'

'Whatever. He was weird.'

'He was NOT weird. He was perfect! Didn't you hear him asking me about what music I liked? He seemed genuinely interested! Even though he had a big queue waiting for him, he took the time to chat to each fan.'

'Who cares what he said? No respectable musician should be taking fashion tips from a canary.'

'I think his yellow shirt was cool,' Nina says defensively. 'It was very bright and happy.'

'It literally damaged my eyes. I thought I'd never see again.'

I can see Nina glaring at me as the woman behind the counter passes over the four tote bags, bulging with the cushions and my other purchases. I pay and then lead Nina over to a quieter corner of the concert lobby, putting down the bags and immediately pulling off my jumper.

'What are you doing?'

'Haven't you ever been to a concert before? I'm putting on my new T-shirt,' I explain, pulling it over my strap top. 'What do you think?'

She glances at it and shrugs. 'You look like you're a big Chasing Chords fan.'

'Just the vibe I'm going for.'

Nina waits as I stuff my jumper into one of the bags and check my phone again. No messages. I don't know why Layla and Sophie aren't replying to me. There's no way they haven't looked at their phones in the last half an hour. Barely a minute goes by without Layla checking her phone. And I don't know why they headed in without telling me. They could have waited for us in the lobby. We're not *that* late; Chasing Chords haven't even started their set yet.

I watch Nina glancing about nervously as everyone bustles past us, chattering excitedly as they show their tickets to the people on the door before heading into the concert. Every time the doors open to let a new group in, Nina jumps at the sudden wave of music that comes blaring through the lobby.

I feel a pang of guilt. Until that Tube incident, where she freaked out, I had no idea that she was so bad with crowds. I kind of get it, too. Being squished in a big group of people jostling you about can be pretty stressful, and I guess someone like Nina just gets swallowed up in it. I've never seen her like that before.

I wish she'd told me beforehand so I could have made sure I was looking out for her a bit more, guiding her more carefully on to the Tube and keeping close to her side, but then she never tells me anything.

'Are you OK?' I ask, tucking my Chasing Chords T-shirt into my high-waisted jeans. 'Do you want to put that book in one of the tote bags?'

She shakes her head. 'I'll hold it, it's all right.'

'Come closer, I need to lean on you,' I instruct, placing my hand on her arm and using my other hand to whip off my shoes.

'What are you doing?' she asks, baffled. 'Did you buy Chasing Chords shoes, too?'

'Don't be ridiculous, Nina,' I snort, crouching down to rustle through my handbag. I pull out a pair of heels and hold them up triumphantly. 'Ta-da!'

'What are those? They look expensive.'

'That's because they are,' I say smugly, putting them down on the floor in front of me and leaning on her again so I can slide my feet into them.

'Mum's going to kill you. You know she's worried about money at the moment and she was just saying last week how you –'

'Calm down, goody two-shoes,' I say, doing up the straps. 'I got them for free.'

'How?'

'The brand sent them to me. All I have to do is post a picture of me wearing them on Instagram and they're all mine,' I squeal, gripping her arm. 'Isn't that amazing?'

I couldn't believe it when I received the parcel in the post from Silhouette, one of my favourite brands, with a note on top of the most beautiful sea-blue shoes I'd ever seen – high slender heels, with gladiator straps up over the ankle – saying that it was their pleasure to send me a pair of heels from their new collection, signed with their handle so that I could tag them on social media. I had screamed so loudly that Mum thought I was being attacked by a pigeon and had come running into my bedroom with a broom to use as a weapon.

My followers were getting higher and higher every day, which encouraged me to post more and more pictures. I had been sent a couple of things before, but just little things, like tea lights and hand cream. I'd never been sent anything like these shoes before and I knew this was the start of something big.

Nina frowns. 'I don't get it. Why would they want a picture of you wearing them?'

I let go of her arm and sigh crossly. Why does she always have to ruin everything?

'Because I have loads of followers who care about what I wear, not that you would know.' I shove my phone into her hand, suddenly feeling irritated by her. 'Take some pictures, will you? We won't get such good lighting in the concert.'

She tucks her book under her arm and holds out the phone awkwardly, pointing it down at my feet.

'What are you doing?'

'Taking pictures of your shoes,' she replies, confused. 'I thought that was what you wanted.'

'I want pictures of me *in* the shoes. Otherwise there's no point in sending them to me, is there? They could just take photos of anyone's feet. Seriously, Nina, it's very simple. Make sure you get some good ones.' I sigh and flick my hair back, putting a hand on my hip.

I scrutinize my photos after she's done and decide that there're one or two in there that I can use.

'I could have done a better job with my camera,' she comments, watching me as I scroll through and patting her bag.

'These are fine,' I say, before picking up two of the bags and gesturing for her to help me carry the rest. 'Let's go in before we miss the start.'

I march towards the doors and show the doorman our tickets, letting him point out our seats where I can see Layla and Sophie next to each other, looking at their phones. They're both wearing the white Chasing Chords T-shirt and I'm very pleased to note that my black version looks way better. As we make our way down the row towards them, Nina gets her foot caught in the handle of someone's bag and knocks a girl's drink all over her.

'I'm so sorry!' she says, as the girl angrily wipes it off her jeans.

'Careful, Nina!' I hiss over my shoulder, relieved that Layla and Sophie are so engrossed in their phones that they didn't see anything.

'There you are,' I say as we reach them, tucking my bags underneath the seats. 'Didn't you get my messages?'

'Sorry,' Layla says, barely looking up. 'I was about to reply.'

Sophie smiles, leaning forward. 'Glad you made it in time. Hi, Nina.'

Nina waves hello awkwardly before leaning back and sliding down in her seat. After everything I'd done for her at the book signing, she could not make it more obvious that she doesn't want to be there. I swivel in my seat so that my back is turned to her.

'So? What do you think of the shoes?' I ask, pointing my feet for them to admire.

'Love them!' Sophie exclaims. 'So cool that they sent those to you!'

'They're nice, but I prefer them in pink,' Layla says, putting her phone down to look at them.

'I can't wait for Chasing Chords to come on,' I say, brushing aside Layla's comment. I know she's just annoyed that she hasn't been sent anything. 'Although I'm more excited for the concert to end.'

'What?' Sophie laughs. 'Why would you want the concert to end?'

'Because of my plan.'

Layla raises her eyebrows at me. 'What plan?'

'I am going to meet Chase Hunter tonight. After the concert.'

Sophie gasps. 'Are you serious? He said he would meet you?'

'Don't be stupid, Sophie. She doesn't know him,' Layla says, rolling her eyes at her before turning to look at me quizzically. 'How are you going to try and meet him?'

'Outside the back door.'

'The stage door is not very original,' Layla says. 'Don't you think everyone else in here will be thinking the same?'

'I didn't say "stage door", Layla.' I lean towards them and lower my voice so only they can hear. 'Everyone else will be waiting by the stage door but I happen to have researched the venue and it turns out the bands don't tend to go out that way. They only go out there to sign things and greet people waiting for them. But there's another door, which they actually use to get to and from their car without being hassled by the press or by screaming fans.'

'Do you really think that's true?' Sophie asks, her eyes twinkling.

'I *know* it's true. Like I said, I've done my research.'

Layla shrugs. 'Whatever, I'm not going to wait around afterwards in the cold.'

Suddenly the lights go down and there's an eruption of screams and applause as spotlights beam on to the stage, lighting up Chase in the centre and the rest of the band around him. I leap to my feet alongside the others, towering over them in my heels, and cheer loudly as the band strike up their first song, one of my favourites.

I quickly reach for my phone and begin filming, making sure that I zoom in on Chase for all the important solo bits.

He is amazing live and I feel a surge of happiness as I realize how lucky I am to have got tickets. I grin at Sophie and Layla as we begin singing along with the rest of the crowd when it reaches the chorus. As the first song comes to an end, the room descends into loud noise as we all scream and stomp in appreciation. Chase thanks everyone for being there and then launches straight into the next song, a new one that they haven't released yet.

I hold my phone up to try and get the best angle for filming, live-streaming it so that everyone who didn't get tickets can enjoy it too. As it goes into a blackout between the end of that song and the beginning of the third, I look around the room in awe at all the hundreds of blinking white lights from phones, twinkling in the darkness.

I'm so engrossed in it all that I forget Nina is even with us, until she leans over to say something in my ear. I can't hear her above the music.

'What?' I cry, careful to keep my phone steady for the video.

'Why do you have to watch the concert through your screen?' she says, pointing at my phone.

'What are you talking about?'

'Just watch the band.' She gestures towards the stage. 'You've filmed every song.'

'Yeah, because I want to share their music and keep the memories safe. And it's proof I was here.'

'You don't need proof. You know you've been here. You're missing so much by watching the entire concert through your phone.' She frowns at Layla and Sophie who are both doing the same, but thankfully can't hear her. 'Music is about enjoying the moment, not about proving to people that you heard it.'

I narrow my eyes at her.

'Thanks for the lecture but I can do what I want. And you know what? You getting that conductor to sign your book –'

'Composer.'

'I don't care!' I snap, making her flinch. 'The point is that you don't need him to sign your book, do you? You could have just met him and said hello, but you wanted him to sign the book so that you could *prove* you met him. Isn't that right?'

She purses her lips.

'Yeah, I thought so,' I huff. 'I know you don't seem to think social media is very important and you like to look down your nose at it all, but I'm actually good at this stuff. I know what I'm doing.'

'It just feels like you're missing out, that's all.'

I look down at my sophisticated new heels and then pointedly glance at her old, scruffy trainers. She follows my gaze and then shuffles her feet, embarrassed.

'Really, Nina?' I smile in self-satisfaction, turning my attention back to filming the band. 'Because from where I'm standing, it looks like you've got that the wrong way round.'

CHAPTER SIX

NINA

I was wrong about Chasing Chords.

All this time I just thought they were a manufactured pop group, dutifully singing songs written for them with no creative bones in their bodies. I know the lead singer Chase has a nice voice – if you live with Nancy, you can't escape his singing blaring through the house thanks to those new speakers Mum got her (she has fully owned up to regretting that decision) – and I know that the band can play their instruments well, just like any other pop group, but I thought that was it. I assumed they were in it for the fame and the money, not for the music. I was wrong.

For the first half of the show, they play all their big hits and everyone in the audience goes crazy, singing along to the lyrics and dancing to the catchy melodies. I try to enjoy it but it's too hot and crowded, and the person next to me is dancing so enthusiastically that I keep having to dodge her arms flinging wildly all over the place.

'Why do you have to watch the concert through your screen?' I ask Nancy, noticing that she's filming every song.

I wish I hadn't said anything. She looks so angry, as though I am trying to tell her what to do. But I'm not. She's been looking forward to this concert for so long that I don't want her to miss out on enjoying the band's performance, just to show off to everyone at school that she'd been to see them. How can she really have fun if she's spending the whole time telling everyone how much fun she's having? It just doesn't make sense to me.

As soon as I see her expression at my comment, I know I've made a mistake.

I've already embarrassed her by spilling that girl's drink at the beginning of the show because I tripped over a bag. The last thing I want is to bring attention to myself, but for some reason my clumsy feet always have other ideas. Nancy NEVER trips over. She's NEVER clumsy. I wish I could be like that.

Instead, I keep embarrassing her in front of her popular friends.

I'm just about to tap her on the shoulder and tell her that I'll go outside and find a cafe to wait for her, when something happens on stage that makes me hesitate.

The vibrant flashing lights change to cover the stage in a simple, natural white, and Chase moves aside so that crew members dressed all in black and wearing headsets can push a piano centre stage, close to the audience.

'I know what's happening,' I hear Nancy announce to Layla and Sophie. 'He's going to play an acoustic song. I know the set list off by heart; there's only a few songs left now.'

Chase sits down at the piano, while his fellow band members sit at the side of the stage, swigging from bottles of water, or go off into the wings.

'This is a song I wrote recently called "Ghosts",' he says into the microphone, and then he brings his hands down to the piano keys and begins to play.

He's good. Really, really good.

I watch him in a trance, amazed at how beautifully he's playing, making it look as though it's no effort at all as he sings, like it's completely natural to him. He looks much more at ease now behind the piano than he was standing up at the front of the stage. He seems much more real somehow.

I tear my gaze away from him and quickly reach into my bag, fumbling about for my camera. I check the settings and the lens, and then zoom in on him, clicking the button quickly, desperate to capture this moment of a musician really connecting with his song.

As soon as the song ends, the room erupts into applause but it's not as frantic and excitable as the response to the band's other songs. He sits back on the piano stool and bows his head, drawing his hands back from the keys to rest in his lap, as though he wishes the song hadn't had to end. It sounds silly: I don't know what it is about him in that moment, but there's something . . . different.

Click.

I check the shot on the screen at the back of my camera. Got it.

Suddenly the crew are on stage again, pushing the piano backwards and clearing the way for the rest of the band to step forward to their microphones, enjoying the screams and whoops from their audience as they move back into position. The lead guitarist announces the song they're about to play, the crowd goes wild, the lights switch to their frenzied flashing mode and Chase flashes a winning smile as he grips the microphone stand waiting for him in the centre, before jumping in the air to the upbeat screech of the next song's first chord.

The moment has passed and everything is back to normal. But I'm glad I caught it, whatever it was.

'Excuse me,' Nancy says, pushing past me on her way out with all her tote bags.

'Wait, where are you going?' I ask, shoving my camera back into my bag.

'There're only three songs left of the set. I need to go and wait for Chase.'

'What? Where?' I say, grabbing her arm in panic. I don't want her to leave me here.

'Don't worry, Nina,' she snaps, shaking me off. 'Just watch the rest of the show and I'll find you later.'

I'm about to ask her exactly where she's going but she's already gone, rushing down the row and disappearing through the doors. Layla and Sophie are swaying along together to the song playing, both filming it on their phones, oblivious to both Nancy leaving and me being left on my own.

Now that the show is drawing to an end, the music seems to be getting louder and the audience is more hysterical. The girl next to me knocks into me so hard mid-dance move that I almost fall over, steadying myself on my seat and causing Layla and Sophie to glance over. Layla smirks and whispers something in Sophie's ear, and they both laugh, watching me.

Why is she here? I bet they're saying. *She is such a loser. How embarrassing that she thinks she's cool enough to come to a concert like this.*

I begin to feel alarmed at how big the crowd is and how, when the concert ends, everyone will be flooding at once through the doors. I'll get caught up in it and I don't know where Nancy is and I have no idea where to go. I feel too hot and my throat is getting tighter and tighter.

I need to get out.

Just as the band announce they're playing their last song, I grab my bag and push my way down the row, ducking my head and elbowing through, to the loud annoyance of everyone I pass, but I don't care. I burst through the doors into the lobby. There are a few people milling about, preparing their merchandise, drinks and snacks stands, ready for the audience to come out. No one pays me any attention.

I begin to panic, knowing that I can't stay here, where everyone is going to pour in any minute, as soon as the song ends. I'll get lost in the crowd. I really need to get some air but, more importantly, I have to find my sister. I try calling her phone but she doesn't pick up. I attempt to steady my breathing, so that I can work out what to do next, but my brain feels fuzzy and it's hard to think straight.

She said she was going to go and meet Chase, which means she must have gone to a stage door somewhere.

I hurry in the opposite direction to the main exit, guessing that the stage doors would be at the back of the building. As I race down the corridor, I have no idea where I'm going, but then I spot some emergency exit double doors that lead to a stairwell.

There's a sudden rush of noise – cheering and stomping – as Chasing Chords finish their last song and exit the stage.

I don't hesitate, opening the doors and hurrying down the steps, my footsteps echoing in the silence off the walls. At the bottom of the stairwell by a door are bits of rubbish and old cigarette butts, which I find strangely comforting because they suggest that this is an emergency exit that doesn't get used a lot. The crowds of people won't be coming this way. I sit on the bottom of the stairs for a couple of minutes, trying to work out what I should do next. Nancy must be outside somewhere; it's no good me sitting in a stairwell all night.

I stand up and push down on the handle bar of the door, emerging into an alleyway. My neck is still damp with sweat from my panic and my ears are ringing. I quickly lean back against the wall and close my eyes, inhaling deeply and telling myself that I'm all right for the moment, that everything is OK now.

'Not hanging around for the encore, then?'

I jump at the voice, turning to see a boy a couple of metres away, sipping from a bottle of water and watching me curiously. I recognize him immediately.

'Were we that bad?' Chase grins, accentuating his chiselled cheekbones, before his expression turns to concern as I have to push my hand against the wall to steady myself. 'Hey, are you OK?'

'S-sorry,' I stammer. 'I just . . . feel a bit dizzy.'

'Here,' he says, rushing over and taking my arm. His hands are warm and strong. 'Sit down. Have some water.'

He lowers me down to sit on the pavement next to him and holds out the water bottle. He's still wearing the same clothes he performed in but he's thrown a hoodie on, zipped up to the top. Up close, his blue eyes are warm and gentle, and he's even better-looking than his framed picture on Nancy's dressing table.

'I can't. It's yours.'

'Trust me, I have a hundred back there.' He laughs, nodding to the building. 'Got to stay hydrated on stage. Drink as much as you like – I promise I don't have any germs.'

'Thanks,' I whisper, taking a sip. 'I'm so sorry . . . This is really, really embarrassing.'

'No, embarrassing is when you faint on stage and as you hit the floor your trousers fall down showing your Batman boxer shorts to the whole audience.'

'That happened to you?' I exclaim.

He nods gravely. 'Oh, yes. I was eight years old but I remember it like it was yesterday. Carly Johnson whistled the Batman theme tune every time I walked past her at school for at least two years after that. I still dream of getting my revenge.'

I can't help but giggle.

'You feeling better?'

'Much better, thanks.' I nod, taking another sip of water.

His conversation is so normal and relaxed that for a moment I forget he's a famous pop star who has hundreds of fans waiting for him inside. I gasp and leap to my feet.

'What's wrong?' he asks, brow furrowed as he stands up.

'You're Chase Hunter!' I cry.

'You've only just realized that? Because, if so, my earlier encore gag must have been lost on you.'

'No, I mean, you can't be out here talking to me. You need to be in there, playing your concert.'

'The concert finished. At least I think it did, otherwise I'm in trouble.' He reaches out to grip my arm. 'I really think you should sit down. You're kind of swaying.'

'I stood up too fast,' I admit, plonking myself down on the pavement.

He sits next to me. 'There's nowhere I have to be, don't worry. I got here just before you did and I'm taking some time out from the madness.'

'Me too,' I say, making him smile. 'You were great, by the way.'

'Thanks. It's always a good sign when you see people bursting through fire escapes just after you've finished a performance.'

'No, that was nothing to do with you! I just hated the noise!'

'What every musician wants to hear.'

Oh my god, why am I insulting a FAMOUS POP STAR??

'I mean, not the noise, I couldn't stand the people!'

He raises his eyebrows.

ARGH, THAT SOUNDS WORSE. SAY SOMETHING NORMAL.

'I like you,' I blurt.

GROUND, SWALLOW ME UP NOW.

I wait for Chase to stand up and walk away, like any normal pop star who is being majorly insulted and creeped out by some random girl on the street would, but instead he does the strangest thing.

He throws his head back and laughs. Like it's the funniest thing in the world.

'I'm so sorry,' I cry, burying my head in my hands. 'This is all coming out wrong.'

'No, it's coming out great!' he says. 'Keep going!'

'What I mean is . . . What I'm trying to say . . . look, can you please stop laughing?'

'Sorry,' he wheezes, before clearing his throat and looking at me with a mock-serious expression. 'You were saying?'

'I meant, this whole concert stuff, it's not really my thing. The crowds and everything; it all made me a bit nervous. But your music is great. I like your *music*,' I add hurriedly. 'That's what I meant by "I like you". You and your band are really good. Does that make sense?'

'That does make sense. In fact, it's not my thing either.'

I blink at him. 'What? But you're –'

'– the lead singer of a famous band. I know.' He shrugs. 'But it's still not my thing. It never was.'

I watch him in silence for a few moments. He's sitting so close that I can see the scattering of freckles across his nose, and his long dark eyelashes.

'I think I actually guessed that about you,' I say eventually.

He looks at me in surprise.

'You seemed different when you played that song on the piano, "Ghosts",' I explain, hoping I don't sound like a weird stalker. 'More into it somehow. I don't know.'

He nods slowly. 'That's my favourite song. I've always loved playing the piano but I don't get to play it as much now in the band. Apparently, those acoustic songs don't really match the band's image.'

'Well, I think it was by far the best song of your set. You were playing it really naturally and the melody reminded me a little of Yiruma's softer songs. Almost soulful in a way. It was nice. You should write more songs like that.' I hesitate. 'You know, if you want.'

'I'll think about it.' He smiles, looking at me strangely. 'You like Yiruma?'

'Of course. What pianist doesn't?'

'So, I'm talking to a fellow musician then?'

My cheeks grow hot and I look down at my feet. 'Not a musician like you. I just play the piano a little.' I pause. 'Well, I guess, a lot really. It's all I'm good at.'

'Me too.'

'That's a lie.' I smile, catching his eye. 'You can play a hundred instruments and you can sing. The only hope I have of getting into Guildhall after school is on the piano.'

'You want to go to Guildhall School of Music and Drama? I've always wanted to go there.'

'Seriously? But you're already so successful,' I point out.

'I don't know. It all happened so fast . . . the YouTube following, the record contract, the concerts,' he lists, his eyes looking forward as though he's still trying to make sense of it all.

'Isn't that what you wanted?'

He opens his mouth to speak and then stops himself, turning to look at me suspiciously.

'Before I say any more . . . you're not a secret teen reporter, are you? Sent by a magazine to trick and lure me into revealing all?'

I laugh and hold up my hands. 'I promise I'm not. This is all off the record. And you don't have to tell me anything if you don't want. We can just sit here.'

'OK then, I'll continue. We're just two people having a deep and meaningful conversation in a creepy London back alleyway,' he says with a lop-sided grin. 'I've always known that I wanted to be a musician, but I still feel I've got so much to learn. And I've always loved writing songs, singing and playing the piano, but now I can't do it for fun. I have to write hit songs, and I can only perform the music the Chasing Chords fans want to hear. All the pressure from management and the label, and these fans going crazy when they don't have a clue who we are as people . . . It's a bit overwhelming.' He hesitates before breaking into a grin. 'I sound like a rambling, pretentious spoilt brat, don't I? I'm so sorry.'

I shake my head. 'No, you don't. That makes sense. Your music is no longer just for you; it's for everyone else. The band, your management team, the fans. That can't be easy.'

'Right. I'm lucky though. Really lucky. I shouldn't complain.'

'You're not complaining,' I assure him. 'You're just talking about it. I wouldn't be able to cope with any of that. I can't even perform to my family, let alone an audience. I can't even work out how I feel when I play.'

'What do you mean?'

'It doesn't matter. It's boring.'

'No, come on,' he encourages. 'I just poured out a load of rubbish to you, a complete stranger. It's only fair you repay the favour.'

Never in a million years did I ever imagine I'd be sitting on a cold, hard pavement talking to Chase Hunter about my problems. *The* Chase Hunter. World-famous, unbelievably good-looking teen musician, Chase Hunter. This just doesn't happen to people like me, who can't handle crowds and who fall over their own feet.

But there's something about Chase. The way he is looking at me makes me feel like he is genuinely interested in what I have to say, even though he must be exhausted from just being on stage, and, except for Jimmy and Mum, NO ONE is ever interested in what I have to say. He is so casual and relaxed, it puts me completely at ease. He's right: we are complete strangers. But it doesn't feel that way. It's just like opening up to an old friend.

And suddenly I find that I have so much to say.

'I'm always happiest playing the piano. But I get complete stage fright at just the idea of performing in front of an audience and if I really want to get a place on the Guildhall summer school, let alone study there after I've finished school, I'm going to have to be able to perform. But I completely freeze and my brain gets all muddled. A little bit like how I felt just then in the crowd of your concert. It feels like I don't belong and I'm getting everything wrong. But when I'm just playing for me, and for no one else, I completely escape into the music and I've never felt happier. It's so weird,' I say with a sigh. 'I don't know how I'm ever going to solve it.'

Chase nods the whole time I'm speaking and then when I finish talking he takes a deep breath.

'Same.'

'Huh?'

'Same,' he repeats. 'I'm the same.'

'I'm sorry – I'm confused. Are you saying that you have a problem performing? Because I just saw you do exactly that and it was like you were born up on that stage, the way you were prancing about.'

'OK, firstly, let's get one thing straight: I do not prance,' he insists, making me laugh. 'Secondly, not everything is what it seems. It may look like I'm comfortable up there but that took time. Like you, I don't really have a choice. After that YouTube video went viral, the band was signed and our audience numbers went from one person – my mum – to hundreds of people. Chasing Chords was just for fun; I had no idea it would become my whole life. I can't let the band down now.'

'So, how did you get over your stage fright?'

'There is a very simple way to getting over it. It's an age-old secret, only known by those in the music business.'

'What is it?' I ask eagerly.

'I can't tell you. Like I said: it's a secret.'

'You're joking.'

'I am. Funny, aren't I? If you are a secret teen reporter, make sure you put that in your tell-all piece. "Incredibly talented and devastatingly handsome Chase Hunter also happens to be a hilarious comedian."'

'I'll make a note,' I say, rolling my eyes. 'So? Are you going to tell me this big secret to stage fright?'

'OK, I'll tell you.'

He leans in to whisper in my ear and a chill runs down my spine as he gets closer.

'Practice,' he says.

I turn my head to look at him and find he hasn't leaned back yet. Our noses are almost touching.

'Practice?' I say quietly, bringing my eyes up to meet his.

'Yeah. That's all it is.'

He's looking at me so intently and we're so close that for a moment I swear he might lean in and kiss me. I feel completely numb and I've stopped breathing.

'THERE HE IS! IT'S CHASE!'

A girl's ecstatic cry echoes down the alleyway and the spell is broken. We instantly break apart and quickly scramble to our feet, Chase holding out his hand to help me up. A group of girls is running full pelt in our direction, all screaming their heads off, all wearing Chasing Chords T-shirts, just like Nancy's.

Oh no. NANCY.

'I have to go,' I say quickly, a wave of guilt hitting me. I don't know how long I've been here and Nancy will have been looking for me. I wrench open my bag and search for my phone, jostling everything else and finally pulling it out from right at the bottom, hidden underneath my Austin Golding book.

'Thanks for everything. It's been . . . amazing meeting you.'

'Wait,' Chase begins, 'how can I –'

But I don't stop to hear the rest of his sentence. I run as fast as I can, away from the screaming girls, round the back of the building, and finally come out on to a main road. I look at my phone and see three missed calls. I quickly call back.

'Nina!' Nancy says, sounding relieved as she picks up. 'Where have you been?!'

'I . . . I got lost.'

'We have to get the last train. Where are you now?'

I read out the name of the road and she comes to meet me, looking relieved to have found me. I'm stunned that she was so worried when I'd been annoying her so much all night. She doesn't even stress when, after a fraught journey involving finding a taxi and running to catch our train, I get to the ticket barriers only to realize that I've lost my purse. Nancy buys me another ticket and we make the train to Norwich with minutes to spare.

'Did you lose your purse in the concert? You can call tomorrow and see.'

I shake my head, racking my brains. Maybe it fell out when I got my camera from my bag in the show? But then I surely would have noticed it on the ground, or Layla and Sophie would have when they went to leave. My bag was closed the whole time I was in the alleyway, except when I got my phone out to call Nancy . . .

But my phone was at the bottom of my bag. And I hurried to get it out, pushing everything else in my bag aside. My purse could easily have fallen out then, without me noticing. That's when I must have lost it.

When I was with Chase.

'Do you know where it might be?' Nina suddenly asks, trying to read my expression.

'No,' I reply hurriedly. 'No idea. Maybe after the concert. When I . . . I was lost. It could be anywhere. Never mind – it's not important.'

'I shouldn't have left you on your own in the concert. I should have known that Layla and Sophie would just go off without you,' she says, looking up at me sincerely.

'No, don't worry. I'm fine. I just got a bit lost and went out through an emergency-exit door. You know what I'm like with directions.' I laugh, trying to brush it all off.

'Well, still . . .' She lets out a long sigh, looking out of the window at the London buildings we're whizzing past. 'It was all for nothing anyway. I didn't even get to meet Chase.'

'Really?' I gulp, pretending to fiddle with my camera.

'I don't know where he went after the show. I was certain he'd be at this door I found out about, but he wasn't. Then I went to the stage door where the rest of the band were taking pictures but he wasn't there either. I wonder where he went. It's so strange that he just disappeared like that. I was so sure I was going to meet him tonight.'

'I'm sorry, Nancy,' I say quietly.

'It's OK, the concert was still amazing.' She shrugs. 'But meeting him would have been a dream come true. Chase and I are meant to be together. I just know it.'

She leans back and closes her eyes, gradually falling asleep. I stare down at my camera screen, admiring the picture of Chase at the piano. I turn the screen off and tuck the camera safely back into my bag, turning to stare out of the window for the rest of the journey.

Tonight may have been a surreal experience, but one thing is definitely for sure.

I can never tell my sister the truth.

CHAPTER SEVEN

NANCY

Chase Hunter @ChaseHunter
A brief encounter yesterday got me thinking. Guys, I need your
help. Anyone know Miss N. Palmer? #FINDTHEGIRL

I rub my eyes. Then I rub them again. I blink several
times. I pinch myself. Hard on the wrist. Then two more
times. It hurts. A lot.

I'm definitely awake.

I look down at my phone and read it again.

Remain calm, Nancy. Just. Remain. Calm.

'AHHHHHHHHHHHHHHHHHHHHHHHHH
HHHHHHHHHHHHHHHHHHHHHHHHHHH
HHH!!!!!'

Mum comes bursting through the door, wearing her
blue dressing gown, her eye mask resting on the top of her
hair which is sticking up wildly in every direction. She
must have just woken up.

'Nancy, what is it?' she cries, rushing over to my bed. 'What's wrong?'

'OHMYGODOHMYGODOHMYGODOH MYGOD!'

Nina suddenly comes through the door, sporting some truly terrible flannel pyjamas with weird birds all over them. If I wasn't so distracted by the best thing that's ever happened to me, I would have instructed her to throw them straight in the bin. But that task would have to wait for another less unbelievable, brilliant, perfect day.

'What's going on?' Nina asks, bleary-eyed. 'I heard screaming.'

'I don't know!' Mum replies, scrutinizing my face and reaching over to put the back of her hand against my forehead to check my temperature. 'She looks as though she's in shock. Was it a nightmare, Nancy? You're OK – it was just a dream.'

'That's the thing,' I say, barely able to breathe. 'I don't think it is a dream. I've checked. And here I am. And here you are. And here Nina is. And here's my phone. It's all real. It's definitely NOT a dream.'

'What is she talking about?' Mum says, looking quizzically at Nina, who shrugs.

'LOOK!' I scream, shoving my phone in Mum's hands before I jump out of bed and dance around my room, continually squealing.

'What is happening?' Nina asks, as I take her hands and swing her round in circles. 'Nancy, stop! You're going to make us dizzy!'

'I already am dizzy! I'm the dizziest, happiest girl on the planet! Nina,' I say, my hands shaking with excitement as I clutch hers, 'he's looking for me!'

'Who's looking for you? What's going on?'

'My plan worked! It genuinely worked! I have no idea how, but it did!'

I skip across the room back to Mum, who's looking at my phone in such confusion that you'd think it was some kind of time-travel device.

'I don't understand all this,' she says, as I take my phone and clutch it to my heart, jumping up and down on the spot. 'What happened at the show, Nina? Did she meet someone? A boy?'

Nina shakes her head. 'I have no idea! I honestly don't know what's wrong with her.'

'There's nothing wrong with me!' I grin, my jaw beginning to ache from so much smiling. 'Everything is right with me. Nina, look! LOOK!'

I hold up my phone and she takes it. She reads the tweet with her forehead furrowed. She gasps.

'See?' I squeal, as she reads it again. 'He's looking for Miss N. Palmer! THAT'S ME!'

'Can someone *please* tell me what is going on?' Mum sighs, leaning back on my bed. 'I have never been so confused in my life and it is not even seven a.m. yet.'

'It's Chase,' Nina says, still staring at my phone, while I open the window and let out a long 'Eeeeeeeeeeeeee!' to the world.

A man walking his dog on the pavement below is so surprised by the sudden burst of noise, he walks straight into a lamp post. I give him a cheery wave as he rubs his head angrily.

'Chase?' Mum asks, her forehead furrowed in confusion. 'What chase? Some kind of police chase? Nancy, I hope you are not involved in any way in a police chase, young lady, otherwise we will be having words.'

'No, not *a* chase. Chase Hunter. The boy. The singer of the band we went to see last night, Chasing Chords,' Nina explains quietly, placing the phone carefully down on my dressing table. 'He's tweeted about a girl he's hoping to find.'

'Not just any girl, Mum,' I add, jumping on to the bed next to her and wrapping my arms around her neck, making her giggle. 'Miss N. Palmer. Do you know what that stands for?'

'I think I've heard that name before . . .'

'MISS NANCY PALMER! THAT'S MY NAME!' I leap off the bed and go to dance around Nina again. 'Chase Hunter is looking for me! I knew this would happen some day!'

'I thought you said you didn't meet him,' Nina mentions, backing into the doorway as I shimmy enthusiastically.

'No, but that's not important! It's FATE.'

'This is a lot of excitement for a Sunday morning.' Mum yawns, stretching her arms out. 'I had better go put the kettle on. I need a cup of tea.'

'Tea? *Tea?* MUM!' I grab my phone and fall backwards on the bed, sprawling out like a starfish next to her. 'How can you think about tea at a time like this?! Chase Hunter of Chasing Chords wants to find me! Look at this hashtag he's created just for me!'

'What on earth is a hashtag? Is it a type of poem?'

'What?! No, it is not a type of poem!' I pass her my phone and point at the screen. 'That's the hashtag: #FINDTHEGIRL. Right there, at the end of his tweet. And it's going viral! Everyone is going to know he's looking for me, Miss N. Palmer. Me, me, *me*!'

I stand up again and dance across the room to the framed picture I have of Chase on my dressing table. I pick it up and give his face a big kiss, leaving a mark on the glass.

'Oh, look and you've replied!' Mum says, still reading my phone. 'You seem to have replied a lot, Nancy. I think you only needed to tell him once that it was you he was after. You've replied dozens of times!'

'What?'

I rush back over to my bed and snatch my phone from her hands, scrolling down from his tweet and reading the replies.

Wait a minute. This can't be happening.

'AHHHHHHHHHHHHHHHHHHHHHHHHHHH HHHHHHHHHHHHHHHHHHHHHHHHHHHH HHH!'

'Nancy!' Nina cries, lifting her hands to cover her ears. 'You're going to wake up the neighbours!'

'I don't care about the neighbours!' I shriek. 'All these girls are pretending to be me! HOW DARE THEY?!'

'I'm lost again,' Mum confesses, slumping back on to my mound of Chasing Chords pillows.

'Look, Nina,' I say, rushing over to her and shoving my phone under her nose. 'Look what they're doing!'

'Wow,' she agrees, scrolling through. 'It would appear that there are a lot of Miss N. Palmers on Twitter. And all of them claim to have met Chase Hunter last night.'

'I suppose Palmer isn't exactly an unusual surname,' Mum reasons. 'When I was younger I did think about legally changing it to Palm-Tree, just to spice it up a little, but your grandfather went berserk when I suggested it.'

'They're obviously lies!' I scream. 'They can't all be called N. Palmer! They're trying to trick him! How could they do that? Some people in this world have NO SHAME!'

'Calm down, Nancy,' Nina says. 'I'm sure he won't believe any of them. He should have known that this would happen.'

Mum laughs. 'It's like a real-life Cinderella!'

'It is NOT funny, Mum,' I huff. 'Everything is a disaster!'

'Oh, I don't think so.' She smiles, pushing herself up off the bed and drifting over to us. She flings out her arms and drapes one round Nina and one round me, squeezing us close to her. 'I think everything is wonderful. A few days ago, you two would hardly speak to each other and you certainly never ventured into each other's rooms. And look at you now, talking to each other as if it's perfectly normal! You see? My cunning plan worked and I see bright things ahead.'

'What cunning plan?' Nina asks. 'I thought Nancy and I going to London together yesterday was a necessity because you had to work. Or was that all a lie?'

'I guess you will never know,' Mum whispers, winking at us and then swanning out of the room. 'I'll go put the kettle on, my darling cherubs!'

'Cherubs?' Nina says, raising her eyebrows at me. 'She truly is loopy.'

'Nina, what do I do?' I beg, clutching her arm. 'If I reply to him now on Twitter, he might think I'm one of the fakers!'

'But if you didn't meet him, how could you –'

'I *know* it's me, Nina. I just know it. Maybe he saw me in the crowd, maybe he's been watching my tweets, maybe he knew I was waiting for him, maybe I bumped into him on the street outside when he was in disguise so he wouldn't be mobbed by crazy fans! I don't know how he came to be looking for me, but I do know that it is fate. It just has to be. Don't you think?'

'I don't know . . .'

'Nina,' I say, taking her hand and leading her over to sit next to me on the bed, 'I know that you don't know him, but I do. I have been in love with Chase Hunter forever. I was the one who introduced his music to our entire school. I am his biggest fan, his most important supporter. Do you really think it's coincidence that the day after I go to his show, he sends out a tweet like this?'

She looks thoughtful. 'What are you going to do?'

'I'm going to devise a plan. And, to do that, I'll need help. I'll text Layla and Sophie to come over as soon as they wake up. Together, we can use all our brain power to work out what my next steps will be.'

'That's a good idea,' she says, before standing up and heading towards the door. 'Well, good luck.'

'What? You're not going to help?'

She stops in the doorway and turns back to face me.

'You . . . you want my help?'

'Obviously! Didn't you hear what I just said? We need to use ALL our brain power. Emphasis on the "all". And, you know, no offence to them, Layla and Sophie are smart but neither of them are a big nerd like you.'

'Thanks. I think.'

'Come on, Nina, I haven't asked you for help in years. And, even when we used to be close, it was mainly me helping you, right? Don't you think you owe me? What about that time I helped you sneak into that posh dinner party Mum's friends next door were holding? Remember?'

'We sneaked into that dinner party because *you* wanted help stealing back that posh box of chocolates Mum brought her hosts as a gift!'

'And didn't I share those posh chocolates with you?'

She sighs. 'I had one or two, yes.'

'There you go!' I nod happily. 'You are welcome! And now I'm calling in a return favour.'

'You're saying this now, but you won't want me around when Layla and Sophie are here,' she says, blushing. 'I'll just say all the wrong things and embarrass you. It's OK – I've got lots of homework to do and piano pieces to practise, anyway. And I should call Jimmy at some point. He'll want to hear about yesterday.'

I think about protesting but I've already tried a lot to persuade her and she's made her answer very clear. So I give up.

'Fine,' I say, lying back on my bed and picking up my phone to message the girls. 'I'll see you later.'

She nods and leaves the room. I just don't get her. No one has *that* much homework. And I heard her playing the piano the other day, and she doesn't need to practise. She's already really good.

It's like she doesn't want to have any friends. And I really could have used her help on this whole Chase thing. I feel a bit deflated about how much she resisted spending the day with me. But THEN I remember that right now Chase Hunter is out there looking for me, and I feel on top of the world again. It's not like Nina and I are friends anyway.

After singing Chase's favourite song, 'Take a Risk', repeatedly in the shower, complete with harmonies, I head downstairs to find that Mum has been out to the shop and bought loads of food for breakfast.

'Wow! Thanks, Mum,' I say, grabbing a croissant and taking a bite. 'Can we save some for Layla and Sophie? They'll be over soon.'

'Layla and Sophie are coming over?'

She glances at Nina, who's reading that conductor's book at the table as she eats her scrambled eggs.

'What?' I ask. 'Is that a problem?'

'No! No, of course not, they're very welcome and they can help themselves to as much food as they like.'

I leave them to it and take my pastry upstairs to my room, so I can start sorting my make-up. I bet that Mum thinks I'm excluding Nina from my group of friends, when really she's the one choosing not to join us. I select my make-up brushes and think about what look I should go for today, just in case the Chase Hunter plan we concoct involves pictures. I apply my foundation and then decide on bright pink lips with simple eye make-up. It's exactly what I was wearing yesterday and I want him to recognize me straight away.

Just as I've started doing my lip liner, the doorbell rings.

'Can someone get that, please!' I call down the stairs. 'I'm in the middle of something!'

I hear footsteps go down the hall and the click of the door coming off the latch and swinging open. There's a pause and then I hear Layla's voice.

'Wow. Nice . . . pyjamas.'

Nina must have got the door. I forgot she was still in those stupid pyjamas and I'm annoyed at myself for not telling her to change before my friends got here. Silly clothes are like catnip to Layla.

'I can't believe this is happening!' Sophie squeals as soon as they burst through the door of my room. She follows Layla up on to the bed, rearranging the Chasing Chords pillows so they can lean back on them.

Layla sits back, catching my eye in the mirror. 'What is your sister wearing? Where did she get those pyjamas?'

'I think they were a gift from Mum.'

'That makes sense. They have similar taste, then?'

'Did you see the tweet?' I ask, eager to steer the conversation away from Nina but also keen to discuss Chase. 'It's amazing, isn't it! What do you think I should do?'

'What do you mean?' Layla asks, looking confused.

'I mean, I can't just tweet him saying it's me, can I? That's what loads of deluded girls have done! I have to do something very different, something very original –' I flick my hair behind my shoulders – 'something very Nancy.'

Sophie giggles. 'You're so funny.'

'I thought you said you didn't actually meet him, though,' Layla says slowly. 'Do you really think he's talking about you in this tweet?'

'Layla, he said "Miss N. Palmer". Of course he's talking about me.'

'It is weird that he said your name,' Sophie enthuses. 'I can't believe you got on his radar! And now he wants to find you!'

'You think he knows about the fan-fiction site?' Layla suggests, finally deciding to be a little more helpful.

'I think it's a combination of the tweets, fan fiction and all-round unconditional support that I have shown him since he started out. He must have seen me in the concert yesterday and put two and two together.' I shrug happily. 'It's fate.'

'I can't believe you're going to date Chase Hunter!' Sophie squeaks, wiggling her feet and receiving a look of irritation from Layla. 'Imagine what's going to happen when you go into school on Monday. I'm so happy I'm your friend!'

I get a flutter of excitement in my stomach as I think about everyone's reaction at school to Chase Hunter tweeting about me.

'Do you think everyone knows?' I ask casually.

'YES!' Sophie shrieks. 'I've already messaged everyone, and we're all talking about it.'

'If he does know it's you from the fan-fiction website, why doesn't he just message you through that?' Layla asks, getting up from the bed to root through my nail varnishes. 'Why tweet about it when he can just contact you directly?'

'That's a good point,' Sophie says thoughtfully. 'He can't have seen the fan fiction, then.'

'What are the chances of there being two Nancy Palmers in the room last night?' I say, growing irritated by Layla's lack of enthusiasm for something so important to me.

Sophie shakes her head and Layla doesn't say anything. She selects purple and blue nail varnish.

'Right. So, it has to be me. Now, how do I get myself in front of him? We have to think of a way.'

'He's in London for the next few weeks,' Sophie points out, as Layla sits down on the floor and rests her hand on the bedside table to start painting her nails. 'Chasing Chords are doing a radio press tour.'

'That's true, so I could try and get access to one of those?'

'But you're not a journalist,' Sophie says slowly.

'No, but I'm a blogger. I could try and get a pass as a blogger!'

'You have a blog?'

'Technically the fan-fiction site is a blog, right?'

'And you've got your Instagram,' Sophie adds excitedly. 'You've got loads of followers! That must mean something!'

'I like your thinking, Sophie. I can just post about going to the Chasing Chords press events and then they'll see those and surely let me in, especially when they see how many followers I have AND how I get sent free products to feature.'

'What free products?' Layla asks, waiting for her nails to dry and starting on the other hand.

'The shoes, remember?' I gesture to where my beautiful heels are neatly placed by the door. 'As soon as I'm face-to-face with Chase, he'll realize who I am and everything will fall perfectly into place.'

'Great plan!' Sophie nods.

'Now that that's sorted, do you think we could get some breakfast?' Layla asks, putting the varnish lid back on.

I spend most of the day hoping that one of them will bring up Chase, so we can talk about him and #FINDTHEGIRL, but Layla hardly mentions it at all and Sophie is so easily distracted that even when we touch upon the subject the conversation keeps going off on a tangent.

When they leave that afternoon I feel a little relieved that they're gone. It means I can go sort out a detailed plan of action and maybe even write some fan fiction. Suddenly I feel very inspired.

'Did you have a nice day with your friends?' Mum calls out as I shut the door.

I go into the sitting room to find her on the sofa, staring at the coffee table, on which is perched one of our large frying pans.

'Yeah, it was great. What exactly are you doing? Why have you put an empty frying pan on the table?'

'Ah! I'm glad you asked!'

Oh, boy. Here we go.

'I've decided to get back into art and one thing I was particularly good at when I was younger was life drawing,' she explains, tapping the sketch pad on her lap with a charcoal pencil.

'Life drawing? Mum! Isn't that drawing . . . naked people?!' I stare at her, horrified.

'My art tutor always said I had a knack for capturing the human form. So, I decided that to ease myself back into my talents I should start with objects. Hence, the frying pan.'

'Let me get this straight,' I begin, leaning on the door frame. 'You're going to draw that frying pan and then you're going to go and draw a load of naked people?'

'Let's see how we go with this pan, Nancy,' she says with a flourish of her pencil. 'We don't want to get ahead of ourselves.'

I wish her luck and then bolt up the stairs, wondering whether Mum was always this weird or whether it has something to do with the countryside air. I stop at my door, overhearing the music coming from Nina's room.

I smile to myself, before creeping up to her door, resting my hand on the handle, waiting for the perfect moment and then I suddenly burst through, letting it knock into the wall, which sends Nina jumping into the air in shock.

'AHA!' I cry, hands on my hips in a Peter-Pan-style stance.

'Nancy!' she yells from behind her keyboard. 'You scared me!'

'I just heard you playing!'

'So?'

'So! You were playing Chasing Chords! That was "Ghosts"!'

Her cheeks redden. 'And? I was just messing around.'

'Admit it!' I grin, crossing my arms. 'You, Nina, the great musician with her superior classical music taste, have fallen in love with Chase.'

'What?' she cries, suddenly standing up. 'I'm not in love with him!'

'His music, whatever. You can't fool me, Nina, I heard you playing it and you wouldn't be playing it if you didn't like it. All this time you've been saying that it's not real music; it doesn't have violins and yellow-shirt conductors, blah blah blah. Admit you were wrong.'

'Fine,' she says, breaking into a smile. 'It's not bad.'

'And?'

'And what!'

'Feel free to thank me for introducing you to the awesomeness that is Chasing Chords.'

She laughs. 'Fine. Thank you, Nancy, for introducing me to Chasing Chords' music.'

'You are welcome. That's another favour you owe me then.'

'I'll add it to the list, behind the posh chocolates.'

'By the way, Mum is drawing a frying pan downstairs.'

'Yeah, I know,' she says. 'Weird.'

I turn to leave, eager to start sorting out my #FINDTHEGIRL plan.

'Wait,' she says, 'I have something for you.'

She moves out from behind her keyboard and shuffles over to her desk, picking up a piece of paper and holding it out for me. It looks like a weird list of names in her scrawled handwriting.

'What is this?' I ask, examining it.

'It's a list of songs I thought you might like,' she explains shyly. 'Now that I've listened to Chasing Chords, I figured it was only fair that you experience some Austin Golding. Who, as you very well know, is a *composer*. Not a conductor. Those are the songs I think you'll like. You can download them or they're on YouTube. My favourite is the top one. See what you think.'

I fold up the piece of paper. 'Thanks, Nina. I'll check these out. That's really . . . cool of you.'

'It's nothing.'

We share a smile and I head to my room. Just as I get to my bedroom door, a voice comes out of nowhere.

'You see?'

'*Mum!*' I yell, turning to see her standing smugly on the stairs with her arms folded. 'Stop *doing* that.'

'It's all going to plan.' She grins, tapping the side of her head. 'A very cunning plan.'

CHAPTER EIGHT

NINA

For a moment, I think about telling her.

But how can I when she's so excited?! Ever since Chase started his #FINDTHEGIRL mission, she hasn't walked anywhere – she's DANCED. She dances around the kitchen to get the plates out for dinner, she dances up and down the bathroom while brushing her teeth, and I can hear her dancing around her room to all of the Chasing Chords tracks. She's the happiest I've ever seen her. I can't be the one to take that away from her. I just can't.

Especially now that we're starting to get on.

It's weird; I always thought I didn't want to be friends with Nancy. Of course I missed how we used to be and, when I really thought about it, I'd get a little sad at how much we'd grown apart. But I always figured it was really for the best because we are so different, and what's the point of forcing a friendship, just because we're sisters?

But, now, just from having to spend some time with her, I realize I haven't missed how we used to be – I've been missing *her*. She may have different tastes in . . . well . . . everything, but she has something about her that is bright and fun. She makes me want to be bright and fun, like her.

And, I'm not sure, but I think she's starting to like me again too.

On Monday morning, when we get to school, Jimmy is waiting for me at the gates. He waves as I get out of the car, and I start walking towards him when I notice something weird. Everybody is looking at me. And I mean, EVERYBODY.

Students hanging around the steps or by the gate stop talking and turn to look in my direction and there's a ripple of excited whispers.

'What's going on?' I ask Jimmy, approaching him nervously. 'Why is everyone looking at me? Do I have something on my face? What's happening?'

Jimmy laughs. 'I think it may just have something to do with the #FINDTHEGIRL thing.'

'What?' My throat and stomach tighten in fear. 'That's got nothing to do with me!'

'Yeah, I know,' Jimmy replies, looking at me strangely. 'They're not looking at you. They're looking at Nancy.'

He nods at Nancy, who is right behind me, flicking her hair behind her shoulders and flashing everyone a pearly white smile. I breathe a sigh of relief.

'Are you OK?' Jimmy asks. 'You've gone really pale.'

'I'm fine,' I say, hurriedly.

Nancy taps me on the shoulder. 'I'm going to go find the girls. See you later, Nina.'

Jimmy's jaw drops to the floor as Nancy flounces off.

'Sorry,' he says in disbelief. 'I think I just hallucinated. Did Nancy just say she would "see you later"?'

'Yeah, we live in the same house, remember?'

'Nina, she never speaks to you. Ever. Especially not at school.' He grabs my shoulders and looks me straight in the eye. 'What's happened? Are you sick? Are you dying?'

'What?' I laugh. 'No! Why would you ask that?'

'Maybe because your twin sister who, for the last however many years, has acted as though she's so much better than you and made it clear she doesn't like being anywhere near you, just spoke to you as though you were . . . a person.'

'I wouldn't look into it too much, Jimmy,' I say with a smile, linking my arm through his and leading him up the steps into school. 'Come on, we'll be late for registration.'

'Did you bring in the Austin Golding book?'

I nod and reach into my bag to pull it out. 'Here. How was the rest of your weekend?'

'This is so cool,' he says, reading Austin's note and passing the book back to me. 'My weekend was good. Dad persuaded me to start a book club with him.'

'A book club?' I laugh.

'Yep!' He smiles. 'We're going through the Man Booker Prize shortlist. Do you want to join? It would bring our number of members up to a grand total of three.'

Even though I have the most amazing mum in the world, I've always been a little envious of Jimmy's relationship with his dad. Jimmy got his love of all things books from his dad, who's a big culture buff and is always taking him to the latest exhibitions in Norwich and sometimes London. Jimmy's mum teases them both about how often they have their noses stuck in a book, but you can tell she's really proud that Jimmy takes after his dad like that. They even look the same, with their untameable dark, curly hair, bold eyebrows and a constantly pensive expression.

Apart from the occasional Christmas card, my dad seems to pretend Nancy and I don't exist.

'I would love to but I think I would get behind on the reading list,' I admit. 'I'm busy with a lot of piano practice.'

'And your family's new-found celebrity status.'

'What celebrity status?'

Jimmy stops at the doorway to my form room and gestures to where Nancy is sitting at the back. She is perched on the edge of her desk, surrounded by the entire class, who are all eagerly asking her questions and squealing loudly at her answers.

'It's like some kind of bizarre press conference.' Jimmy chuckles, watching as she selects the next person to offer a question. 'She must be loving this attention. Do you really think it's her that Chase is looking for?'

'Why wouldn't it be?' I reply, swallowing the lump building in my throat.

'On the phone yesterday you said she didn't meet him. Seems odd that he'd send out a tweet like that about her if she didn't.'

'I don't know. Fate? That's what she keeps saying.'

He snorts. 'Well, whatever happened, I think it's safe to say things are going to be a bit different around here now.'

'In what way?'

'Because if it really is her, then you should prepare for a load of crazy to come your way. The press has gone wild about the #FINDTHEGIRL campaign. I know you don't do social media, but you might want to have a little look online at how much attention Chase is getting about the whole thing. It has gone viral; everyone is talking about it. Once they find out that Nancy is the girl, then the spotlight is coming her way.' He glances back at Nancy, who is busy listing the reasons why she and Chase are perfect for each other. 'For someone like Nancy, this is a fairy tale come true.'

By the end of the day, I know that Jimmy is right. Everyone is talking about it, including the teachers, and we even spot Nancy signing an autograph for a Year Seven student at lunch. Wherever she goes, she's followed by adoring fans constantly asking her how she's going to tell Chase that she's the one, and every time she walks into a room it descends into whispers. On my way to the music room, I get accosted by a group of girls a few years below asking me what Chase is like and whether I'll be moving away to be with him.

'I'm Nina,' I squeak, backing away from them. 'Wrong twin.'

When we get home from school that evening, I run up the stairs and shut myself in my room, sitting down at my desk, trying to process everything. I pick up my phone and type #FINDTHEGIRL into the search engine. Instantly, hundreds of results come up, from national newspapers to celebrity gossip sites to every social media platform, most of which I've never even heard of. I have no idea how to really work any kind of social media, so I click on the top result, a celebrity gossip column that went live yesterday evening:

Hunter is on the hunt: pop star launches global search for mystery girl!

Chase Hunter, lead singer of YouTube sensation Chasing Chords, has launched an online campaign in a desperate attempt to find a girl who apparently 'got him thinking'. The pop star sent out a tweet Sunday morning, asking his millions of followers to help him find a Miss N. Palmer, which quickly went viral, and he has since been inundated with replies from girls claiming to be The One. It is believed that Chase met the lucky girl after the Chasing Chords London gig on Saturday night and, according to a source close to the band, although he didn't catch her first name, Chase has been besotted ever since. 'He won't stop talking about his mystery girl,' reports our source. 'He has never met anyone like her before and he's determined to track her down. Although she hasn't reached out to him yet, he won't be giving up any time soon.' All we have left to say is . . . good luck with the Chase!

I read to the end of the story and immediately turn my screen off, sliding my phone away from me across the desk. I feel sick with nerves at all the attention and am very grateful that no one has any idea about the truth. I don't want to be any part of this.

The thing is, when I think about how lucky it is that no one will ever find out it's me, I also get a sharp, painful pang. Because that means Chase will never find out either.

I still can't believe he started #FINDTHEGIRL just for me. When Nancy first showed me the tweet, I was completely in shock. *How did he know my surname?* But then I remembered that my bank card was in my purse. He must have picked it up when it fell out of my bag.

I sit at my desk, biting my nails and thinking about the news story. Did he really say those things about me? That he's never met anyone like me before? That he's not going to give up until he tracks me down?

I know gossip websites make things up all the time, and what kind of friend close to Chase would listen to him talk about how he feels, and then immediately get on the phone to a journalist so they can report it? And anyway I'm not entirely sure it's even *me* he's talking about. He could have been chatting to one of those girls who ran up to him after I left, and maybe he thinks the purse belongs to her.

BUT if it is true and if he is talking about me and if he really did say that he'd never met someone like me before . . .

Well, I wish I could tell him . . . likewise.

My door swings open and Nancy marches in, interrupting my thoughts. She seems to have forgotten how to knock.

'Hey, what are you up to?' she asks, plonking herself down on my bed.

'Homework.'

She raises her eyebrows. 'Yeah, I can see you're getting a lot done with nothing on your desk.'

'I was just about to start,' I say, quickly grabbing the nearest textbook and opening it on a random page.

'Whatever. I just thought we should chat about how crazy school was today.'

I nod.

'My throat feels hoarse from all the talking I've been doing,' she continues dreamily. 'Everyone is so excited about me and Chase. I can't wait to finally see him.'

'You've worked out a way to meet him?'

'Yes and it is, if I say so myself, totally genius. He's doing a radio press tour in London and I'm going to go meet him at an event. There's one this coming weekend, so I'm off to

London again. I wonder what I should wear. I should start planning my outfit ASAP.'

'Don't you have to get a ticket or something?' I say, trying to keep the sense of panic out of my voice.

'It's for press members only so I'm going to be attending as a blogger.'

'A blogger? What's that?'

'Oh, Nina, you are so funny.' She laughs. 'I have a website for all my stories about Chasing Chords. Technically, it's a blog, so I'm sure they'll let me in on that.'

'What do you mean, stories about Chasing Chords? Like, news stories?'

'This is so typical,' she grumbles. 'Everyone worships my Chasing Chords fan-fiction site EXCEPT my sister who doesn't even know it exists. Come on, I'll show you. You can do your homework later.'

I follow her to her bedroom and she pats the space on the bed next to her, getting out her laptop and resting it on the duvet. As she loads the site, I look around her room. Every time I come in here, I think this is what it must be like to sit inside a marshmallow.

'Here!' She slides the laptop towards me and watches for my reaction. 'What do you think?'

Across the top of the website, it reads 'CHASING CHORDS FAN FICTION' in bright blue font and below that is a picture of the band, then an 'About the Author' bit with a photo of Nancy, followed by a long list of story titles, each one with a small blurb underneath. I scan through the top few titles: 'Breaking My Heart', 'Centre Stage', 'For a Song', 'Friend or Foe'.

'Nancy,' I say, scrolling through in confusion, 'what on earth is this?'

'I told you. It's fan fiction. I've been writing short stories about Chasing Chords for ages. They're all completely different situations. And most of them are about Chase, although I do try and give the other boys some screen time. Their stories just never seem to turn out as well, and my stories about Chase are always the most popular ones. See, look at how many clicks this story "Word for Word" has got. It's set in New York and, while he's on tour there with his band, Chase finds this diary in an old, second-hand bookshop. He starts reading the diary and gradually falls in love with its writer, but he has no idea who or where she is, so he makes it his mission to find her.' She grins. 'It's almost the same as real life!'

I tear my eyes away from the screen to blink up at her. 'You wrote all these?'

She nods. 'Yeah. Sophie and Layla are supposed to contribute stories too, but they never do.'

'But there're so many.' I shake my head, clicking on to the latest one. 'When did you write all this?'

'When do you think? Evenings, weekends. Whenever I have a bit of spare time and the inspiration hits me. Sometimes it's the middle of the night. Whenever I think of a story idea, I try to imagine it as a big Disney movie starring me and Chase – and maybe Zac Efron can do a cameo too, for a love triangle or something – and if I think it would make a good film, then I know I'm on to a good story.'

'I can't believe you spend your time writing stuff like this.'

'Because you think I'm not very clever?'

'What? Nancy, no!' I put my hand on her arm. 'I think you're very clever. You've always been clever. I just thought that you only spent your time hanging out with all your friends. I had no idea you were so passionate about writing.'

'I'm not passionate about writing; I'm passionate about Chase,' she corrects, and I feel a stab in my stomach for lying to her. 'I think he may have read some of these stories and that's why he wants to find me. So, do you want to read one?'

'Am I allowed to?'

'Sure!' She beams, hopping off the bed. 'I'll go and get us some snacks. Do you like popcorn?' She hesitates. 'I should probably know that about you.'

'I do like popcorn,' I say. 'Mum bought some of those microwavable bags.'

'I know. She bought them for me.'

'I thought she bought them for *me*.'

Nancy laughs and skips down the stairs. I sit silently on her bed, reading 'Word for Word' and, although at first

I find it hard to get my head round the fact she's writing fiction about a real person she's never met, soon I'm completely lost in the story. I don't even hear her coming back in the room.

'Do you like it?' she asks, carefully putting the bowl of popcorn on the duvet between us.

'I love it!' I look up at her. 'Nancy, this is really good.'

'You can read more if you like. Here, this is one of my favourites,' she says, eagerly leaning over to click on the link to another story. 'Chase finds a haunted house. I wrote it on last Halloween and completely freaked myself out.'

We spend the rest of the evening trawling through Nancy's fan fiction and stuffing ourselves with popcorn, while Nancy provides commentary on each story as we go. As I climb into bed, I realize that we didn't bicker once the whole evening.

'All right, I've been patient all week,' Jimmy announces on Friday afternoon, finding me at my locker at the end of school. 'It's time to come clean.'

I think he's talking about #FINDTHEGIRL and I drop all my books in panic.

'Come clean?' I squeak, crouching down hurriedly to pick them up.

'Yes. What is going on with you and Nancy? Something's changed between you two.'

PHEW. I stand up, breathing a sigh of relief.

'Don't try and deny it,' he continues. 'I've been a first-hand witness to such events as Nancy saying she will "see you later" in the mornings; I've overheard her asking you if you favoured salt over sweet popcorn – obviously sweet, who has salty? – and what do I hear this morning, you ask? Well, let me tell you. My dear pal, Jessica Hawks, telling someone in class that apparently Nina Palmer can play Chasing Chords songs really well on the piano. Do you want to know who told her? Miss Nancy Palmer, of course.'

He leans on the lockers and watches me expectantly.

'Out with it,' he instructs.

'We're just getting on a bit better, I guess. It's nice.'

'But how did this happen?' he asks curiously. 'Don't get me wrong; I think it's good that you can be in the same room without constantly rolling your eyes at each other. It has to be very relaxing for your eyeballs these days.'

I burst out laughing.

'But seriously, Nina, did something happen that day in London? Because ever since the weekend, things have changed.'

'I think we've just started seeing things from each other's point of view,' I suggest. 'That's all.'

'Hey!'

Jimmy spins round to see Nancy approaching us, carefully holding three tubs of ice cream.

'They've just brought out loads of ice cream in the canteen as a Friday treat. You two want some?'

Jimmy stares at her. 'You . . . huh?'

'Here, can you take them? They're getting difficult to balance.'

Jimmy quickly takes two of the ice-cream tubs from her. 'Thanks, Nancy.' I smile warmly.

'No worries.' She digs into her tub with the plastic spoon and then pauses to nod at the stack of books I'm holding from my locker. 'I've been enjoying studying *Jane Eyre*, have you? You like classic books, don't you, Jimmy?'

Jimmy is so stunned that he can't seem to speak, so he just nods.

'Jane Eyre is so cool,' Nancy continues. 'I love how she doesn't let anyone mess with her. She sticks to her principles and she's very caring, even though she has a rubbish childhood. I've been doing some reading on the author Charlotte Brontë and apparently –'

'Nancy, what are you doing?' Layla's voice makes Nancy jump.

'Hey, there you are!' she replies, looking flustered as Sophie and Layla walk over towards us. 'Did you see that they were giving out ice cream in the canteen?'

'Yeah!' Layla snorts. 'But it looks gross.'

Nancy lowers her ice-cream tub as though ashamed of enjoying it.

'So, are you coming with us?' Layla asks Nancy, folding her arms before her eyes flicker disapprovingly towards me. 'Or are you busy?'

'We're having a film night with Mum,' I explain, jostling the books in my arms and putting them away in my locker. 'It was Nancy's idea. I'm sure that if you wanted to join, you cou–'

'Actually, Nina,' Nancy interrupts, her cheeks growing pink under her flawless foundation, 'I'm going over to Layla's tonight.'

'We're having a Disney marathon,' Sophie adds, clapping her hands together.

'Oh! Right. Cool.'

There's a long silence as I wait for Nancy to say something. Maybe even invite me to join them. But she doesn't say anything.

'Have fun at the movie night with your mum, though!' Layla smirks, twirling a lock of her hair round her fingers.

'Oh, no, if you're not home, Nancy, I'll head out. I've been meaning to go to the record store anyway.'

'Record store?' Layla raises her eyebrows as Nancy shifts uncomfortably next to her. 'Aren't they just dusty places for old people? Do they even still exist?'

'The one in our village is actually very famous for its collection of vinyl and when it almost closed down there was this huge petition that –'

'I'll see you at home, Nina,' Nancy interrupts sharply. Layla stifles a giggle.

'Right.' I nod, getting the picture. 'Come on, Jimmy.'

I turn on my heel and quickly race down the corridor, Jimmy rushing to keep up with me.

'Are you OK?' he asks, shooting me a sympathetic look as I text Mum to let her know I'm heading out for the evening.

'Of course.' I shrug. 'Why wouldn't I be?'

'It's just . . . Nancy was –'

'Obviously, we were wrong about Nancy and me being in a better place. But it doesn't matter. Anyway, I'll call you later.'

I hurry away from him, through the school gates and down the road towards the bus stop, anxious to get to the calm of the record store.

I had no idea what was about to happen.

CHAPTER NINE

NANCY

I can't stop thinking about Nina and that look she had on her face.

There's no real reason why I should feel guilty. It's not like I did anything wrong.

Yeah, OK, so I probably shouldn't have said to Layla that I'd come round to hers when I'd already planned a movie night with Mum and Nina. But, in my defence, it's REALLY hard to say no to Layla and what was I supposed to say? 'Sorry I can't come; I'm hanging out with Nina this evening'?! She would think I'd lost the plot. I saw the way they looked at Nina when they saw me talking to her and Jimmy at the lockers. I couldn't bear for them to look at me like that.

But those stupid puppy-dog eyes of Nina's were burning into my brain. Surely she can't care *that* much about missing a movie night with me? A few days ago she hated even being in the same room as me, so changing plans can't have been too disappointing.

And WHY did she have to ramble on about that stupid record store?! This is the thing with Nina: she's never been good at reading situations. Mum always says, plonk me in any room with anyone and I'll be just fine. I work out the vibe and then I fit in comfortably, no matter what (except maybe if I was in a room of diehard comic-book weirdos – or pigeons). I'm basically a chameleon, you know, those lizards that blend in with their background.

Nina, on the other hand, can't read the vibe of a room AT ALL. There she was standing in front of Layla and Sophie, talking about vinyl. VINYL. Layla couldn't stop sniggering and do you know what Sophie said after Nina walked off? She said, 'Isn't vinyl some kind of nasal spray? *Ew.*' That's how irrelevant vinyl is to the world these days! Sophie thought it was a brand of NASAL SPRAY.

Although, to be fair, Sophie also thought Jane Austen and Jane Eyre were the same person.

But still, it was obvious that her audience wasn't exactly on board, so I don't know why Nina thought it was a good idea to go on about that dusty old record store. I had to cut her off. If I'd let her go into detail about it, Layla would have made fun of her FOREVER.

And I don't want that. I don't want anyone making fun of Nina. Except maybe me, you know, when she wears those stupid pyjamas and stuff. But that's allowed, because I'm her twin.

It's been a long time since I've felt protective over Nina. But, at the moment, I do.

'I can't believe your sister is spending her Friday night at a record store,' Layla says, as we get to the school gates and stop to wait for her mum to pick us up. 'She is so sad.'

A group of giggling girls in the year below us stop to wave at me and I happily wave back. Even though I haven't managed to see Chase yet, my #FINDTHEGIRL fame at school is still going strong.

'Does Nina have a record player?' Layla asks.

I shrug. 'She must do, I guess. But she has records up on her wall too, so maybe she's getting them for that.'

As soon as the words are out of my mouth, I regret them. Layla's expression lights up as though I've just given her plenty of ammo for a future attack.

'She has records up *on her wall*?' she echoes, a Cheshire-cat grin spreading across her face.

'Yeah, it's quite cool actually,' I reply quickly. 'Some of them are signed. She's going for a vintage look, I guess.'

'It doesn't sound cool to me,' Layla says, folding her arms and raising her eyebrows at me. 'It sounds weird. Why would anyone stick a load of old, dusty records on their wall?'

My phone beeps loudly in my bag and I reach to get it, pleased for an excuse to move the subject away from Nina's odd decorating habit.

'It's Chase!'

'WHAT?' Sophie screams. 'HE'S MESSAGED YOU?!'

'No, no,' I say, reading my phone. 'I get notified any time he or the band tweet.'

'I think I just had a minor heart attack,' Sophie wheezes, leaning on Layla's shoulder. 'I really thought he'd just messaged you.'

'Why would he be messaging her?' Layla sighs, shaking her off grumpily. 'He doesn't *know* her. Anyway, what film shall we start with tonight? And I think we should start talking about the school talent show this year and what we're going to do.'

'I saw this really cool thing on TV last week,' Sophie says enthusiastically. 'This guy was plate spinning! Maybe we should do something along those lines.'

While Layla tells Sophie how stupid her idea is, I read the Chasing Chords tweet over and over again. My heart begins beating really fast.

Chasing Chords @realchasingchords

Excited to be here in Norwich tonight, what a cool city! Gonna go see some sights xx

Norwich. NORWICH. Why would they be in Norwich? Oh my god.

He found me.

Yes, I don't exactly live in Norwich, but I live VERY close to it. And I know their schedule off by heart, and they're meant to be in London for the next few weeks. Not Norwich. So why would they come to the city all of a sudden? WHY? It has to be because Chase has realized that this is where I live. It has to be because of his #FINDTHEGIRL mission. He could have seen all those tweets I sent him and worked out that I'm just two hours from London. And then he got on a train . . .

Butterflies are flitting madly in my stomach and I realize that I've stopped breathing.

'Nancy, are you OK? You've gone super pale,' Sophie says, furrowing her eyebrows at me.

'Actually,' I whisper, my heart thudding against my chest, 'I don't think I am OK.'

'What's wrong?'

'I . . . I don't feel so good,' I say, quickly coming up with a plan. 'I think I might be sick.'

Layla takes a quick step back from me.

'I don't think I should come tonight,' I say, clutching my stomach as convincingly as possible. 'Just to be safe.'

'Good idea.' Layla nods vigorously, as her mum's car pulls up along the road.

'You guys go ahead. I'll call Mum and get her to come pick me up.'

'Are you sure?' Sophie says, worried. 'Do you want us to wait with you?'

'No, don't worry. Mum will be here in a minute.'

Sophie tells me to get better soon and then the two of them scurry off towards Layla's mum's car. I wait for them to drive off and turn the corner, before jumping up and down on the spot ecstatically.

Chase has come to find me and he is SO CLOSE. I can't believe we're finally going to come face-to-face.

I fumble with my phone, my hands shaking with excitement, and go on to my maps, working out the best way of getting to Norwich from the school. Easy. There's a bus that goes straight there from down the road. I run to the bus stop and wait, praying that one will come along soon. Chasing Chords might only be in the city for one night. This might be my only chance.

FINALLY a bus trundles towards me (OK, so I was waiting two minutes max but it felt like FOREVER) and I sit down, nervously checking my make-up in my compact mirror. I'm annoyed that the first time Chase sees me I'm going to be in my school uniform, but I can't do anything about that now. I didn't exactly have the time to go home and change.

I tap my nails on my knees impatiently as we head towards Norwich, wondering why this bus has to pull over every THREE SECONDS to let people on. And some of them really take their time getting on, fishing around in their bags for their bus pass or some change. What is wrong with them?! Don't these people have any sense of urgency?!

Nancy

HELLO! I want to yell. KEEP MOVING. I'M ON MY WAY TO MEET THE LOVE OF MY LIFE.

I'm pleased at least that Layla and Sophie aren't here. I could have told them about the tweet, and they might even see it themselves later, but they would have slowed me down and I didn't fancy an entire journey of Layla's doubting, snide comments. If I was going to catch Chase's eye, I had to be at my most confident and that's not going to happen with Layla telling me that the whole #FINDTHEGIRL situation seems impossible.

I check on Twitter and see that someone has just posted a selfie with the band in The Ashby hotel.

'That must be where they're staying!' I cry loudly, making the old lady next to me jump. I turn to her and point at my phone because there's no one else to show it to and I'm SO EXCITED I MIGHT BURST.

'LOOK!! I've just worked out where Chase is staying.'

'Who?' she mutters, looking at me weirdly.

'Chase!! The love of my life! You see, we've been looking for each other and I've just found out which hotel he's staying in. That's why I'm going to Norwich.'

'Oh!' She blinks at me. 'How . . . nice.'

'It is nice, isn't it! You see, we've never actually met before . . .'

And, once I'm off, I can't stop, pouring out my heart to this random old lady sitting next to me on the bus so that when we reach the last stop in Norwich city centre, she

139

knows my entire life story and I know that her name is Rose, that she has four grandchildren and that she's been having trouble with her back recently, but the physio says she'll be just fine if she keeps up her strict morning exercises.

'Good luck with that dishy Chase!' Rose smiles as we get off the bus. 'He reminds me of a young James Dean.'

'Don't forget those morning leg extensions!' I reply, waving back to her as I follow my map towards the hotel.

The Ashby is one of the poshest hotels I've ever seen, with all these large imposing columns and a big arch over the doorway. A group of reporters are outside, chatting and holding their cameras in wait. Clearly I wasn't the only one who saw that Chase was at the hotel. I dodge around them and suddenly feel very self-conscious when the porter tips his hat at me and opens the door into the reception.

It suddenly occurs to me that I hadn't planned what I'd do once I actually got to the hotel.

I was going to have to wing it. I stride up to reception confidently.

'Can I help you?' The lady behind the desk smiles.

'Yes, you may. I'm here to see Chase Hunter.'

'Chase Hunter?'

'Yes, that's right.' I nod, flicking my hair back. 'He's staying at this hotel. Could you give his room a call and say Miss N. Palmer is here to see him? He'll know what it's about.'

Her expression changes quickly from polite to stern.

'I'm afraid you're mistaken. Mr Hunter isn't here.'

'Yes, he is. And I need you to call his room and tell him that I'm waiting for him. He's expecting me!'

'I'm sorry, miss, but I can't do that. If you could kindly leave the hotel . . .'

'Excuse me, but I am Miss N. Palmer!' I huff, crossing my arms stubbornly. 'And Mr Chase Hunter, one of your guests, is expecting me. I don't appreciate being spoken to like some kind of silly school student!'

I hesitate as her eyes flicker to my uniform.

'OK, yes, I am a school student, but I'm not a silly one. And Chase is going to be VERY cross when I tell him that –'

'Excuse me, miss.'

I look up to see the porter has now come inside the reception and is gesturing towards the door.

'Let me help you out. Thank you for your visit today.'

'This is ridiculous!' I cry, causing everyone to look at me.

'Kindly keep your voice down, miss,' he says in a strained voice, 'and we can discuss this outside . . .'

'I'm not going to discuss this outside. I'm going to discuss this right here, right now!' I shout, stabbing at the reception desk with my finger as though I'm in some kind of dramatic court scene in a movie. 'This is OUTRAGEOUS! I demand that you call Chase Hunter and tell him to come down right this instant!'

A thought does fleetingly cross my mind that I should probably stop yelling in the middle of the hotel and just leave, but I'm too invested in the act now to bring it to a halt, so I decide to just go with it.

What's the worst that can happen?

'Miss, if you refuse to leave the hotel, I'm going to have to call the police,' the reception lady hisses through gritted teeth, before attempting to smile reassuringly at the other guests in reception who are staring at me.

OK, prison would be quite bad.

'FINE!' I yell. 'I'll leave, but you should know that Chase is going to be livid!'

I turn on my heel, scowl pointedly at the porter and march right on out of there, chin held high. The paparazzi all glance up hopefully as I push open the hotel door but when they see me they all glumly look back down again.

I run round the corner of the building and crumple into a heap on the pavement, leaning back against the wall. If only I had a change of clothes. I should have known they would never believe someone who has clearly just come straight from school.

Well, I'm not giving up that easily. I'll have to stay here for when Chase leaves the hotel or comes back to it. Either way, I'll be ready, waiting.

I get out my phone to scroll social media while I wait and then groan when I see how low my battery is. Typical. I let out a big sigh and wrinkle my nose as I glance up and down this side road at the big bins all around me. What am I doing here? This is ridiculous. I should wait out front with the reporters.

Just as I'm about to stand up, a door next to me swings open and bashes into my arm.

'OW!' I cry, falling back on to my bum.

'I'm so sorry! Are you OK?'

'NO. What were you –'

I stop when I look up into the dark brown eyes of Miles, the Chasing Chords drummer.

'I didn't see you there,' he says, offering me his hand to pull me to my feet. I stare at him, my jaw dropping to the floor. 'I wasn't expecting anyone to be crouched by the bins.'

'I . . . uh . . .' I shake my head, completely star-struck.

Obviously Miles is no Chase, BUT he is still in the best band in the world and, because he's the drummer, his arms are all muscly. Even though everyone knows he's really hot, he's even better-looking in person with his dark, mysterious eyes and thick dark hair. I can't believe he's here in front of me, a real person.

'You're . . . you're . . . Miles,' I manage to croak.

'Yeah. Look, are you OK? Because I'm kind of in a rush.' He glances nervously behind me. 'The press has been swarming the hotel for hours and I don't want them to see me sneak off.'

'Right . . .' I nod slowly. 'Right.'

'OK then, glad you're all right. Sorry about nearly taking you out with the door. Have a great day!' He winks, puts on a pair of sunglasses, pulls up his hood and then begins to walk quickly away from me in the opposite direction to the main road.

I stand there staring at him for a few seconds and then it's like my brain suddenly kicks into gear again. *It's Miles. From Chasing Chords. He'll know where Chase is.*

'Wait!' I cry out, my voice echoing down the side street as I run to catch up, falling into step alongside him.

'Did you want a picture? That's fine but, like I said, I've got to move quickly before –'

'I don't want a picture. I mean, I would quite like a picture, I'm a really big fan, but that's not why I'm here. Following you. I need to speak to Chase.'

'Oh?' he says, staring straight ahead of him as he walks.

'Yes, I'm Miss N. Palmer. The girl he's been looking for.'

He bursts out laughing. 'Of course you are. Haven't you heard? Every girl is.' He shakes his head. 'Look, I'm sure you're really nice and everything, but just drop the act, OK? I've got to go.'

'No, I swear, I really am Miss N. Palmer!' I quickly reach into my bag and pull out my bank card. 'See?'

I wave it in front of his face as he stops to cross a road. He looks at it and then shrugs. 'So you have the same name. It turns out it's really common. I don't know what

Chase was thinking with that stupid tweet. We've been hounded by Miss N. Palmers ever since.'

'You have to believe me! He must know I'm from around here! Why else would you be here?'

'To check out a studio and meet a producer here we're hoping to work with. Please stop following me.'

'No! Not until you listen! I need you to tell Chase!'

'All right then.' He sighs, coming to a sudden halt on the pavement and making me stumble backwards. 'What's the secret?'

'Huh?'

'The secret. What is it?'

'I don't know what you're –'

'Chase told us all about it. He told Miss N. Palmer – the *real* Miss N. Palmer who he met that night – a secret. Right before she ran away, he let her in on a big music industry secret,' he says tiredly, as though he's had to say this a hundred times before. 'If you really are her, then you can tell me what it is. So, go ahead.'

I desperately try and rack my brains for something Chase has said in his interviews, his tweets, anything that might give me a clue. But my brain is frazzled from everything that's happening and I can't think of a thing.

'That night was kind of a blur and I –'

'I thought so. Bye now.'

He strides off and turns the corner, but I can't let him get away that easily. I run up to him again.

'Look, I'm not going to tell you what to do but –'

'Wow, you are so persistent. Am I going to have to call my security or the police or something?'

'It wouldn't be the first time I've heard that threat today.' I hesitate. 'OK, that sounded really bad but I promise you I'm not a weirdo.'

'I'll take your word for it,' he says, taking a sharp left.

'The thing is, I know Chase must have had loads of girls telling him that ... Hey, where are you going?' I ask, looking about us at the quiet, narrow alleyway we're walking down. 'What is this place? I think you're lost.'

'Nope. I'm good.'

'You know,' I say, an idea popping into my head, 'you owe me.'

He stops at a weird door that I never would have noticed and leans on it, facing me.

'I owe you?' he says, taking off his sunglasses.

'That's right. You almost killed me.'

'When?' he says, stunned.

'Hello! The door? Of the hotel? You swinging open that door so irresponsibly could have had very dangerous consequences. As it is, I have excellent balance.'

The corner of his mouth twitches.

'I guess that was very lucky,' he says.

'And don't you think it's weird that I was crouched by that very door that you came out of at that very moment at the hotel? That HAS to be fate!'

'Apparently, empty alleyways *are* the perfect way for us pop stars to bump into mysterious soulmates. According to Chase anyway.'

'So, you agree it's fate that you met me?' I ask hopefully.

'No. I'd call it more like . . . unfortunate timing. But, hey, when it comes to this whole #FINDTHEGIRL campaign that Chase launched in a moment of crazy, I'd give you "A" for effort.'

I narrow my eyes at him. 'You used to be my second favourite in Chasing Chords but now you're down to seventh.'

'There are only four of us in the band.'

'I've included your manager, producer and your cat, Buttercup, in that list.'

He grins. 'Buttercup will be flattered.'

'Whatever.' I glance up at the building we're next to. 'So, what is this place?'

'I can't tell you. It's a secret.'

'Another secret? How many secrets can one band have? It's obviously that studio you were talking about but, don't worry, I won't tell the press.' I let out a long sigh. 'Well, you can't say I didn't try. But, before I go, you should know that I'm not giving up on finding Chase.'

'I don't doubt it.'

'You should also know that you look much better in the grey T-shirt you wore for last Saturday's show than that awful button-down floral shirt you had on for the latest music video, no offence. And your drum solo in "Light the Way" is very good,' I add, just so things are left on a positive note.

'Thanks, Miss N. Palmer.' He smiles, opening the door. 'I'll take that all on board.'

He shuts the door behind him and I walk back down the alleyway, towards the centre of town, dragging my feet. When I get to the right bus stop, I sit down on the bench and put my head in my hands. I check the tracker apps on my phone, and then I scroll through Twitter and check his Instagram to see if there are any updates hinting at his whereabouts. Nothing. My heart sinks as I shove my phone back into my bag.

If Chase told this girl a secret, then I guess it can't be me he's looking for after all. I feel completely deflated as it dawns on me that maybe I'm not #FINDTHEGIRL. When everybody else finds out about this, I'll be a laughing stock at school.

I can't let that happen. I have to find a way of meeting Chase so that he can realize it should have been me all along. I can't give up.

If only Chase had been the one to come out of that door, instead of Miles. If only I knew where Chase was right at this moment.

Everything would be different.

CHAPTER TEN

NINA

I remember the exact moment I first stepped into Neptune Records. We were still new to Norfolk and Mum took us on a day out to explore our new village. We were strolling down the high street and Nancy started to have a strop because we'd just left the sweet shop and she wanted more lemon sherbets but Mum wouldn't let her go back. While Nancy yelled and Mum put her foot down, I happily wandered into the mysterious-looking shop we were standing next to.

The door was quite heavy for me at the time and it had one of those old bells at the top, so when I walked in, it made it ring, notifying the woman behind the counter that she had a customer. The door shut behind me, closing out any street noise and the sound of Nancy and Mum arguing, and everything was silent. It was so peaceful in there and it smelt like a room of dusty old books.

'Hello there,' the woman had said, coming out from behind the counter and smiling down at me. She was wearing a loose black T-shirt, skin-tight black jeans with studs down the sides, biker boots, bright red lipstick and her hair was a big wild mess of blonde curls. She looked amazing.

'I'm Haley, it's nice to meet you. Have you ever heard a vinyl record before?' she had asked me, as I stared at the rows and rows of colourful record sleeves.

I had shaken my head. She had smiled in response and walked back behind the counter, moving the needle of her record player on to the vinyl.

By the time Mum came marching into the shop with Nancy in tow, I was sitting up on the counter nodding along to the music while Haley told me about the artist. Mum said she'd never seen me look so at home before.

I come to Neptune Records almost once a week, sometimes more if I'm feeling particularly anxious about something. I feel safe in there, hidden from the craziness of the world. Haley is still there and her face brightens up every time I walk in.

'Hey, Nina,' she grins as the bell rings above my head. She's wearing a Beatles T-shirt today and her trademark red lipstick. 'How's your week been?'

'Interesting,' I reply, pleased to see there's no one else in there.

'How intriguing. Pray tell. Anything to distract me from doing these accounts.'

'It's a long story. You want any help?'

'With the accounts?' She raises her eyebrows at me. 'Nina, you may not have noticed but you're a teenager. Let's protect you as long as possible from having to come near any kind of tax paperwork. So, no, I don't need any help. But I could use a distracting story.'

'I heard a new band this week,' I begin, pulling a vinyl from the nearest stand and brushing the dust off the cover. 'They were actually quite good.'

'A new band? Like, new to the world? Or new to you?'

'New to the world by your standards.' I smile, putting the record back in its alphabetical slot. 'I thought they would be like any other boyband, but I actually liked some of their songs. Weird, right?'

'Don't you go knocking boybands,' Haley says sternly. 'The Jackson 5 brighten the gloomiest of days.'

'Well, I wasn't expecting to like them, that's for sure. They're called Chasing Chords.'

She looks thoughtful and then shrugs. 'Haven't heard of them. Should I check them out?'

'Maybe just listen to one song, "Ghosts". It's written by the lead singer. It's –' I search for the word, smiling as I remember sitting on the pavement with Chase – 'different.'

'If I didn't know any better, Miss Palmer, I'd say that someone has a little crush,' she grins, winking at me. 'Good-looking, is he, this lead singer?'

'What? No!' My cheeks immediately start burning. 'I mean, I don't know. I just like his music.'

'Sure, sure.' She shoots me a knowing smile. 'Nothing wrong with crushing on a pop star. I remember the first time I set eyes on Kurt Cobain.'

She sighs and her eyes glaze over.

'I'm going to leave you alone with your daydream,' I say with a laugh, 'and I'm going to go get lost in your shop.'

'Do your thing.' She nods, gesturing to the stacks of records dotted around. 'I'm here if you need me.'

I head to the back and start flicking through a row, admiring the covers, pulling them out to read the list of songs on the back. Already I feel better about today. Nancy's harsh words to me in front of her friends are fading into the distance. I don't know what I would have done if this place had closed down like it almost did. It was a horrible time for Haley, but the whole village clubbed together to petition to make the shop a community landmark. The shop has an impressive history – Haley's father had run it before her and over the years lots of celebrities had visited. Luckily the council took notice and Haley was able to find the funding to keep the shop going.

I pull out a Stevie Wonder record. My dad loved Stevie Wonder. That song, 'Isn't She Lovely', came on the radio once and Dad turned the volume right up and grabbed Mum's hands, pulling her towards him for a dance around the kitchen. She shrieked with laughter and Nancy and I had giggled, watching them twirl happily around us.

'Have you heard that one?' Hayley asks, interrupting my thoughts and making me jump.

'I don't think so,' I reply, hurriedly.

'Shall we put it on?'

'It is a Friday, after all,' I say. 'Perfect day for a bit of Stevie Wonder.'

'Every day is a perfect day for a bit of Stevie Wonder.' She laughs, ruffling my hair, before heading back to the other side of the room and placing it carefully on to her record player.

As the music starts, Haley gets back to her paperwork and I continue browsing, swaying gently to the song. I'm so lost in my task of finding a new record to add to my collection that when the bell goes above the shop as someone strolls in I get a fright, dropping the record that was in my hands. I quickly bend down to pick it up, putting it back in its place before turning round to see who disturbed me.

I don't recognize him at first – whoever it is has their hood up over a cap. It's only when he pulls it down that I gasp. Chase Hunter.

What on EARTH is he doing *here*?!

I do the only thing that I can do in this situation: I drop to the floor.

I kneel, safely hidden behind a row of records at the back of the shop. I can't believe this is happening. He's supposed to be in London, not a tiny village in Norfolk! Maybe I imagined it. Maybe it's not him. Maybe it's just someone who looks like him. That makes more sense. I peer over the top of the row as he takes off his cap and goes over to the counter. There's no mistaking those cheekbones.

It is definitely him.

I duck down again, frozen in panic. What do I do? WHAT DO I DO?

'Hey,' I hear Haley say. 'Welcome to Neptune Records. Are you looking for something in particular?'

'Just browsing,' he replies. 'I've been wanting to come to this shop for a long time.'

'Well, I'm pleased you found us. Take as long as you need to have a browse, I won't be closing for a while.'

'Thanks,' he says and then it's silent as I assume he begins to look around him.

I have to get out of here. I can't handle meeting him again. Not after the #FINDTHEGIRL thing. I don't even know what I'd say! My face is so hot, it feels like it's on fire, and my stomach is churning with nerves. I decide that the best thing to do is to scout the shop and see where he is. Then I can casually peruse my way to the exit without bumping into him. I lift my head up over the records, spotting him right by the door.

WHY IS HE IN MY EXIT ROUTE?!

'You OK?'

I'm so surprised by Haley's voice that I tumble backwards on to my bum. She's standing with her arms folded, looking down at me.

'Oh hi, Hales! Didn't see you there,' I croak, leaning back on my hands and sliding my legs straight out in front of me.

'What are you doing on the floor?'

'I . . . I'm stretching.'

'Stretching?'

'Yeah, my knee has been playing up,' I say quietly, before sitting up and attempting to touch my toes. I barely reach past my calves. 'Got to keep my exercises up, you know? Don't want it to get worse.'

'Why are you whispering?'

'I'm not whispering,' I whisper.

'You are whispering,' she whispers back. 'You know what this looks like to me? It looks like you're hiding.'

'Why would I be hiding? Don't be silly, Hales. It's perfectly normal to do exercises on the floor of a shop when your knee is bad.'

'So you don't know that boy then?' she asks, nodding towards the front of the shop.

'What boy?' I squeak.

'The boy in the shop who you're hiding from.'

'There's a boy in the shop? I didn't notice.'

She smiles and holds up her hands. 'All right, I won't get involved in whatever teen angst this is.'

She gives me a thumbs up and then leaves, going back to her counter. I roll my eyes at myself, mortified that I was caught and then bring my focus back to how I am going to escape this situation. I have to start making my way towards the exit, crawling. If I angle my head low enough to the ground as I go, I can just about make out his shoes, watching him tap his foot to the beat of the song playing, careful to avoid his path. I finally make it to the row leading to the door and wait patiently for him to move far enough along.

Haley can see me now and is watching with a very amused expression on her face. I catch her eye as I shuffle along on all fours and she shakes her head at me, chuckling to herself.

As his shoes move away towards the back, I make a dash for it, scrambling to my feet and pelting to the door.

Unfortunately, I misjudge the aisle space between the stand at the front of the shop and the row of records next to it, bashing my shoulder into the stand and making it wobble. Records at the top of it topple forward right on to my head. I yelp and duck as Chase runs over to steady the stand and stop any more from falling.

'Are you OK?' he asks before gasping when he sees my face. 'YOU!'

I quickly bend down to pick up the records and I consider shoving them in his arms and then racing out of the door before he can work out what's going on. But something stops me. I straighten up, holding all the fallen records, and begin sliding them back into the stand.

'Sorry, Haley,' I say, blushing furiously. 'I'll put them back in order.'

'No problem,' she says, watching us carefully.

'I can't believe this,' Chase says with wide eyes as he shakes his head. 'It's *you*.'

'Oh, hey,' I say breezily, barely able to look at him. 'What's up?'

'*What's up*? Are you kidding me?! After everything I've done to find you, you're asking me "what's up"? Why didn't you contact me?'

'What do you mean?' I say, deciding to pretend I know nothing about the hashtag. There's no way I can admit to him that I was scared. Or that my sister is madly in love with him and I couldn't hurt her by telling her the truth. 'How could I contact you? We didn't swap numbers.'

'You mean, you don't know about #FINDTHEGIRL? On Twitter?'

'I don't have Twitter. Or any social media.' I shrug. 'Why? What's Find the Girl?'

'You don't have social media,' he says slowly. 'I guess that makes sense. It's not important. I just . . . well, let's just say I was trying to find you after the concert.'

'Oh. Sorry.'

'I can't believe I've bumped into you in here. This is so *weird*.' A grin spreads across his face. 'My uncle has always said this shop is magic.'

'Your uncle knows this place?'

'Yeah, that's why I'm here. Apparently my dad used to hang out here all the time.'

'Does he still come here now?'

He hesitates, shoving his hands in his pockets. 'I don't know. He left when I was younger.'

'Sorry,' I say quietly.

'It's OK. When he was around, he got close to my mum's brother and, according to him, Dad loved this place. I've been wanting to come here for years.' His expression breaks into a smile and he shakes his head again in disbelief. 'I can't get over that you're here. The world is so crazily small sometimes.'

'I live in this village. This is my favourite place.' I pause, bringing my eyes up to meet his. 'I thought you were in London.'

'We're in Norwich for a couple of days. There's a famous music studio here that my uncle was keen to take us to. Apparently one of the producers is an old friend of his. He told me that the record shop he always talks about was in a village close to the city, so as soon as I got some free time tonight I hopped in a taxi and came here.' He takes a step forward. 'And here you are. It's like . . .'

'Fate?' Haley suggests in this soft wistful voice.

I spin round to see her leaning forward across the counter, with her head resting in her cupped hands, watching us dreamily. I shoot her a look and she quickly straightens up, rustling her papers.

'Sorry! I was just . . . uh . . . well, nothing to see here. You guys carry on chatting. I . . . uh . . . I've got to check something in the stock room.' She walks towards the door at the back and, as she reaches it, she turns and gives me a massive wink.

Wow. She could not have been less subtle.

'A friend of yours?' Chase asks.

'Not any more,' I reply, making him laugh. 'So, you've come to the right place. For records, I mean. This is the best record store in the country. Probably the whole world.'

'You sound like you know what you're talking about. Any recommendations?'

'Let me see.'

He follows me over to an aisle where I begin searching for something to give him, but it's hard to concentrate when I can feel his eyes on me the whole time.

'So, you . . . you were looking for me?' I eventually work up the courage to ask, as casually as possible.

'Yeah. I was. I liked talking to you that night after the show.'

'Me too,' I admit quietly. He takes a step closer to me and a tingle runs down my spine. I feel nervous but excited at the same time, like the feeling I get right before I play a new piece I've been practising to Mr Rogers, but if you multiplied that feeling by a billion.

'I found your purse on the ground after you ran away from me.'

'I didn't mean to run away. I was late to meet someone. And you were busy with all your screaming fans.'

'I was busy shouting out for you to stop.' He leans forward and pulls out an LP by Led Zeppelin, flipping it over to read the back. We're standing next to each other so close that his arm brushes mine as he goes to put it back and this rush of tingling runs up my arm and down my spine. I'm suddenly so aware of everything I do. 'I was hoping to find you on social media but that was a disaster.'

'Really?' I ask innocently. 'What happened?'

'You do not want to know.' He sighs and I suppress a smile. 'And it doesn't matter. I'm just pleased I found you.'

'Yeah.' I smile, catching his eye. 'Me too.'

'Fate, huh?' He nods, reaching to look at another record. 'I never really believed in it before now.'

As we go along the aisle, pointing out our favourite artists, telling each other about songs we like, I wish that the day never has to end. I wish that I could just stand in Neptune Records with Chase Hunter, talking about music and talking to him forever. I've never met someone I felt so at ease with. I always feel embarrassed and awkward about myself, but Chase makes me feel like I'm interesting. Like he wants to know what I think about things. Even though he's a world-famous pop star, he acts like he's just a normal teenager, as though he hasn't got millions of fans singing along to his songs and people writing fiction about him in their spare time.

I feel so guilty about lying to Nancy and I keep telling myself that I shouldn't be talking to him. She would kill me if she found out. But at the same time I just want to be around him.

His phone rings just as he's in the middle of telling me a story about the time he was on holiday and stepped on a jellyfish, and he sighs when he sees who it is.

'I have to take this.'

'Sure.' I smile, glancing out of the window to see that it's got dark outside.

As he picks up, I suddenly hear a loud male voice go, 'Where the hell are you?' and Chase flinches at the volume, rolling his eyes at me and turning away to speak.

'You need to come back to the hotel,' the booming voice says, now a little more muffled up against Chase's ear. 'You're meant to be at this charity event in an hour. And it's black tie.'

'All right, calm down – I told you where I was heading,' Chase says. 'I'll make my way back.'

'I've already sent a car. It will be with you in five minutes.'

Whoever it is hangs up and Chase turns to face me.

'My uncle. Aka my manager.' He smiles. 'He's actually very nice in person. He just gets a little . . . stressed.'

'I can imagine it's a stressful job,' I reason.

'Especially when I disappear to record stores in random villages.'

'You had better go, then.'

'Yeah,' he says, nodding. 'Hang on a minute.'

He walks to the alphabetized aisle and begins looking for something. I stand awkwardly, waiting for him to leave, not knowing what to do with myself. What I do know is I really don't want to say goodbye.

'Aha,' he says suddenly, pulling out a record and moving over to the counter.

Haley shoots out from the storeroom as soon as he gets there, meaning she was lurking right next to the door the whole time. I am going to kill her.

'Excellent choice,' she says, as she puts it through the till. 'I like a man with good taste.'

I roll my eyes and wait next to the stand of records by the door, twirling it round absent-mindedly. A car horn beeps outside the shop and my heart sinks.

'Here,' Chase says, coming back over to me and holding out the record. Our fingers brush as I take it from him, and my breath catches in my throat. Our eyes meet. 'I think you'll like this.'

And then, without another word, he pulls open the door, making the bell clang loudly, and walks out, the door slamming shut behind him.

I stand in silence as I hear a car door open and close, before it pulls away. My heart is slamming against my chest. He didn't even say goodbye. Hot tears prickle in the corner of my eyes. I tell myself to stop being so silly.

Who was I kidding?

He's *Chase Hunter*. A celebrity. I can't believe I thought that he might . . .

'So, who was that?' Haley says, catching me off guard.

'Oh, um, no one,' I say, hiding my face and pulling open the door. 'Anyway, better get home. See you later, Haley!'

The whole journey home I run through the evening in my head, wondering what I might have done wrong. He went to all that effort to find me, then we bump into each other in the shop and he doesn't even say goodbye? It just seems so odd. But what was I expecting? For Chase Hunter to ask to see me again? It's embarrassing that I even let myself hope that. He probably wanted to be left alone in the shop and there I was, chatting away to him like we were friends. He must have been wishing the whole time I would leave. I acted just like one of his deluded fans.

I tell Mum I'm not hungry when I get in and go upstairs to my room, shutting the door behind me and slumping down on to my bed. I stare down at the record he gave me.

At first I think about chucking it away. It's just a reminder of how stupid I was. But I can't bring myself to do it, so after a long, deep breath, pulling myself together, I slide the vinyl out from the sleeve.

A piece of paper flutters down on to the ground, folded neatly into a square.

I pick it up, thinking it must have belonged to the previous owner of the record, and open it curiously.

They say third time's a charm. There's something about you. I would love to see you again. Chase x

Underneath is his number. I stare at it, hardly daring to believe what I'm reading. I take out my phone and tap in his number, save him as a contact under 'CH' and then begin typing a message. I stop, my finger hovering over the send button. I can't do this to Nancy. Can I? It would ruin everything and we're only just starting to talk again.

But then I remember the way she looked at me when I said I was going to the record store. How embarrassed she was to be seen with me in front of her cool friends. She doesn't know the real Chase; she's in love with the image his management have created. His brand. They would have nothing in common, not in real life. She thinks records are a relic of the past. Chase knows their real value. Like I do. We have a connection. I can't ignore that.

I press send, put my phone down next to me and wait, biting my nails nervously. My phone beeps within seconds and I almost knock it to the floor in my hurry to pick it up.

You got my note then?

Yes. Very smooth

I thought so. Quite proud of
myself actually. So, I have some
interviews tomorrow, but did you
want to maybe meet up on
Sunday? For a coffee or
something? I need to return your
purse after all . . .

Nina

I stop breathing. He wants to see me again. Chase Hunter really wants to see me again. This can't be happening. My fingers are shaking as I reply.

> That sounds great. I'm free
> on Sunday

Cool. Anywhere local you like?
Somewhere quiet would be good

> There's a beach near where I
> live . . . It's empty around
> this time of year. It has a
> nice cafe nearby

Perfect. Txt me the name of it
tomorrow morning. Just on my
way to the charity gala

> Hope it's fun!

I'm a bit distracted. Can't seem to
get you out of my head

I feel like I might explode with happiness. As I try and work out how to reply, he messages again.

Find The Girl

Just before I go, can I ask you
something?

Of course!

What does the N. stand for?

What?!

Miss N. Palmer. I feel like I know
you so well, I can't believe I
forgot to ask you your name

Oh! Haha. It's Nina

Nice to meet you, Nina

Nice to meet you, Chase

That's it then. Mission completed

What mission?!

Haven't you heard? I found the girl

CHAPTER ELEVEN

NANCY

Sophie

SOS. Can I come round to one of yours??? Layla, are you awake?? Can I come over???

Nancy

What's wrong?? Are you OK?

Sophie

I had an accident

Nancy

OMG what kind of accident?????? Are you OK?? What's happened?

Sophie

I'm fine. It's the plates

Nancy

What plates?? What are you talking about??

Sophie

The china plates

Nancy

What china plates??

Sophie

In the locked cabinet in the sitting room. I thought the reason my parents never used them was because they didn't like them. But it turns out they never used them because they were extremely precious china plates given to them as a wedding present

Nancy

OK . . . what about them?

Sophie

Well, you know I had that spinning plates idea for the talent show?

Nancy

Oh god

Sophie

I thought I'd give it a go
That guy made it look so easy

Nancy

I'm scared to hear the rest of this

Sophie

I just wanted to try it out. See if I was a natural

Nancy

And . . . are you a natural?

Nancy

Sophie

No. No, I'm not

Nancy

How many did you try with before you worked out you weren't a natural?

Sophie

Five

Nancy

FIVE???

Sophie

It was a six-piece set

Nancy

Did any of them survive?

Sophie

The sixth one did

Nancy

Your dad is going to kill you

Sophie

That's why I'm hiding under the sofa

Nancy

Which sofa???

Sophie

The one in the sitting room. I can see his feet pacing up and down as we speak. He's telling Mum that they should send me to boarding school in Canada

Nancy

You didn't clear the mess up in time then?

Sophie

No. They walked through the door, just after try number five. I ducked under here as soon as I heard them coming in

Nancy

What are you going to do?

Sophie

Wait until the coast is clear and then escape to your house?

Nancy

Fine by me!

Sophie

Mum is saying that she thinks I get it from Dad's side of the family

Layla

OMG it's Saturday morning, I was TRYING to have a lie in

Sophie

Sorry, Layla, did I wake you??

Layla

Yes

Sophie

I've had a bit of an emergency

Layla

I can see

Sophie

What shall I do???

Layla

I don't know. I'm turning my phone on silent

Nancy

Maybe just tell your parents you're really sorry?

Sophie

Uh oh

Nancy

What???

Sophie

They can see me

Nancy

Under the sofa?

Sophie

Yes

Nancy

That's not good

Sophie

They're telling me to come out from under the sofa

Nancy

Really not good

Sophie

They're now telling me to get off my phone

Nancy

Maybe you should??

Sophie

I'm pretending I haven't noticed

Nancy

That they can see you?

Sophie

Yep. They're both on the ground now just staring at me. I'm playing it cool

Nancy

Say you're sorry

Sophie

Uh oh

Nancy

What now???

Nancy

Sophie

Dad is reaching under the sofa. I think he's going to try and take my . . .

Nancy

Hello?? Sophie??? Are you there??

Did he confiscate your phone??

Sophie??

Hope you're OK

I just had an idea by the way . . . as good as the spinning plates idea is, I think for the talent show we should do a dance? Our routine last year went down really well and I think we could win again with a new one

What do you guys think?

Oh yeah, neither of you can answer

I'll start thinking up a routine today anyway

You guys, stop talking so much!

LOL

I'm hilarious

OK I'm going to go now

Getting tired of all your chatter ;)

xx

*

'Can you PLEASE stop laughing?'

I cross my arms in a huff as Nina leans on the arm of the sitting-room sofa for support, clutching her stomach in fits of giggles. Today she's wearing a set of pyjamas with snowmen waving candy canes all over them. I had no idea that she had such a collection of flannel nightwear. I'll have to raid her wardrobe when she's out and get rid of all these offensive pieces.

'I'm . . . s-sorry,' she wheezes, through tears of laughter. 'I just wasn't expecting to come in here and see . . . *that*.'

She explodes into a fresh new round of infectious giggles. I can't help but smile, even though I try my best to stay grumpy at her.

'Stop laughing!' I say, still grinning, as she sits down. 'It's not supposed to be funny.' Mum works at the shop on Saturdays, so we have the house to ourselves.

'What are you *doing*?' she asks.

'What does it look like I'm doing?'

'Some kind of elephant impression?'

'Very funny. I happen to be choreographing a very important dance for the school talent show and you just barged in on me coming up with some moves for the introduction.'

'I see.' She smiles mischievously. 'And is the dance completely inspired by animals, or just the intro?'

'You know,' I say, sitting on the armchair opposite and narrowing my eyes at her, 'I think I preferred it when we weren't talking. Have you always been this sarcastic?'

She laughs. 'I'm sorry for interrupting your rehearsal. How was your movie night?'

'About that –' I shift uncomfortably, lowering my eyes to the floor in embarrassment – 'I'm really sorry for snapping at you yesterday. After school, in front of Layla and Sophie. I was just –'

'You don't have to explain,' she interrupts, blushing. 'I shouldn't have rambled on about the record store. I forgot who I was talking to.'

'Layla can be a bit funny about things. I didn't want her to . . . well, never mind. I'm sorry anyway.'

'Forget it,' she says quickly, brushing it aside. 'So, how many Disney films did you manage to squeeze into one night?'

'Actually,' I confess, 'I ended up skipping Layla's. I had a complete disaster.'

'What happened?'

'You'll laugh at me,' I say, already feeling my cheeks growing hot. Nina is going to think I'm a complete lunatic when I tell her what happened.

'I promise I won't,' she says sincerely, holding up her hands.

'OK, well, I saw that Chasing Chords are in Norwich this weekend. Can you believe it?'

'Really?' she says, looking down at her hands.

I sense that suddenly she's not so interested in hearing my story, probably because she's been so stressed out by all the attention I've been getting since #FINDTHEGIRL began. I was standing in the lunch queue the other day and that friend of hers, Jimmy, was in line behind me – he told me that Nina has been acting strange all week, a little more nervous than usual. He thinks it's because everyone keeps asking her about me and Chase.

'She hates all the attention,' he'd confided. 'But I suppose it's unavoidable when a pop star tweets about your twin sister. So, it's really you that Chase is looking for?'

'Yes, of course,' I'd said very confidently. His expression when he asked me the question annoyed me. As though he was doubting me or something.

Even though I might not technically be the person who inspired #FINDTHEGIRL, I'm still the one Chase is meant to be with. He just doesn't know that yet.

Not that I care what pretentious Jimmy thinks. But I do care a little bit that Nina is uncomfortable with the situation. It's not really fair on her when she's so shy. Still, as soon as I find Chase and sort this whole thing out, I can make sure that Nina is protected from all that. All the attention will be on me anyway, so she'll be all right.

It won't be long now.

'I saw on Twitter that they were in Norwich this weekend, so I pretended to Layla and Sophie that I was sick,' I explain, enthusiastically continuing my story even though I notice she's avoiding eye contact. 'Then I went to see Chase.'

She snaps her head up. 'You *what*?'

'What was I supposed to do, Nina? They're in Norwich and they're supposed to be in London doing a press tour. But it all went wrong. Chase wasn't around. I have no idea where he was all evening. I found the wrong band member. I went to the hotel they're staying in to tell Chase that I was right here, his soulmate. But the snobby receptionist wouldn't tell him that I had arrived, purely because I was in my school uniform. Which is total discrimination and I'm considering suing.'

The corner of Nina's mouth twitches as though she's trying to hide a smile.

'Then I bumped into Miles, you know, the drummer? And he didn't believe a word I said about me being the girl Chase is looking for because, apparently, they've had so many fakes come forward. And yes, OK, so I might not have met Chase that night in London as far as I'm aware BUT that doesn't mean we aren't meant to be together. Sometimes you just know. Anyway, Miles wouldn't listen to a word I said and in the end I gave up and came home. Can you believe that Miles brushed off that I might be the one? He just made fun of me. And after my years of dedication to his band. Luckily I've already started taking my revenge. In the new story on my blog that I uploaded this morning, you will see that his character has an unfortunate run-in with an angry colony of bees.'

Nina bursts out laughing. 'I can't wait to read it.'

'It's a new favourite.' I grin. 'Anyway, even though last night didn't go to plan, I'm not giving up on Chase that easy. I have Plan B.'

'What's Plan B?' she asks, looking worried again.

'Don't worry, Nina, I'm not going to humiliate myself this time. I'm going to be much more prepared this afternoon.'

'This afternoon?'

'Yep. According to my updates, they have Norwich radio interviews all this morning but then they're free this afternoon. So, I'm going back to the hotel and I'm going to talk my way in.' I hold up my phone and wave it at her. 'I bet Chase was in that hotel last night, keeping a low profile thanks to all the fake Miss N. Palmers.' I roll my eyes. 'But today we shall finally meet.'

'Nancy, I don't think you should –'

'Nina, I know what I'm doing. I just have to dress the part. Yesterday my school uniform ruined everything. Today I'll be more sophisticated. As soon as he meets me he'll realize.'

'Why don't you stay here instead?' Nina asks, looking up at me hopefully. 'We can do something together. We haven't done that in ages and I –'

'Nina,' I say, holding up my hands and stopping her, 'I know what you're going to say. And I have been meaning to say the same. It's been really great getting to know you again.'

She hesitates before saying quietly, 'It has?'

'Sure! I felt really bad last night about not inviting you to the Disney movie night, and for being mean to you. The main reason I felt bad is because it's actually been really nice being able to chat again. You know, like . . . friends. Sort of. You know what I mean.'

She nods slowly.

'And I know that you're trying to protect me, right? By telling me I shouldn't go today. You don't want me to be rejected or publicly humiliated.'

Her gaze falls to the floor. I get up and walk across the room to sit next to her.

'I'm not stupid, Nina. I know that you're not sure I'm the one Chase is looking for. I can see it in your face every time I mention #FINDTHEGIRL. You go all red and change the subject. And your friend Jimmy, he doesn't believe me either. But you have to trust me. I just *know*. And I can't not try. Especially when he's probably going back to London tomorrow.' I reach out and take her hand. 'Thanks for looking out for me. I'll remember you when I'm a famous celebrity girlfriend.'

She doesn't say anything and I know it's because she's embarrassed, so I decide we've had enough serious chat for a Saturday morning and jump up and clap my hands, shooting her a big grin.

'You can help me pick out my sophisticated outfit later. Right now I need to get down to some awesome choreography. This talent-show dance isn't going to create itself.'

I pick up my phone and turn Little Mix back on, their latest single blasting through the house at full volume.

'I'll leave you to it.' She smiles, getting up to leave.

'You know, I could use some help,' I say, making her stop at the door. 'Considering you've been so willing to offer your criticism already. So, that swaying arms move looked like an elephant, huh? I got that one off YouTube. Maybe I got it wrong.'

'I was only teasing,' she says. 'But . . . can I say something?'

'Look, I've only just started choreographing, so it may look all over the place now, but you just wait, I'll –'

'No, I wasn't going to say something about the dance. I'm sure it will be great, but I just wondered if you'd thought about your other talents for the show. Instead of a dance, like you and your friends always do.'

I blink at her. 'Huh? What other talents?'

'Your nails,' she says, nodding at my hands.

'My nails?!' I burst out laughing. 'Nina, I can't enter a talent show with my *nails*. What would I do? Just stand there waving my hands about?'

'But you're so good at them! I don't know . . . You could put together a presentation with all the amazing creations you've come up with. It's art! Like that time you did the Minnie Mouse bows and ears all over them. That was amazing.' She shrugs. 'I don't know; it was just an idea.'

'Wait a second.' I raise my eyebrows at her. 'You noticed the Minnie Mouse bows?'

'They were hard to miss,' she points out. 'I always notice your nails. I've just never said anything before. I should though. They're really cool.'

'Oh. Thanks.' I smile warmly at her, stunned that she ever paid any attention. 'But I think I'll stick with the dance for the talent show. A presentation won't get me to that top spot.'

'You're probably right. Well, good luck!'

'Wait,' I say, not wanting her to leave quite yet. 'Don't you want to help?'

'You can't be serious,' Nina says laughingly, fiddling with her pyjama sleeve. 'You know I'm useless at dancing.'

'Hello!' I grab her hands and drag her to the middle of the room. 'I'm a choreographer! I can teach you some moves if you like. It's all in the hips. Come on, give it a try.'

I begin shaking to the beat, making Nina giggle.

'I can't do that!'

'Yes, you can. Everyone can! Come on, Nina,' I encourage, poking her hip.

'Nancy, I can't stand here dancing. What if someone sees?!' She blushes, covering her face with her hands.

'Who is going to see? We're the only ones in the house, you weirdo. This is a perfect opportunity for you to shake off those Nina-style inhibitions.' I wiggle my bum at her to make her laugh. 'I know you can do it!'

She sighs and then begins a tiny little bop.

'Very good! An excellent tip is to pretend you're in the music video.'

'How is that an excellent tip?' she cries. 'That's literally my worst nightmare.'

'Are you kidding? I was born to be in a music video.' I hop up on to the coffee table and Nina screams with laughter as I shimmy across it, before sliding into a sexy hair swish move.

The door swings open mid-swish and Mum walks in holding a shopping bag.

'Mum!' Nina quickly turns the volume down on the speakers. 'What are you doing home? Who's looking after the shop?'

'I just closed it for an hour to pop home with some lunch for you and pick up some paperwork I forgot.' She glances from Nina to me on the table and back to Nina again. 'What's going on in here?'

'Nancy is choreographing a dance for the school talent show,' Nina says, giggling.

'I was just teaching Nina some of my signature moves,' I announce, putting my hands on my hips and feeling a little out of breath.

'Really? A dance lesson? Well!' Mum drops the shopping bag dramatically. 'Turn that volume up, my cherubs!'

Nina does as she says and Mum leaps up on to the sofa and starts hip rolling. Nina's jaw drops.

'Mum,' she cries in disbelief, 'what are you doing?'

'I second that question!' I laugh, staring at her.

'When it comes to groovy moves, you should have come straight to me,' she responds, swaying her hips from side to side, and waving her arms about. 'You're looking at the 1988 East Anglia Amateur Dance Competition Mambo Champion, ladies.'

'Mum, you're going to put your hip out!'

'Rhythm is in our blood!' she declares, taking a breather as the song finishes and there's a pause before the next one. 'You should have seen your grandmother take to the floor.'

The next song comes on and I leap from the table across to the sofa to Mum's delight. She throws her arms around me and we dance together, jumping up and down to the beat.

'Nina!' I laugh, stretching my hand out to her. 'Get up here!'

She shakes her head stubbornly at us. 'No way. I'm very happy where I am.'

'Come on, Nina!' Mum cries, lifting her arms up in the air and waving them about madly. 'Just let the rhythm take over your body.'

Nina looks at me in horror and I laugh, shrugging. 'What she said! Come on, I know you want to.'

I jump down and grab her round the waist, making her shriek as I drag her up on to the sofa.

'Yes! That's my girl!' Mum smiles, grabbing her hands. 'Look at you go!'

Eventually Nina goes, 'Oh, all right then,' and Mum and I cheer loudly as she launches into some very enthusiastic dancing herself.

I'm having so much fun that I lose track of time and suddenly realize that I have to get going soon. As Mum and Nina collapse into a giggling heap on to the sofa, I turn off my music and check the band's social media in case there's been any updates. I'm not risking Chase not being there again. But there are no changes; they've been updating with photos of them at the radio station and then in the car on the way back to the hotel.

'Let's go, Nina,' I say, gesturing for her to follow me. 'We have to get ready.'

'Ready for what?' she says, leaning her head on Mum's shoulder.

'To meet Chase! I need you to help me pick the right outfit.'

'What's going on, Nancy?' Mum asks, before stretching her neck from side to side. 'Ouch, I think I felt a pang when I did all that head banging.'

'I'll explain later, Mum. Nina and I are going out this afternoon but we'll be back for dinner.'

'Hang on,' Nina says confused. 'What do you mean, *we're* going out?'

'You're coming with me. It's all decided.'

'What? No!' She shakes her head vigorously. 'I can't go!'

'Why not? I need some moral support after last night, and Layla and Sophie won't be able to come. Layla is having lunch with some family friends, and Sophie ... well, it's a long story involving china plates.'

'Sounds mysterious,' Mum comments, before Nina cuts across her.

'No. No, I can't go.'

'Nina!' I sigh in frustration. We're having such a nice day and I don't want her to ruin it. 'I know you don't have anything else on today. You said earlier you wanted me to stay in with you. And you don't need to worry anyway – this event is not going to be a big stampeding crowd, OK? It's just a posh hotel. While I chat with Chase, you can read your Alfred conductor book or something. I just want some company there and back; you can help me build up my confidence before I find him.'

'I can't,' she says, colour draining out of her face. 'I don't want to go, Nancy. I won't go.'

Seriously. She is such a drama queen.

'I don't understand why you're so against it,' I huff, folding my arms. 'I thought I explained to you why I had to do this. I thought you'd want to be supportive.'

'I do want to be supportive!' She stands up to face me. 'And I'll help in any other way I can. Just please, please don't make me come with you to the hotel.'

Mum shoots me a knowing glance and Nina's looking at me so pleadingly that I decide to give up. 'All right, all right, I won't make you go. You don't have to make such a fuss about it. I just don't understand why you're so against it.'

'I . . . I can't explain it,' she says quietly. 'I wish I could.'

'Whatever. You can at least help me pick what to wear.'

'Absolutely,' she says, nodding over-enthusiastically.

'Can I come help, too?' Mum asks, clapping her hands together. 'I give excellent fashion advice.'

'You mean, like that time I was going to the school bonfire night and you offered me your umbrella hat?'

'What's wrong with an umbrella hat? They are very practical and lots of fun!'

After I've forced Nina and Mum – who joins us in my room with popcorn, deciding she's going to give her advice whether we like it or not – to sit through an hour of outfit changes and make-up and hair decisions, I finally have the perfect look of skinny black jeans and heels, with a crisp white shirt, natural make-up and my hair up in a messy bun.

'You know,' I say thoughtfully, spraying perfume on my wrists, 'it's probably a good thing you're not coming today, Nina.'

'Because I'd embarrass you,' she offers, prompting Mum to throw popcorn at her head.

'No!' I sigh, swivelling round to face them. 'I was going to say because of the identical-twin thing.'

'What do you mean?' she says, throwing the popcorn back at Mum.

'Chase might have fallen in love with you instead by accident. Although maybe not in those pyjamas.' I giggle, making her blush. 'So, what do you think?'

'You look lovely,' Mum nods. 'Sure you don't want to complete the look with an umbrella hat?'

'Thanks, Mum – I'll pass.'

'I'd better get back to the shop.' Mum yawns, sliding off the bed.

'You work too hard,' Nina says, looking at her sympathetically. 'I wish you had the weekends off.'

'I've just had a lovely hour's lunch break with my girls,' Mum replies cheerily. 'It's been very refreshing. And I've got tomorrow off with you.'

'Do you want to drive me to Norwich, by any chance?' I ask hopefully, making her laugh.

'Nice try, Nancy. Afraid you'll have to get the train. But what I will do is walk you to the station. How about that for service?'

I roll my eyes. 'Great. Thanks, Mum.'

'Come on, then. Are you ready?'

'Yes, I'm ready,' I say, checking my outfit one more time and catching Nina's eye in the mirror's reflection. 'It's time for Plan B.'

CHAPTER TWELVE

NINA

I don't see him straight away. I glance around the beach cafe at the few people sitting at the tables and think that maybe I got the time wrong, or maybe he's changed his mind. But then I notice someone on the bench outside, alone, their back to the shop and their hood up, looking out towards the sea.

'Hey,' I say, sliding up next to him.

'Hey, Nina.' Chase smiles, his blue eyes shining. Waves of excitement are tingling through me. He makes my brain go so muddled that I can barely think straight. In a good way. He holds out a cup and my purse for me.

'I believe this belongs to you.'

'Thank you.' I laugh, shoving the purse in my bag and taking the cup from him.

'I was going to get you a coffee but then I had no idea what sort of coffee you would like. And then I thought I'd get you a tea, but it turns out there are about a hundred different teas you can choose from too. So I stood there panicking for a while, then decided to play it safe and get us both hot chocolate.'

'Excellent decision. My favourite.' I wrap my hands around the warm foam cup. It's a freezing cold day and, even though I've got a scarf on and my coat zipped up, my hands are like ice blocks.

He holds his hot chocolate up to tap the side of my cup. 'Cheers.'

'Cheers,' I say, taking a sip. 'Thanks for coming out here. If you want, we can try and find somewhere a bit warmer. I guess there's a reason why no one comes to the beach in winter!'

'Are you kidding? This place is perfect for today. I was just thinking that before you got here. I love the sound of the waves; it's so peaceful. Good recommendation. So, you live around here?'

'About twenty minutes away,' I explain. 'You should see this place in the summer; you wouldn't recognize it. There're people everywhere, it's completely packed, and this cafe always has a queue.'

I look over my shoulder at the almost-empty cafe and the owner behind the counter, reading her book.

'Despite the weather, I always prefer it at this time of year,' I continue, taking another sip of my hot chocolate. 'You feel like you have the place to yourself.'

'Just what I was thinking. And, let me tell you, that is rare for me,' Chase adds, looking down at his lap. 'Yesterday was very overwhelming.'

'The radio interview?'

'All of it. We took a picture with someone in our hotel the day before and they tweeted it so everyone knew where we were staying. The place was crawling with fans trying to get in. It got a bit out of hand. Pretty stupid of us not to think about that when we took the picture.'

I purse my lips, thinking about Nancy. She had come home yesterday afternoon in a terrible mood, flouncing through the door, stomping up the stairs and slamming her bedroom door. I'd been in the middle of playing a song on the piano with my headphones on, but I felt the door slam, it was so loud. I had waited a few minutes to approach her room and then knocked timidly.

As soon as I'd walked in, Nancy had exploded into a rant about how The Ashby had something against her, they didn't have one ounce of compassion, and how dare they accuse her of being a crazed fan.

'There were so many people trying to force their way into the hotel that I could barely get in the door and, when I finally got in, that horrible receptionist was there again and she insisted that she recognized me from Friday evening,' Nancy had wailed from her bed. 'How did that happen? I look completely different to how I looked on Friday! And then when I tried to persuade them I was in fact a journalist and had booked an interview with the band, she told security that I wasn't press, that I was still at school. No matter what I said, they kept looking at me as though I was an idiot even though I have a perfectly upstanding blog, with thousands of followers, and enough of a social media presence to be sent beautiful new shoes. I showed them all the pages but they would barely look at them! What is wrong with these people? Why don't they get it? The doorman escorted me out of the building! In front of everyone! It was HUMILIATING!'

'I'm so sorry, Nancy.'

'It's like fate is teasing me,' she had continued angrily. 'Bringing me so close to my one true love. How can Chase realize I'm the one if I can't get to him to tell him so? Fate isn't working! I HATE FATE!'

She had sulked and raged for another half an hour before calming down and telling me that she was now going to get to work on Plan C. When I had gone back to my room, I had a text waiting for me on my phone from Chase.

I felt so anxious about the situation that I had listened to 'Ghosts' four times before replying.

And now here I am.

'It must be really strange the way people think they know you,' I find myself saying out loud to Chase, huddled on the bench as the sea breeze whips my hair around my face. 'They have this idea of you, and in their heads they're convinced they know you.'

'Exactly.' He nods, lifting his eyes to meet mine. 'I'm just glad to be here today. With you. So, finish that hot chocolate.' He stands, does his jacket up over his hoodie and holds out his hand. 'Shall we go for a walk along the beach?'

My heart beats so hard against my chest when he takes my hand, linking his fingers through mine and pulling me gently to my feet, that I think it might just explode right out of my chest. While my hand is freezing from the sharp wind, his is warm and he grips my hand tight as though he's afraid I might pull it away.

It sounds weird but I've never held hands with a boy before. As in, a boy I like in that way. I've held hands and linked arms with Jimmy plenty of times, but in a non-romantic way of course. No one has ever wanted to walk along next to me and hold my hand, as though he's showing the world that we're a team. Chase pulls his hood down as we traipse down the walkway leading to the sand, and he smiles broadly, taking in deep breaths of the fresh air. I notice he has the cutest dimples when he smiles.

'What is it?' He laughs, looking at me with a raised eyebrow as we get to the sand and he throws our empty cups in the bin.

I realize I've just been staring at his dimples without saying anything that whole time.

'Uh . . . nothing . . . I just . . . you . . . well . . . I . . . uh . . .'

Oh god, I've forgotten the art of language.

It's just so hard to concentrate with his dimples right there in front of me and the hand-holding thing. I can't tell him I was staring at his dimples! That sounds weird. I try to quickly think of something interesting to say. ANYTHING.

'Pebble!' I blurt out as I see one lying on the sand.

Pebble? *PEBBLE?* What is WRONG with my brain?!

'Huh?'

'A pebble,' I say, pulling my hand away from his so I can bend down and pick it up in an attempt to explain myself. 'Are you any good at skimming stones? My mum taught us how to do it when we first moved here and now, whenever I see pebbles, I'm always looking out for good ones. And this one looked OK . . .' I glance up and notice him giving me a strange look. I drop the pebble and straighten up, feeling like an idiot. He must think I'm mad. 'Sorry, it's stupid. I don't know why I said all that. Ignore me.'

'Stupid? No way!' He crouches down to pick the pebble back up and examines it closely. 'I don't want to brag but when it comes to skimming stones I am the champion.'

'Really? You're being serious?' I say, stunned that I haven't completely ruined everything with my pebble outburst.

'This is a good one, you're right. Smooth and flat. We shouldn't waste it. You want to do the honours?'

He holds the stone out in his palm.

'And risk making a fool of myself in front of the self-proclaimed champion? No thanks.'

He grins, showing off those brain-frazzling dimples. 'Prepare to be amazed.'

He steps back and then does a run to the edge of the tide, ducking down slightly and flicking the stone forward. It spins through the air and lands with a distinctive plop into a small wave. I burst out laughing.

'OK, so I'm a little out of practice,' Chase says, turning back to me. 'Any chance we can pretend that didn't just happen?'

'I thought it was very impressive, *champion*.'

He narrows his eyes at me mischievously and I see him glance at a large piece of stray seaweed lying near his shoe.

'Oh no,' I warn, shaking my head at him. 'No, no, NO!'

But he's already picked it up and he comes running straight at me, gleefully holding it out in front of him and chases me for a few metres before he hurls it up into the air, but, instead of throwing it forward at me, it just goes straight up and down again, landing with a splat on his head. I laugh so hard that I have to clutch my stomach.

'That went exactly how I planned it,' he says, peeling the seaweed off his head and tossing it on the sand.

'That seaweed look really suits you.' I giggle, wiping the corner of my eyes with my coat sleeve. 'You should wear it to your next concert.'

'I'll consider it. Might be a good publicity stunt actually.' He grins, coming over and falling into step with me as we continue along the beach. 'This is a lot of fun. I miss having weekends.'

'You don't get days off?'

'Not really. Being in a band is great, don't get me wrong, but you don't get much down time. My uncle doesn't really believe in taking a break. I had to beg him to let me have today to myself. I got lucky though – that producer friend of his asked him to a fancy lunch, so I got permission to do my own thing.'

'Is it weird having your uncle as your manager?'

He nods thoughtfully. 'Yeah, it is weird. Mark is brilliant at what he does, I guess, but it's a lot of pressure on me and the guys.'

'So, was he your manager before your song went viral on YouTube?'

'No, he was furious about that.' Chase laughs, stopping to pick up a shell and inspect it before dropping it and moving on. 'He was in the business already ... he's quite well known; he's worked with a lot of high-profile musicians. He couldn't understand why I hadn't gone to him and told him about my band or sent him any of my songs. When he saw the response on YouTube and realized that it was me, he drove to my house and told Mum off for not telling him about his nephew's "musical ambitions".' He shakes his head. 'When I told him I had just been playing in the band for fun, he just looked at me like I was crazy, said my life was going to change and that was it.' He shrugs. 'The next thing I know we have a record contract, Uncle Mark is my manager and I can't go anywhere without someone taking a picture. I never get time like . . . well . . . this.'

We walk in silence for a bit as I think about what he's just said, then I say softly, 'What do you want to do?'

He looks at me quizzically as though I'm speaking to him in riddles. 'What do you mean? You already know what I do. I'm in a band.'

I grab his arm and stop him. 'I have an idea. Lie down for a second.'

'What, now?'

I laugh, sitting down on the sand and lying back. 'Just lie down, come on.'

'OK, crazy person,' he says, lying down next to me so we're both staring up at the grey sky. 'A jellyfish had better not creep up on me when I'm down here not paying attention to the sea. I don't know whether you remember that story I was telling you, but those jellyfish are evil, they can come out of nowhere and –'

'I won't let a jellyfish attack you, OK?' I laugh, turning my head to look at him.

'OK, I trust you.' He smiles, those dimples making my whole body feel like a jellyfish. 'So, why exactly are you making me lie down on the cold sand? Is this some sort of weird Norfolk tradition?'

'I want you to look up at the sky,' I instruct, watching him as he smiles quizzically at me and then does as he's told, turning his head to look up.

'Done.'

'Now, I want you to forget that you're Chase Hunter of Chasing Chords.'

'Riiiiiight?'

'I want you to just be Chase. A boy I met in London. And now have bumped into again. And we've been chatting and I've told you about Guildhall. That I want to go there.' I look up at the sky too, watching the clouds swirl above us. 'I remember when I was little, we went to the Barbican theatre. Have you ever been there?'

'No, I haven't.'

'Well, we went there once before Dad left. It's amazing. And on our way there from Liverpool Street station we walked past Guildhall School of Music and Drama. I remember it so clearly. I looked up at that building and thought to myself, I hope I end up here one day. And that hasn't changed. I really hope I can get a scholarship to study there and learn more about music, which is what I love. And then . . .'

I pause.

'And then?' Chase prompts.

'And then . . . I don't know. Maybe I'll be a concert pianist. Part of an orchestra maybe. In a West End show pit
orchestra or a symphony one. Or if I could learn how to
compose music, maybe I could be like Austin Golding. Or
maybe I'll have nothing to do with the piano at all and I'll
become a professional cloud watcher.'

Out of the corner of my eye, I can see him smiling.

'So, what you're telling me,' he says slowly, 'is that you
don't know what you want to do. But you hope it has
something to do with music. Which is what you love.'

'Guess so. What about you?' I ask.

'Me?'

'Yeah. You're not talking at a press conference. Or to a
Chasing Chords fan. Or to your family or friends. You're
just talking to me. That girl you met in London and have
bumped into again. What do you really want?'

He takes a deep breath. 'I guess . . . I like writing songs.
I kind of get lost in the zone when I'm writing a song. It's a
weird rush of adrenaline when I finish writing one, and I
can play it. The process can be frustrating and tiring and
lots of hard work but . . . I just love it. I definitely couldn't
not be a songwriter, if that makes sense.'

'It does,' I say softly.

'I don't even know if I want to be in a band.'

His hand reaches out across the sand and his fingers find
mine, entwining them. I turn to look at him and see he's
already watching me.

'I've never told anyone any of that,' he tells me, our eyes locking.

'I can keep a secret,' I assure him.

'That wasn't what I was saying.'

I'm so lost in his deep blue eyes that when a seagull squawks loudly next to my ear, I'm so shocked that I scream and scramble to my feet, making Chase burst out laughing.

'I'm s-sorry!' he says through laughter as I scowl at him. 'But you should have seen your face!'

'That seagull came out of nowhere!' I claim, feeling my cheeks grow hot. 'I thought it was on my head!'

'Honestly, don't be embarrassed,' he says, still chuckling, as though he can read my mind. 'That was nothing compared to the seaweed-landing-on-my-head moment. And, frankly, I was impressed by your ninja-like instincts. I don't think I've ever seen anyone move so quickly in my life.'

'Well, I hate pigeons,' I say, still shivering at the idea of that bird near my head. 'We have always hated them, ever since this time that Nanc–'

I stop myself. As Nancy comes into my brain, I feel a stab of guilt. 'Never mind,' I say, quickly. 'I just hate them. And now I hate seagulls too.'

'I will protect you from all seagulls, if you protect me from all jellyfish.'

'Deal.'

'Shall we walk back to the cafe?'

'Yeah, it's getting even colder,' I point out, as he picks up another shell, inspects it and clutches it in his hand. 'Hang on, don't move.'

'Why?' He looks panicked. 'IS THERE A JELLYFISH?'

'No! There's not a jellyfish.' I giggle, reaching into my bag for my camera. 'It's just a good shot with that lighting and the sea behind you.'

'What? Nina –'

'Just stay right there,' I order, pointing the lens at him and taking a picture. 'Perfect! The real Chase.'

I look up from my screen to see that his expression has darkened. His eyes are hard and accusing.

'Chase, are you –'

'I can't believe you. You've tricked me, haven't you?'

'Tricked you, what are you talking about?'

'You just happen to have a professional camera like that on you?'

'I –'

'Did my uncle put you up to this? Did he arrange for you to be in that record store? Let me guess, that photo is going to be on Instagram in the next five seconds with the caption "The Real Chase".'

'What? I don't even have Instagram!'

'I trusted you,' he hisses, turning from me and striding across the sand.

For a moment, I stand frozen to the spot completely stunned at whatever has just happened and then I feel something bubbling inside of me, a need to be heard for once and not just shoved to the side under everyone's shadow. This is important to me.

'Hey!' I yell, catching up with him and standing in his path. 'How could you think I would do that to you? I have been nothing but honest with you. I'm not going to put that picture on social media. I've told you before, I'm not on social media. I don't even know how to work Instagram or put a caption or whatever you were saying. I'm just into photography as well as music and my mum bought me this camera for my birthday. It's a hobby. You think you're the only one who has put themselves out there today? I trusted you, too.' My eyes begin to well up as I stare him straight in the eye. 'I like you. Not because you're in a band or you're famous or any of that. But because you actually listen to me. I just like *you*.'

His expression immediately softens and he takes my arms as I lower my gaze to the sand, trying to blink the tears back.

'Nina, I'm sorry. I freaked out about the photo. It's just . . . I've been let down by people before. Trusted the wrong people and then seen my secrets splashed about online the next day. I'm sorry. That was completely my fault and I overreacted.'

'I would never do that to you.'

'I know,' he says softly. 'I'm sorry. I really am. I was being stupid.'

'Yeah,' I sniff. 'You were.'

He grins. 'Hey, at least I got you to admit you like me. So, that's a win.'

'I'm not sure I like you any more.'

'Whatever, you said it twice. That seagull over there is my witness.'

'I hate seagulls.'

'I know,' he says, as he brushes a stray curl away from my face. I feel his hand slowly move to my chin and he gently lifts my face so that our eyes meet. He closes his eyes and kisses me, wrapping his arm around my waist and pulling me towards him. My first kiss. And it's perfect.

Suddenly I don't care about seagulls. Or jellyfish. Or the fact that my fingers have turned blue from the cold. Or anything, in fact.

I only care about this moment and how I never want it to end.

CHAPTER THIRTEEN

NANCY

Something is different about Nina.

I first notice it the Sunday she comes back from her day out with Jimmy at the beach. She decides to go meet him for the afternoon to take arty photos of sand dunes or whatever, even though it is cold and grey outside.

'You're mad – it's freezing out there,' I say from the sofa before she leaves, as she wraps her scarf tightly around her neck.

'That's why it's the best time to go to the beach,' she replies, smiling. 'It's deserted.'

By the time she gets home it's dark and I've had to listen to HOURS of Mum droning on about what it's like having an artist's eye. Apparently, to artists, there is beauty in everything, including a kettle.

'Look at those lovely curves,' Mum says, lifting the kettle high into the air. 'And the way the light glints off the handle.'

I'm so grateful when I hear Nina's key turning in the door, I dart into the hallway and catch her just as she is coming in. She has her back to me and is shutting the door very slowly and carefully as though she doesn't want to disturb anyone in the house, and then her phone buzzes in her pocket. She takes it out, looks at the message and turns round with this dopey grin on her face. She sees me standing there, watching her, and yelps loudly.

'Nancy! You scared me.'

'Take your time, why don't you. How long does it take to photograph a couple of sand dunes?'

'I had to get the right lighting,' she says defensively.

'Whatever. We waited for you to put on the Sunday night film. I was thinking maybe we could watch one of the Mary-Kate and Ashley Olsen classics. I highly recommend *Holiday in the Sun* or *Winning London* but I told Mum it's your choice.'

I still feel a bit guilty about the way I snapped at her on Friday evening in front of Layla and Sophie, so I'm attempting to make it up to her by choosing some of our favourite comfort films from when we were little. Growing up, we'd get a lot of Mary-Kate-and-Ashley themed presents, I guess because of the twin parallel. We LOVED those films. I still have a box under my bed with all our old Olsen twin annuals, but I've never told Nina that I kept them.

'We haven't watched one of those films for years,' she says, putting her phone away.

'Yeah, well, I thought it was about time.'

The three of us settle down to watch *Holiday in the Sun* and that's when I really notice something is up with her. She has her phone resting in her lap for the whole film and keeps glancing at it. For most people, that's normal behaviour. But for Nina, it's *weird*. I may not know her that well these days, but even I know that Nina is barely on her phone. She has no social media at all and she rolls her eyes at me maybe five hundred times when she sees me messaging at the table.

And it isn't just on Sunday that she acts strangely. The whole week she is constantly on her phone or has it near her. And when I ask her why she's checking her phone a lot, she gets defensive and changes the subject. I find it confusing at first and then I think maybe it has something to do with her music, because what else would she be acting so strange and jumpy about? Maybe she's applied to that Guildhall summer course already and is waiting to hear back, which is why she won't let her phone out of her sight. It seems very early to have applied for something that isn't for months, but still. It's the only thing that makes sense.

I don't want to embarrass her and come right out with it, so one day I decide to give her a sneaky bit of encouragement without making it obvious that I know.

'Nina, you're *really* talented at the piano,' I say over dinner when there's a lull in conversation.

She pauses with her fork midway to her mouth.

'What?'

'I don't know anyone our age as talented as you are at music,' I continue casually, trying to ignore Mum beaming at me from her seat. 'And anyone who doesn't realize that or, hypothetically, turns you down, say, for a place on a course or something, is MAD.'

She blinks at me. 'Uh. Thanks.'

And then I stealthily change the conversation so it sounds like it was just a fleeting thought that I'd said out loud. It was the perfect confidence boost, even if I do say so myself. And I'm pretty sure it works because not only is she being weird with her phone but she is also a lot *happier*. She used to hardly say a word at meal times but now she chats away happily and the way she holds herself is different.

'Have you been working on your posture?' I ask her one morning as we walk from the car into school.

'No.' She laughs. 'Why?'

'You look taller.'

'We're exactly the same height.'

'I know. But you look taller today.'

'Thanks!' She smiles and then skips off to go meet Jimmy.

I'm not joking. SKIPS. Nina never skips anywhere. She usually drags her feet and is slightly hunched forward, as though she's constantly apologizing for being present. Now she's skipping off to meet her friend as though it's the most natural thing in the world.

I consider that maybe I'm overthinking things but then Layla mentions it and I KNOW I'm not making it up.

Layla is rarely interested in anyone except herself, so Nina's change must be obvious.

'What's with your sister?' she says the morning of the skipping incident.

'Did she trip over again?' I ask, craning my neck to see her across the classroom.

Usually when I look at Nina from my desk, she's sitting quietly with her headphones on and her face buried in whatever book she's reading, hidden from everyone as much as possible. But now she's standing at the front telling Timothy Davies something that is making him laugh so much that he's clutching his stomach and gesturing for one of his friends to join them so she can tell the story again. She's got her signature blush going on, so I know she's not completely at ease with being the centre of attention, but she never used to join in with pre-morning-registration chatter, let alone lead any of it.

'She looks different,' Sophie observes. 'Has she changed her hair?'

'I don't think so,' I say.

'Her face seems brighter somehow too. Has she started using foundation? Or that new shimmer highlighter you were telling us about, Nancy?'

'She wouldn't know how to use products like that,' Layla sneers, watching as Nina cheerily goes to sit in her seat. 'She has no idea about make-up.'

'I know!' Sophie says suddenly, her eyes widening. 'It's her smile.'

'Her smile?'

'Yeah.' She nods confidently. 'That's definitely it. Something's different about her smile. Did she get her teeth whitened?'

'No, but I think you may be right in a way, Sophie,' I say thoughtfully. 'I think we're seeing her smile a lot more.'

I decide that it's about time I ask Nina if she did get a place on some kind of prestigious piano course and get to the bottom of this whole smiling business, so I catch her at lunch when she's eating with Jimmy and ask her to help me pick out an outfit that evening. That way we'll have some nice bonding time together and I can find out what's going on.

'Wow, what a fun evening ahead for you,' Jimmy says drily. 'If only I wasn't going to see my grandparents tonight, otherwise I would be there in a heartbeat.'

'Nobody asked you for your opinion, thank you,' I huff. 'Nina will love helping me pick out outfits. I trust her to tell me what looks good and what doesn't. Right, Nina? It will be fun!'

'Is this for another Chasing Chords thing?' she asks nervously, her smile fading.

'No, not today.' I sigh. 'I actually need your help for the talent show.'

'Let me guess,' Jimmy smirks, pushing his food around his plate. 'You, Layla and Sophie are doing a dance again this year?'

'As a matter of fact, we are,' I say, folding my arms.

'How original.'

I narrow my eyes at him. 'And let me guess: you and Nina plan to spend the whole time moaning about how the school talent show is simply another popularity contest.'

'Exactly.'

'Well, instead of continuing that honourable tradition this year, Jimmy, why don't you spend your valuable time encouraging your best friend to show off her incredible talents?'

'Are you talking about Nina?' he asks, surprised.

'Do you have any other friends?'

'Touché,' he says with a grin.

'Me? What about me?' Nina asks, already looking panicked.

'You should enter the talent show this year. Play the piano.'

'What?' Her jaw drops. 'I can't do that.'

'Why not?'

'Because she gets terrible stage fright,' Jimmy explains. 'She hates performing.'

'Yes, I know that, thank you very much.' I roll my eyes dramatically, making Jimmy smile. 'But you have to get used to performing to an audience, Nina, especially if you really want to go to that Guildford place –'

'Guildhall.'

'Whatever. You're going to need to practise.'

She's just looking at me blankly, so I pull out the chair next to Jimmy, sit down and continue.

'Practice. Just like Chase. You remember him, the lead singer from Chasing Chords? He gets really bad stage fright. He mentioned it once ages ago in one of his early interviews. So you just need to, you know, channel your inner Chase Hunter and get up there. You can't hide from the stage for the rest of your life when playing the piano is what you love. Don't you agree, Jimmy?'

'I hate to say it,' he says, looking at me strangely, 'but I think I do.'

'Great, so we're all agreed that Nina will enter the talent show this year.' I nod firmly. 'Hey, you should play that "Ghosts" song that Chase wrote! The one you were practising after the concert? That will appeal to the crowd rather than all those songs you normally play written by dead people. OK, then,' I say brightly, pushing my chair out and standing up. 'My work is done here.'

'But –' Nina begins.

'And, in return for my wisdom, tonight Nina can help me pick out a flattering outfit for the *amazing* and *original* dance I've choreographed,' I say, looking pointedly at Jimmy.

'I'm sure this year's dance will be an absolute hoot,' he says, giving me a thumbs up. 'It's always a crowd-pleaser.'

I roll my eyes at him one more time and then leave them to their lunch, heading to the sign-up board to write down

Nina's name before she can change her mind. I have to say, I feel very pleased with myself for helping her realize her dream.

I should totally be a life coach.

When Mum picks me up after school, she tells me that Nina texted her to say she's got an extra piano lesson and so she'll get the bus home later. I can't help but puff up with pride, knowing that she must have booked an extra lesson with that hot-but-nerdy piano teacher of hers so that she can tell him about the talent show and start working on her performance.

I get home and lay out all the dance outfit possibilities, covering my entire bed and then move on to cover all the floor space too.

'What's going on in here?' Mum asks, popping her head round the door as she passes on the way to her room. 'Are you doing a wardrobe clear-out?'

'I'm going to pick out what I should wear to the talent show this year. It has to be glitzy enough for the stage but classy at the same time, and obviously I have to be able to move freely in it,' I explain, glancing around at the piles of clothes everywhere. 'Lots of boxes to be ticked. Nina will have the answer, though.'

'Yes, you can certainly rely on her,' says Mum, smiling. 'But, you can also come to me at times like this because I have something PERFECT for the occasion.'

I groan as she scampers excitedly away down the corridor to her room, digs around in her wardrobe, and then re-emerges in my doorway holding what can only be described as a parrot costume.

'Mum,' I gasp in horror, taking in the mound of multi-coloured feathers. 'What is that?'

'Fabulous, isn't it,' she says dreamily, stroking the feathers and holding it up against herself. 'I wore this dress to my sixth form dance. That was quite a night. I had my first kiss and the moon was shining and –'

'MUM. Firstly, please stop talking about the moon and kissing. Gross. And, secondly, I don't know what that thing is, but it is NOT a dress.'

'Of course it's a dress, darling.' She chuckles. 'I'll leave it here –' she hangs it on the top of my door – 'and you and Nina can decide, but, really, I think this should be a front runner.'

I shake my head as she leaves and then I watch YouTube videos on my laptop, waiting for Nina to get there. After an hour and a half of waiting, I decide to call Nina to see where she is but it goes straight to voicemail. I leave it for another ten minutes then I try again, but no luck.

'Mum, do you know where Nina is?' I ask, coming into the kitchen. 'Shouldn't she be home by now? Her piano lesson isn't this long, is it?'

'Ah yes, she texted me about an hour ago, saying she was going over to Jimmy's for a bit,' she says, loading the dishwasher. 'Something about a school project. She's so hard-working.'

'Oh,' I say, trying to hide my disappointment.

'What's wrong?'

'Nothing. It's just . . . she said she'd help me pick out an outfit this evening. I was waiting for her.'

'She must have forgotten,' Mum says, looking at me sympathetically. 'I'll text her now but I think her phone battery has died. She told me it was running out so not to worry if it went straight to voicemail.'

'No, don't text her. It's not important.' I hesitate. 'Mum, do you think Nina has been acting a bit strange lately?'

'She's definitely come out of her shell a little more and she's certainly a lot busier than she used to be with all these after-school activities. She's been doing a lot more photography. She keeps heading to that beach for some really beautiful shots. I wonder if I should look into getting her some more photography equipment for Christmas; what do you think?'

'Sure, good idea, Mum.'

My heart sinks as I turn to head back upstairs. I'm hurt that Nina forgot she was supposed to be helping me, especially when I had been so positive with my talent-show idea, encouraging her to face her fears and show everyone how good she is.

I put on the Chasing Chords album to lift my spirits as I start putting the clothes back in my wardrobe but it doesn't help. Hearing Chase's voice just reminds me that I still haven't managed to get through to him. None of my genius plans have worked. I keep trying to talk to people at school about him, reminding them that I'm soon going to be dating THE Chase Hunter, but I'm starting to get the feeling that nobody is that interested any more. Like it's old news.

I'm so engrossed in how sad it is that I was so close to having my dream come true that I don't notice Nina come in. She sits down on the bed next to me, jolting me out of my thoughts.

'Hi,' she says, glancing at the pile of clothes I'm holding. I'm pleased to see that she looks ashamed.

'Hi,' I reply coldly, standing up and going over to my wardrobe.

'Nancy, I'm so sorry,' she says, reaching over to my phone to pause the music so I can hear her. 'I completely forgot.'

'Whatever. It's fine.'

'It's not fine. I should have been here but I lost track of time. I was just with Jimmy and –'

'You could have texted.'

'My phone died. But I really am sorry, Nancy. I promise, tomorrow we can spend the whole evening going through your clothes and picking your outfit. And, to make it up to you, I can cook you . . . cheese-and-potato pie?' she says hopefully.

'I've told you, I don't eat cheese any more.'

'You ate macaroni cheese the other day.'

'That was different.'

She sighs. 'Nancy, please forgive me. I feel terrible and I really want to make it up to you. It's completely my fault and I don't want you to be angry with me. I like it when we're getting on. I really am sorry.'

I hesitate. 'Fine. You're forgiven. But I have a dance rehearsal tomorrow so you can help me pick an outfit at the weekend.'

'Thanks, Nancy. You're the best.' She grins and then nods towards Mum's dress still hanging on my door. 'So, are you sure you haven't already got a winner?'

That night I lie in bed, staring at the ceiling, with something niggling in the back of my brain, which is stopping me from sleeping. I can't seem to get Jimmy out of my head. Not in THAT way (EW!) but something about him is bothering me. I toss and turn for ages when suddenly it hits me.

'He said he was going to see his grandparents,' I say out loud into the darkness, remembering his rude sarcastic reply when I first asked Nina to spend the evening picking out an outfit.

How could Nina be hanging out with him when he was with his grandparents all night? Maybe she knows his grandparents well and she would rather spend the evening chilling with them than with me.

That can't be right.

Either way, it seems a bit fishy and judging by Nina's recent behaviour something is DEFINITELY going on with her, so I make the decision that I will do a little bit of investigating. She's hiding something.

The next day I ask to go to the toilet in the middle of my maths lesson and then creep along the deserted school corridor to Nina's locker, checking that no one else is around. To open her locker, I need to know her four-digit code so I try and get into Nina's brain to work out what it might be.

'If I was a big nerd,' I whisper to myself, 'what code would I use?'

I whip out my phone and quickly google Austin Golding's birthday, then I key that in but it's not right. I put in 1234, just to see if she'd been lazy with her code, but that's not it either. I sigh and check my watch. I don't have much time before my maths teacher will get suspicious. This is a LOT harder than I thought it would be.

An idea pops into my brain.

When we first moved to Norfolk, Nina and I were exploring our new house and we found this weird dusty old key with '9481' engraved on it in the bottom of an old chest of drawers. It didn't seem to be the key to anything in the house so we both found it really mysterious and would make up silly magical stories about the key opening doorways to other worlds and stupid stuff like that.

Since then, 9481 had been my code to everything. Maybe it was Nina's too.

I tell myself not to be so silly and push the thought aside. It was way too long ago to be important and Nina's probably forgotten all about it anyway. She wouldn't have that as her locker code.

Would she?

I put the number in apprehensively and hear the click as the door opens. I'm so shocked that she remembers that key, too, that I just stand there staring at the locker door. But then I realize I don't have much time and I quickly start searching around to see if I can find any clues, but there's nothing. Just a pile of books and some sheet music.

I'm still thinking about the magical 9481 key when school ends. I can't believe she has had the same code as me all this time. Even though we'd grown apart, we'd both kept it. Thinking about it makes me feel all warm and fuzzy. I wish I could ask her about it but then she'd know I'd been snooping.

Layla and Sophie stand waiting for me as I push all my books back into my locker before we go to our talent-show dance rehearsal.

I suddenly hear Layla say, 'There's Jimmy – let's ask him.'

'Ask Jimmy what?'

She gives me a strange look. 'Weren't you listening to a word I was just saying?'

'Sorry, I was distracted by something.'

'Hi, Jimmy,' she says, stepping into his path as he makes his way down the corridor.

'Layla,' he replies through gritted teeth. 'What can I do for you?'

'Oh, we just had a couple of questions we wanted to run past you,' she says, twirling her hair through her fingers. 'About your little friend Nina.'

Jimmy glances at me and I shrug.

'What about her?'

'We noticed she is a lot happier at the moment and we wondered if it had something to do with l-o-v-e,' Layla says, her eyes glinting. 'Guess you two finally declared your feelings for one another.'

'Sorry to disappoint you, but, no, we're just friends.'

'I think it's really sweet that you two are an item. You're both so . . . weird.' She smirks. 'It's a good match.'

'Thank you, Layla, because I really value your opinion. Bye now,' he says, side-stepping her and striding down the corridor.

'What a loser,' she says. 'Shall we go to rehearsal?'

'Can we rehearse another day? There're a couple of things I need to do,' I say, watching Jimmy at his locker.

Layla and Sophie agree to postpone rehearsal and head home, while I hang back pretending I've forgotten something and then, when they're gone, I rush over to Jimmy.

Layla had put an idea in my head that I hadn't even considered and I wanted to see if I was right.

'Hi,' I say. 'Are you OK?'

'Fine, thank you,' he snaps, not looking at me.

'Jimmy, it's about Nina . . .'

'Seriously? Nancy, I just said –'

'I know you're not together; that's just stupid. Layla has no idea what she's talking about. And sorry, by the way, for her being so rude to you. She can be . . . temperamental.'

He raises his eyebrows at me. 'You shouldn't be apologizing for your friend's behaviour. I don't know why you hang out with someone like that.'

'Is Nina in love?'

He turns to look at me. 'What did you just say?'

'Hear me out,' I say quickly, leaning on the locker next to his. 'She's been a lot more confident in herself. And she's always checking her phone for messages; plus, she's going out a lot more. When Layla just said about the love thing, it made me think. It makes sense that all of this strange behaviour is down to the fact that she's met someone she likes!'

'I . . . I'm not sure.'

'You're not sure? That means *you* think she's met someone!' I gasp triumphantly. 'She just hasn't told you.'

'I seriously don't know if it has anything to do with a boy. But –' he hesitates – 'there's definitely something different about her. It might be something else, something completely different. We can't be –'

But then he stops, spotting someone over my shoulder. I spin round and there is Nina, with her headphones on, heading out and down the school steps. She hasn't seen us. I turn to face Jimmy again with a big smile on my face.

'Thanks, Jimmy. I gotta go.'

I run out of the door and I'm about to catch up with Nina and ask her to tell me all about this mystery boy but then I remember that she's super shy and I don't want to embarrass her. Especially if she's not ready to tell people about him.

But I also REALLY want to know who this guy is and I am WAY too excited to head home, knowing that she might be on a date with her mystery boy. So, instead of asking her about him, I do the next best thing.

I follow her straight to the source.

I know. I'm a GENIUS.

She's texting someone as she gets on a bus to Norwich, the same bus I got that day to The Ashby. I follow her on to it, going into full stealthy spy mode and pulling my coat hood up over my head, careful not to look at her directly.

It feels like I'm in my very own Mary-Kate and Ashley movie and I am LOVING it.

Following her off the bus, after a while I start to recognize some of the streets she's walking down. This is the same route that the Chasing Chords drummer, Miles, went when I bumped into him. I stay a few metres behind her all the time and can't believe it when she takes the turning down that same gross alleyway. I stop at the corner and peer round the wall, watching as she makes her way towards the door Miles stopped at. She calls someone on her phone and the door opens, shutting behind her as she steps inside.

That is so *weird*.

My inkling about that door had been correct – after my chat with Miles, I went home and googled that street and it turns out it's some kind of famous recording studio, just like I'd guessed. But I'd been on that studio's website and there is no chance that Nina could afford to use it; it was a really posh, professional one.

Maybe the boy she was seeing had an internship there? It would make sense for her to date a musician. Maybe he was helping her make her very own recording. Maybe she was going to be a famous piano star! And, if she has access to that studio, MAYBE she'll bump into Chase and she can tell him about me!!

Mum calls and I tell her I'm on my way, heading back towards the bus. For the entire journey home, I look out of the window dreamily, thinking about Nina and her exciting secret.

And I just can't stop smiling.

CHAPTER FOURTEEN

NINA

'So, when are you going to tell me about this boy?'

Jimmy's question comes out of nowhere and I'm so shocked that I slam my hands down on the piano keys, causing a horrible clashing of chords.

'Wh-what?'

He comes to sit down next to me on the piano stool. 'The boy you've been sneaking around visiting? Come on, Nina –' he nudges me – 'you can tell me.'

I stare at him, trying to think of something to say. He holds my gaze patiently.

'OK,' I confess, 'there is someone.'

He grins. 'I knew it. That's so exciting!'

'How did you work it out?'

'I had my suspicions,' he admits. 'Then a couple of days ago Nancy said something that . . . well, it kind of confirmed what I'd already been thinking.'

'Nancy said something?' I croak, alarmed. 'What did she say? How does she know?'

'Relax – she doesn't know. She just noticed you'd been a bit happier, that's all.' He smiles. 'So, why didn't you tell me?'

'I . . . well, it's very new and it's a bit complicated. Nothing to do with you, I swear – I've been wanting to tell you for ages. It's been horrible keeping it secret.'

'Why is it so complicated?' Jimmy's forehead furrows.

'I can't explain it but maybe –' I take a deep breath – 'maybe you could meet him? I'm meant to be seeing him this evening after school. You could come along too if you wanted?'

Jimmy's face instantly brightens. 'I would love to meet him!'

The bell rings, signalling the end of lunch break and Jimmy hops up from the stool, grabbing his books and heading towards the door of the music room.

'I've got to hurry before Mr Barber tells me off for being late again, but I'll meet you by your locker after school, right?'

'Jimmy,' I call out just as he pushes open the door. He stops to look back at me. 'You have to promise me you won't freak out when you meet him, OK?'

'Why would I freak out?' He laughs. 'Don't worry, Nina. Remember I once had to help you when you got stuck climbing through the library window. I'm sure I can handle meeting your boyfriend.'

As he leaves, I stare at the piano keys wondering if I've done the right thing. Chase and I had promised to keep everything secret, because it was so much easier that way. The idea of Nancy noticing that something was different about me made me feel completely on edge. I couldn't risk her of all people finding out about Chase.

But it had been getting more and more difficult to hide it.

Chase had been coming to Norwich from London as often as possible just to sit in various cafes, talking over hazelnut and cinnamon hot chocolate. He'd managed to persuade his uncle to work with the producer in the Norwich studio on some of the songs for the new album, so that he'd have an excuse to come even more often.

Trying not to be recognized made it all more fun – Chase had to wear his cap and hood up most of the time, and if we noticed someone looking our way with interest he'd stand up quickly and wrap his arm around me or link his fingers through mine and lead me out of wherever we were, running down the road giggling. Then he'd always stop when we were a safe distance away and he'd pull me close to him, kissing me right there in the middle of the pavement, with people bustling past us, no idea that a world-famous pop star was right in front of them.

Chase makes me feel happier than I've ever felt in my entire life. I can talk to him about anything – music, family, friends, silly stories from our childhoods, the future – and he makes me laugh so much that after seeing him my jaw aches from all the smiling. And I sometimes catch him smiling at me in a way that makes my breath catch in my throat and I go all tingly, like bubbles are fizzing up from my toes right through to the tips of my fingers.

Hours fly by without us noticing and suddenly it's time to go and we both have to rush off. He always calls as soon as he gets on the train back to London and I'm on the bus home, and then we just continue where we left off. I step off the bus and walk as slow as a snail to the front door, desperate to stay on the phone with him for as long as possible.

I know I can't keep it secret forever.

It feels as though a huge weight has been lifted off my shoulders now that Jimmy knows and, more than anything, I want him and Chase to get on.

I text Chase to ask him if it's OK for Jimmy to finally meet him and whether he'd mind Jimmy tagging along to the studio with me this evening.

> Great idea! I've heard so much
> about him, I feel like I already
> know him. Can't wait to see you
> xxx

I breathe a sigh of relief that he's not mad but then as the afternoon draws to a close and suddenly school has finished and Jimmy and I are sitting on the bus, heading to town, I feel sick with nerves. Jimmy asks me a hundred questions about him on the way there – *What's his name? Where does he go to school? Where does he live? How did you meet?* – and I have to keep brushing him off, saying he'll find out when we get there.

'How mysterious,' Jimmy teases, waggling his eyebrows as we get off the bus. 'I literally have no idea what to expect.'

I lead Jimmy through the centre of town and down the side street, pressing the studio buzzer nervously. Jimmy will be the first person to know about us; I haven't even met the rest of Chase's band yet. Chase made sure we'd be alone this evening, asking to have the studio to himself to write some songs. It is one of our favourite places to meet, away from all the noise and chaos of town.

And I really like to press all the buttons on the mixing console in the control room and pretend to be a hotshot producer when Chase isn't looking.

'Where are we?'

'You'll see. Jimmy, before you meet him,' I begin, hearing the door unlock, 'promise me, you won't say anything about Nancy.'

'Nancy?' Jimmy looks confused. 'What do you mean?'

'I just . . . I haven't told him I'm a twin and I'd rather tell him some other time. Please don't mention her, OK?'

He nods. 'OK, that's weird, but whatever you say.'

'Thanks. You'll understand why in a bit.'

I push open the door and usher him through, closing it quickly behind us.

'What is this place?' Jimmy asks, glancing around him as he climbs the stairs. 'I'm not going to lie to you, Nina, but I'm kind of creeped out.'

A voice comes floating from the door at the top of the stairs.

'I was, too, when I first came here.'

Jimmy stops, his hand frozen to the bannister. Chase is now standing in the door frame, beaming down at us. I feel my heart flip just at the sight of him.

'You must be Jimmy,' he says, grinning. 'I'm Chase. I've heard a lot about you. Come on up.'

Chase turns to go back into the control room, the first room you come to at the top of the stairs, and Jimmy doesn't move, his mouth opening and closing like a fish until I prod him sharply in the back.

'Nina,' he whispers, drifting up the stairs and then stopping to stare at Chase sitting at the mixing desk. 'Is that . . . who I think it is?'

'Yeah.' I nod slowly, squeezing his arm. 'Yeah, it is.'

'You're dating . . . Chase Hunter?' he says under his breath. I've never seen his eyes so wide; they're as big as saucers. 'Wait.' He tears his eyes away from Chase to look at me. 'Miss N. Palmer. You're . . . oh my god . . .' He shakes his head. 'The whole time, it was you!'

'It took me a while to track her down,' Chase adds, hearing the end of Jimmy's shocked ramblings. 'So, do you want a coffee or tea or anything? There's Coke in the fridge, too, if you want.'

'I'll get them,' I say quickly, smiling at Chase. 'You guys chat.'

Chase winks at me and I hurry through to the small kitchen area down the corridor. I grab some cans from the fridge and then put on the kettle, waiting a few minutes before ambling back down towards them. I can hear their muffled voices and I tense, trying to work out if they're getting on. Suddenly I hear Chase burst into laughter.

'You got stuck in the library window?' Chase asks, as I come back into the room.

'That's the story you decided to lead with?' I ask Jimmy accusingly, passing him a Coke.

'I just wanted to make sure Chase knew the real you.'

I go to stand next to Chase, grinning as he puts his arm around my waist and pulls me into him, kissing my cheek.

'This is so surreal,' Jimmy says, beaming at us. 'But at the same time it really makes sense. You just . . . look right next to each other. And I guess there's the whole extraordinarily musically talented thing that you have in common. Have you ever heard Nina play, Chase?'

He shakes his head, letting out a long sigh. 'She refuses.'

'Well, maybe tonight is the night.'

'What?' I glare at Jimmy. 'No way.'

'Nina, the talent show is just days away.' Jimmy cranes his neck over my shoulder to look into the live performing room. 'Are you allowed to use that piano?'

Chase looked at me, baffled. 'Talent show? What talent show?'

'Nina has entered the school talent show for the first time ever. She'll easily win.' Jimmy grins as I shoot daggers at him. 'But she has to get over her stage fright.'

'That is brilliant news!' Chase exclaims. 'About the talent show, I mean, not the stage fright. But I already told you how to get over that side of things. The first night we met, remember? It's all about practice.'

'No, no,' I protest, while Chase grips me by the shoulders and steers me out of the room towards the piano in the recording space. 'I can't.'

'Why not? This is the perfect opportunity. It's just me and Jimmy.'

'We're your perfect audience; already your biggest fans,' Jimmy adds, gazing around at all the instruments in awe. 'And, by the way, this is the coolest place ever.'

'I know, right? Some amazing artists have played here.' Chase drags out the piano stool, fixing it to the right height for me. 'And now we have one more.'

I swallow the lump in my throat and sit down.

'I can't do this. I'll muck it up. I already can't remember a thing.'

'Nina,' Chase says gently, crouching down to my eye-level, 'at some point, you're going to have to face this fear if you want to get into Guildhall summer school. Don't play to us, pretend we're not here. Just play for yourself, like you would normally do.'

He kisses me gently on the cheek and then disappears back through the door. Jimmy follows him out, giving me a thumbs up as he goes. The door closes and it is complete silence. I stare at the piano keys, wishing they would just play themselves.

Chase's voice suddenly comes through a speaker, giving me a fright.

'Whenever you're ready, Nina. You can do this. Remember, just play for you.'

I nod and take a deep breath, trying to slow my brain down. Chase and Jimmy are right. I have to find a way of playing in front of an audience. I lift my hands to the keys and, after a few moments trying to ignore the tingles in my fingers, I start to play my favourite song from *Half a Sixpence* 'If the Rain's Got to Fall'. At first, I'm terrified, aware that I'm being watched but then, as I keep playing, I get lost in the music until I've forgotten that it's a performance at all.

When I finish the piece, there's a moment of silence before clapping and loud cheering comes blasting through the speakers. I blush, turning to look at them through the glass window. Jimmy is doing a victory dance around the mixing room and Chase is watching me, a smile spreading across his face.

Nina

'Nina Palmer,' he says, leaning forward to press a button so that his voice fills the studio, 'you really are something else.'

*

Good luck today! Wish I could be
there

                          Thanks Chase, I wish that
                          too. A lot

How are you feeling??

                          Like I'm about to throw up

You'll be amazing

                          I think I've forgotten how to
                          play the piano

Nerves are good, you want the
adrenaline when you're on stage

                          I don't know how you do this
                          all the time. Got to go, I'm
                          up next! xxx

Thinking of you xxx

*

'As soon as your sister and her friends are off the stage, we'll move the piano forward into the centre and you just go ahead and do your thing, OK?'

My mouth is completely dry and I can feel the sweat forming on the back of my neck.

'Nina,' prompts Timothy, who is helping backstage at the school talent show and appears to be taking his job very seriously judging by his headset and new black polo neck. 'Did you hear what I just said?'

'Yes,' I croak. 'Sorry, I'm a bit nervous.'

'Don't be. Nancy told me that you're going to blow everyone away with your performance.'

'She said that?'

'Yeah.' He smiles. 'She thinks you're going to rob her of first place. I've got to go. Don't go anywhere, OK? You're up straight after them.'

He gives me an encouraging pat on the arm and then marches off, talking into his headset: 'No, Freddie, I said green *lights*, not green tights! Why would I want green tights all of a sudden? Look alive, Freddie, look alive!'

I sidle up to the edge of the curtain and, carefully staying hidden, peer out as Nancy, Layla and Sophie enter from stage right, waving to the audience. Everyone erupts into cheers and whoops. I join in on the applause and give Nancy a thumbs up as she glances at me. She shoots me a smile, getting into position as the lights go down and the music starts. She looks amazing in her glittery sequin dress and she's done the most incredible stage make-up, with heavy black eyeliner, dramatic false eyelashes, and plenty of glitter gems around her eyes, so she's almost unrecognizable.

I can make out Jimmy sitting in the front row, distracted from Nancy's dancing as he fiddles with my camera. I frown, hoping he's not pressing all the buttons and breaking it. He begged me to borrow it so that he could take some pictures of my first piano performance and I eventually caved because (a) he was so persistent and (b) he'd been amazing about the Chase thing.

As Nancy struts forward into the centre of the stage, I see Jimmy lifting the camera and taking some pictures. Nancy sees him too and, at the end of the song, strikes a dramatic pose perfectly directed towards the camera, making Jimmy laugh and he takes plenty of shots. The audience erupts into enthusiastic applause as Nancy, Layla and Sophie take their bows and blow kisses.

'Here we go, Nina,' Timothy says behind me, making me jump. 'Get ready to go.'

I feel my throat close up as they run off into the wings and Timothy walks on with his fellow stagehands to help push the piano to the front. My piano teacher, Mr Rogers, is in the audience, and as he spots the piano being moved he sits up in anticipation. I'm frozen to the spot and start to panic as the hall descends into a hush.

I grip the shell in my pocket. It is the one that Chase picked up right before our first kiss on the beach. He gave it to me afterwards and I've been carrying it around with me ever since.

'Please welcome Miss Nina Palmer to the stage,' Mrs Smithson announces, leading a polite round of applause and gesturing for me to come out from behind the curtain.

I walk forward slowly, my feet like lead. My clammy hands are shaking as I sit and everyone waits patiently while I rearrange the stool to the correct height. I'd been told to announce which song I would be playing but I can't do it. I'm too terrified to say anything at all. I glance out to the audience but the lights are shining so brightly on me that it's like looking directly into the sun, and I blink madly, blotches forming in my vision. I turn my focus back to the piano. My body feels paralyzed.

Oh god, I don't know whether I can do this.

I look up and there's Nancy in the wings. She's smiling at me and nodding, as though she knows what I'm thinking.

You can do this, she mouths.

I inhale deeply, rest my hands on the keys and I start to play. I didn't go with Nancy's suggestion to play 'Ghosts'. Instead I've chosen to play Yiruma's 'River Flows in You'. I keep my head down and try to lose myself in the music, ignoring the warmth of the spotlight on my face, pretending I'm in the studio playing to Chase.

Time seems to stop. The fear begins to ebb away and I forget that I'm being watched by hundreds of people. It helps that the bright spotlights mean I can't see the audience – I'm shielded from all those pairs of eyes watching. And the music starts taking over the stage fright. My fingers stop shaking as the song calms me. I think about Chase and about how we talked about this song when we first met.

The song comes to an end and I play the last notes, slowly taking my foot off the pedal. Silence roars through the hall. As soon as the music stops, I'm back to the harsh reality of being on stage. Immediately I descend into a panic and feel sick.

They must have hated it. My cheeks burn and I'm too scared to look out in case they start laughing at me. I have to get off the stage.

But then something amazing happens.

They start clapping. *Really* clapping. And suddenly everyone in the audience is up on their feet, cheering, whistling and whooping loudly for me. A standing ovation. For *me*. Nina Palmer.

I sit in a daze, wondering what on earth is going on and whether any of this is real, until I spot Nancy mouthing something else at me.

Bow! Bow! She's laughing, gesturing for me to stand up.

I stumble out of my seat and nod my head awkwardly at the cheering audience, amazed at their reaction. The harsh spotlight blinding me thankfully changes into a warm light coming up on the rest of the hall.

And that's when I see him. *Chase.*

He's there, right at the back of the hall, hood up and cap on, trying to blend in. As if he could. But no one is looking behind them, so he's safe for now. I can't believe he came! He's clapping with the rest of the crowd and beaming at me.

The lights change for the next performance and I hurry into the wings where Nancy is waiting for me. She pulls me into a big hug and I rest my head on her shoulder.

'Nina!' she screams in my ear. 'You were AMAZING!!'

'I couldn't have done it without you.'

'Yes, you could.'

I stand with her and all the other acts in the wings, waiting for the last performance to come to an end before we are all called back on stage for another round of applause and for the winner to be announced. Knowing Chase is out there and I can't go see him is torture, but I also start to panic that Nancy might spot him in the audience. I needn't have worried. I scan the audience and can't see him anywhere. He must have left.

'What performances we've been treated to tonight!' Mrs Smithson is saying into a microphone, letting the applause die down. 'And now the judges have decided on their winner.'

The hall descends into an anticipating hush and Mrs Smithson pauses for effect.

'The winner of this year's talent show is ... NINA PALMER!'

Wait.

What?

I feel numb as everyone bursts into a fresh round of applause and Jimmy leaps up from his seat crying, 'YES! GO, NINA!' before lifting my camera and taking photos.

'You did it, Nina!' Nancy says in my ear, squeezing my hand and jumping up and down on the spot. 'Go on! Go collect your prize!'

She pokes me in the back with her sharp manicured fingernail and I trip over my own feet as I go towards Mrs Smithson, while the other acts pat me on the back and yell 'Well done!' in my ear. Mr Rogers beams up at me from the audience.

'What a talented musician you are,' Mrs Smithson enthuses as she hands me a little silver trophy. 'I'm very proud to be your form tutor. None of us had any idea.'

I thank her, not entirely sure what is going on or what I should be doing. Luckily I have Nancy directing my every move, coming over to lead me to the front of the stage and telling me to bow again before leading me off, instructing me to wave to my 'adoring crowd'.

'Now, for the celebrations!' Nancy squeals, giving me another hug. 'We're all going for milkshakes so go get your coat.'

'We are?'

'Yeah, it's tradition. Everyone from the school goes.' She rolls her eyes at me. 'You would know this if you didn't avoid the talent show every year. I'll go call Mum and tell her the good news. She's going to be so proud of you! Go and get your stuff and I'll meet you by the door with the others.' She starts to move off and then stops, coming back to give me another hug.

'You so deserve this,' she whispers before she leaves.

I get my bag and coat from behind the stage, thanking everyone as they congratulate me on my way. I pick up my phone and see a message waiting for me from Chase.

> From the moment we met, I knew
> you were a winner . . .

I quickly type back before anyone can see.

> I can't believe you came to
> watch!!! What if someone
> had recognized you??

> You're worth the risk . . . And
> who cares?! YOU WON! I'm so
> proud of you. You were amazing

> I want to see you!! Where
> did you go? I have to go out
> in a minute, apparently it's a
> tradition! I wish I could
> come find you

Don't worry about it. Go have
fun!! You deserve it xxx

I feel deflated that I can't run straight to wherever he is but I don't have long to think about it because soon Nancy returns, telling me off for lingering and yanking me towards the door. I manage to send a text to Jimmy letting him know where we're going and begging him to come meet us there – I'm not sure I can handle it on my own. He replies instantly saying he's on his way and I breathe a sigh of relief.

'What was that song you played?' Layla asks, as I sit down at the edge of the booth Nancy has chosen in the milkshake bar. 'It was pretty.'

'Um, it's called "River –"'

'Michael from the year above just texted me back,' Layla squeals suddenly, interrupting my answer and shoving her phone in Sophie's face. 'He's going to come here, too. Can you move? I need to slide out and check my make-up in the toilets.'

Nancy comes over with our milkshakes just as they leave, which is lucky because I don't know anyone else at the table and none of them are the least bit interested in talking to me.

'Where is Layla going?' Nancy asks, sliding my milkshake across to me.

'To check her make-up.'

'Again?' She raises her eyebrows. 'Let me guess, did Michael from the year above text back?'

'He's on his way,' I tell her.

'She's going to be impossible now.' Nancy sighs, taking a sip of her strawberry milkshake. 'She won't shut up about him.'

The girl sitting at the other end of the booth gets Nancy's attention and I sit awkwardly in silence, stirring my milkshake, trying and failing to add to the conversation. When Jimmy comes up and crouches down next to me, I hug him so gratefully that I almost knock him over.

'Nina, I'm so proud of you!' He laughs when I pull away. 'You were amazing. The best pianist I've ever seen.'

'I'm the only pianist you've ever seen,' I giggle.

'Not true. I once saw someone play "Chopsticks" on one of the pianos they have at St Pancras station. It was simply majestic, but you even had the edge on that guy.'

'Thanks, Jimmy. You're the best.'

'Hey, can you come with me to the toilets?'

'What?'

'Just trust me. Unless,' he says, lowering his voice so no one can hear, 'you want to stay here with this group. After all, I can tell you're having a REALLY good time.'

'Let's go.' I grin, sliding out from the booth and following him towards the back.

'OK, you go that way,' Jimmy says, pointing at an emergency exit door next to the toilet.

'Huh? But, Jimmy –'

'Didn't I tell you to trust me? You can thank me later.'

I give him a strange look and then shrug, pushing through the door and emerging out on to the road. I don't really feel like thanking Jimmy, considering it's freezing out here and I haven't got my coat on.

A hand comes out of the darkness and grabs my arm, making me scream.

'Shhh! Nina, it's me!' Chase laughs, stepping forward and pulling his hood down.

'You gave me a heart attack!'

'I'm sorry – I wanted to surprise you.'

He brings me towards him, letting me wrap my arms around him inside his coat, and I rest my head on his chest.

'Congratulations for tonight.'

'Thanks,' I say, my voice muffled into his hoodie. 'I can't believe you were there.'

He lifts my chin up to look at him. 'I wouldn't have missed it.'

He closes his eyes and kisses me just as the door creaks open behind us.

'Sorry to interrupt, lovebirds, but I'm afraid your small window of opportunity is almost up. A couple of people have asked where you've gone, Nina. I've told them you'll be back in a minute,' Jimmy says apologetically, before saying goodbye to Chase and heading back into the warmth.

'I don't want to go,' I say, clinging to Chase.

'I wish I could come with you, but I can't go in there.'

I play out in my head what would happen if Nancy and the rest of her friends saw Chase Hunter walk into the milkshake bar.

'Yeah, not a good idea,' I agree. 'There are some diehard Chasing Chords fans lurking. You wouldn't stand a chance.'

'Before I go, can I say something?' he asks, holding my cold hands in his.

'Of course.'

'You can't laugh.'

'Why would I laugh?'

'I don't know,' he says shyly, looking down at the ground. 'It just sounds weird saying stuff like this. It sounds like it should be lyrics in a cheesy song.'

'Try me.'

'I've never felt this way before, Nina,' he says, bringing his eyes up to lock with mine and making me feel giddy. 'I just wanted to let you know that . . . I'm falling for you.'

'That's good,' I whisper back, pressing my forehead against his and closing my eyes. 'Because I've already fallen for you.'

The rest of the night in the milkshake bar is a blur and I hardly hear a word of any of the excitable, loud chatter going on around me. I'm too happy to concentrate on anyone or anything else. All I can think about is me and Chase, and our perfect bubble of happiness.

But it was about to burst.

CHAPTER FIFTEEN

NANCY

The other day in English class, we got to the bit in the book when Jane Eyre finds out Mr Rochester has been lying to her, and our teacher asked us to get into pairs and talk about a time when we have felt betrayed. It would help us understand, he said, the pain and confusion Jane is feeling, hurt by someone she trusted and loved.

I turned to Sophie. 'I know EXACTLY the time I've felt most betrayed.'

'Was it when your dad left?' she asked carefully.

'Nope,' I replied firmly, the anger already bubbling within me as I thought about it. 'It was *Summer Cowley*.'

When Nina and I were eight years old, we were friends with a girl at our old school named Summer Cowley. She was loud and confident, and always the centre of attention, so I was of course immediately drawn to her. Her mum worked for an accessories company, which meant that Summer had the coolest stuff and if you were friends with her she'd let you borrow some of it. When

I got close to Summer, Nina got upset about it because it was obvious that Summer didn't really like Nina; she just let her hang around with us because she was my sister.

We would have sleepovers all the time and Summer was good at sports, so both of us were on the netball and tennis teams, while Nina would watch our matches from the sidelines with Mum. For my birthday, Summer got me a friendship bracelet and I was so proud of it that I didn't even think about the fact that she hadn't got anything for Nina. As far as I was concerned, I had two best friends and everything was great.

Then, one day, our teacher asked us to vote for a class captain to lead a school project. I obviously wrote Summer's name down on my piece of paper and put it in the teacher's hat, giving Summer a knowing nudge.

'And the captain of the project will be,' the teacher announced after counting the votes, 'Nancy Palmer!'

I was surprised but also really pleased because I'd never been captain before. Nina gave me a cute little round of applause along with everyone else in the classroom, but then I saw the look on Summer's face. She wasn't clapping. She looked horrified. I asked her if she minded that I'd been voted captain and she promised that she didn't. She said she didn't want to be captain, anyway.

But she started being a bit different with me at school and I worried that I'd upset her.

'Don't be silly,' Mum said when I mentioned it to her. 'Summer's your friend!'

Then, right before the end of term, I noticed that kids in my class were whispering a lot around me and, when I asked what they were talking about, they wouldn't tell me. I didn't care that much though because I was captain of the project, so that made me the most popular girl in class. I thought maybe they were whispering about Nina and they didn't want to tell me in case it got back to her. I remember wishing that Nina would act a bit cooler because it made me look bad.

'See you on Monday – your birthday!' I said happily to Summer, as the last class on Friday finished.

She didn't say anything, giving me a little wave before linking arms with another girl in our class and walking out with her, talking in low voices. I couldn't work out why my best friend was being so cold with me and I desperately wanted to make it better. I decided I would ask Mum to take me to the shops the next day to pick something special for Summer's present. Maybe another friendship bracelet.

'Hey, Nancy,' Nina said, sidling up to me as I stood still, puzzled at Summer's weird behaviour. 'I need to tell you something.'

'What?'

She blushed and looked down on the floor, biting her lip.

'What is it, Nina?' I asked impatiently. 'Do you not like the bit of the school project I assigned you? You're best at research so I thought that –'

'It's not about the school project. It's about Summer. She asked to speak with me privately today.'

'She did? About what? She didn't ask to speak privately with me.'

'She wanted to invite me to her party tomorrow.'

I stared at her. 'Her party? What party?'

'She's having a birthday party this weekend because it's her birthday on Monday.'

'No, Nina, I already asked her about her birthday and she told me that her parents were taking her to the theatre.'

'I think she just said that so you wouldn't find out.'

'Find out what?'

Nina looked pained. 'That she's having a big birthday party at her house and she's invited everybody in the year.' She lowered her voice so much that I could hardly hear her add: 'Except you. She asked me not to tell you about it, but I think it's really mean and I don't keep secrets from you. And of course I would never go anywhere without you.'

'Summer is having a birthday party and she hasn't invited me? But we're best friends!'

'I know. I think it's horrible of her.'

I stood at my desk in shock. 'But . . . why would she do that?'

'I don't know,' Nina said quietly, shaking her head. 'Did you have a fight?'

'No! No, we haven't had a fight. It's because I got voted captain and she didn't.'

I was so hurt, I started crying right there in the classroom and Nina gave me a long hug before taking me to the toilets to get some tissues. I told Mum everything when she picked us up and she sat with me on the sofa all evening while I cried some more. From that day on, I vowed to never be friends with Summer again and I threw away her friendship bracelet defiantly with Nina as witness. Luckily we moved away soon afterwards so I didn't have to see her again, but anytime I thought about her I would relive that stab of hurt and humiliation that she made me feel that day.

Never in my life have I felt so betrayed.

Until today.

'I am so tired,' Sophie yawns, sitting down at her desk and swivelling in her seat to look back at me and Layla. It's morning registration and Mrs Smithson isn't here yet.

'How come?' I ask brightly.

I'm in a good mood because it's Friday AND in the car on the way to school Mum put on that song from *Half a Sixpence* that Nina and I love, and the three of us sang along to it at the top of our lungs. Mum was so out of tune that Nina and I couldn't stop laughing. It was a good start to the day.

'I was up all night watching the new Chasing Chords music video on repeat,' Sophie admits. 'And then I watched the making of the music video and then I just kept clicking on the next video that popped up afterwards and I ended up falling asleep with my phone on my face.'

'Is their new video good?'

My question causes both Sophie and Layla to look at me like I've lost my mind.

'What?'

'You haven't seen the new Chasing Chords video yet?' Layla asks slowly, as though she hasn't heard me right. 'But it was released last night.'

'Yeah, but last night Nina made me watch this weird old film that no one has ever heard of and it was actually quite good, so I forgot to check their video out before bed. What's it like? How does Chase look?'

Sophie shakes her head. 'What's happened to you?'

I laugh. 'What do you mean?'

'Nancy, you are Chasing Chords' number one fan!' she cries.

'Usually by now,' Layla chips in, 'you'd know everything there is to know about the music video and you'd be going on and on about the inspiration behind the song and what each lyric means. We wouldn't get a word in edgeways.'

'Well, like I said, I was busy,' I say, getting a little defensive. 'I'll watch it now. I'm still their number one fan; I just had other things to do.'

'Have you gone off Chase or something?' Layla asks. 'Is this because you're not the girl he's looking for?'

'Firstly, I *am* the girl he's looking for. And secondly, I will NEVER go off Chase. I will watch the video now and I can promise you that at lunchtime I will be telling you everything you need to know about this song, OK?'

Layla raises her eyebrows and shrugs, picking up her phone to check her Instagram.

I put my earphones in and click on the link to Chasing Chords' new video. I feel annoyed that my friends are questioning my loyalty to Chase and his band just because I didn't watch his new music video as soon as it was uploaded.

And, yes, fine, normally I would have been counting down the minutes until the video was released and then I would have watched it a million times before researching everything about it, trawling through their vlogs and interviews, so that at school I was the one who knew all the facts BUT Nina had been droning on about this movie for ages and then when we put it on she was really excited to point out interesting bits about it as it played, so I felt I couldn't just get out my phone and watch a music video right in the middle of it. I didn't want to upset her and make out like I was bored.

I'm still being extra nice to her in the hope that she might talk to me about her mystery boyfriend. I know there is no point in forcing her to reveal all about him; Nina wouldn't like that and I don't want to make her feel uncomfortable. I'm a very patient person and I feel happy in the knowledge that she'll tell me all about him when she's ready.

I just wish she'd HURRY UP.

Anyway, by the time I'd got to bed I'd actually forgotten the Chasing Chords video had been released and I was so tired I didn't check my social media before bed, so I didn't see any of the reminders.

'As usual, it's genius,' I declare, putting down my phone and taking out my earphones. 'Miles looks good in that jacket.'

'Miles? Don't you mean Chase?' Sophie says, looking confused.

'Chase is the hottest by far, obviously, that goes without saying.' I sigh, frustrated that I'm having to explain everything today. 'Miles just looks good, too, that's all. Have you guys noticed how he's wearing a lot of grey T-shirts these days?'

'You said that yesterday,' Layla mumbles, scrolling through her phone.

'I just think it's very noticeable. Someone *must* have pointed out to him that he looked good in them and also told him that he should avoid floral shirts,' I say smugly.

I wish I could tell Layla and Sophie that I am that very person and that Miles and I have met, but if I told them that I would have to admit how I bumped into him outside the hotel trying to get Chase's attention. It's too embarrassing to tell them the full story.

'The band has stylists.' Layla shrugs. 'It will be one of them. And who cares anyway?'

'Well, I think he looks great. But, of course, Chase looks the best. It's so obvious what this song is about, too.'

'It is?' Sophie asks, leaning forward eagerly. 'Is it about Miles's cat?'

'What? Why would the song be about his CAT?'

'He loves Buttercup.'

'Yeah, I know, but he's not going to write a song about Buttercup, is he?' I roll my eyes. 'Sophie, you know that Chase writes all the songs.'

'But there's that lyric about "hiding in the shadows, away from the light",' Sophie points out. 'That's what cats do. They hide in shadows. There's a cat on our road who always sits behind the bin and then meows really loudly every time I walk past and makes me jump.' She shudders. 'I think that cat is out to get me.'

'Sophie, he doesn't mean it *literally*,' I say, shaking my head at her. 'What Chase clearly means is that this person he's singing about is hidden from the spotlight. The spotlight that he is in. Get it?'

She looks confused. 'So, they're . . . not in the band?'

'They're not famous. They're too shy to come out of the "shadows" and into the spotlight of fame with him. This song is very obviously about #FINDTHEGIRL.'

'You think he's written this song about you?' Sophie gasps.

'Yes.' I clutch my phone to my chest. 'And it is perfect.'

'Wow,' she says dreamily. 'Chase Hunter has written a song about you. That's AMAZING.'

'It's because he still hasn't found me. I'm in the shadows, you see? But this song proves he's not given up on finding me and I've not given up either. In fact, this weekend I am planning on –'

'Oh my god,' Layla says suddenly, staring at her phone. Her mouth is wide open and she looks in complete shock. 'What the . . . ?'

'What's wrong?' Sophie asks, looking at Layla in concern. 'Is everything OK?'

'It's Chase and . . . NINA!'

Layla screams my twin's name so loudly that everyone in the classroom stops talking to turn to look at us. Mrs Smithson has just walked in and, as Layla yells, she jumps, spilling her coffee all down herself.

'You have GOT to be kidding,' Mrs Smithson growls, reaching for a tissue. 'Why does this keep happening?!'

'What about Nina?' I ask Layla, glancing over to where my sister is sitting with her headphones on, oblivious to anyone shouting her name across the room.

'There's a picture of her with Chase Hunter!' Layla tells the whole room, causing everyone to gasp. 'And it's all over the news! It says that she's the one from the #FINDTHEGIRL Twitter campaign! Look!'

Nancy

As Layla shoves her phone in my face, everybody else in the class gets out their phones and immediately starts typing into them.

'Layla, don't be so –'

I stop as I look at her screen. I snatch it from her hand to look at it more closely.

'Ouch!' she huffs, rubbing her hand. 'Your nails are so scratchy.'

But I'm not listening to a word she says. Because I'm looking at a picture of Chase Hunter, the love of my life, walking hand in hand down the street with someone who looks identical to me and Nina. And she has headphones round her neck.

I swipe to the next photo and it's Chase with the same girl, but in this one they're kissing.

This can't be right. It just can't be. It doesn't make any sense.

My heart is slamming hard against my chest and I can feel the heat rising up my cheeks. I scroll down to the news story below the pictures.

Has she FINALLY been found?

Ever since Chasing Chords heart-throb, Chase Hunter, tweeted about meeting a girl after his London concert and used the hashtag #FINDTHEGIRL, which immediately went viral, girls all over the country have been claiming to be Miss N. Palmer. But

there seems to be only one girl who has captured this
musician's heart – spotted walking in Norfolk holding hands,
Chase appears to be besotted with this mystery blonde, who
many are speculating is the girl Chase has been looking for.
'I've never seen Chase this happy,' a source close to Chase
EXCLUSIVELY revealed. 'They've been keeping their romance
low key, but it's obvious to all of us that Chase has found the
girl of his dreams.'

I read it again and again and again until the words all
blur together. I look at the pictures, zooming in carefully. I
can hardly breathe. This just can't be right. There must
have been some kind of mistake. This HAS to be fake.

Layla coughs pointedly. 'Can I have my phone back please?'

I hand it back to Layla in a daze and I stare at Nina.
Everyone is staring at Nina.

'But . . . but . . . I thought it was *you*?' Sophie whispers,
looking at me wide-eyed for an explanation. 'This whole
time, it was *Nina*? That doesn't make any sense.'

'She was there that night of the concert,' Layla enthuses.
'And her name is Miss N. Palmer! "N" didn't stand for
Nancy. It stands for Nina!'

Nina pulls her headphones down from her ears, noticing
that Mrs Smithson is now in the room. Only then does she
realize that the room is eerily quiet and everyone is staring
at her. She glances around nervously and then looks at me.
I glare back.

How could you?

'Nina, look this way!' Layla calls out over the silence, holding up her phone and taking a photo of her. 'Perfect.'

'What?' Nina squeaks, with a terrified expression. 'What's going on?'

'You're dating Chase Hunter!' Timothy grins, moving from his desk to crouch down next to hers and snapping a selfie with her before she has any clue what's going on. 'That's so cool!'

I watch as all the colour drains from her face.

'What?' she whispers.

'There're pictures of you all over the internet,' a boy on the other side of the classroom shouts out. 'It's definitely you, Nina. Look, you've got your headphones on in this one.'

'I've tweeted your picture and tagged Chase, the band and a couple of the gossip sites that have been writing about you.' Layla smiles triumphantly, holding up her phone to show the class. 'Now, everyone will know the mystery has been solved. I can't believe this whole time Nancy thought Chase was looking for her, when in fact it was YOU! And you've been dating him! So, Nina, what's he like?'

The room explodes into noise and Mrs Smithson does her best to bring the class back under control, instructing us to please sit down, but there's no hope. No one is listening to her. It's complete chaos. Sophie and Layla have already got up to join everybody else in clustering around her desk at the front, bombarding her with questions and taking selfies. Nina is frozen to her chair like a rabbit caught in the headlights, unable to say anything or answer anybody's questions.

I stay seated on my own at the back.

I feel like I'm in some kind of dream; an alternative universe where everything is upside down. In the real world, *I'm* meant to be the one who dates the globally famous pop star. Not my shy, socially awkward, nerdy twin sister. This can't be right. Like Sophie says, it doesn't make sense.

Or does it?

As I sit there, watching everyone fight for her attention while I'm left behind, everything seems to fall into place. A shiver runs down my spine.

I think back to how she acted when she first saw that #FINDTHEGIRL tweet. While I danced around all day, she was thoughtful and distant, unwilling to help me work out a plan to get to Chase and tell him that I was the one he was looking for. She started playing Chasing Chords songs all the time; I'd heard her, shut away in her room, practising 'Ghosts' over and over. The song Chase wrote and played on his own.

That's why her confidence had grown. Chase Hunter, the famous pop star, has brought my twin sister out of her shell. He hasn't been coming to Norwich because he knows I'm here. It's because he knows Nina's here.

And then there was the total secrecy shrouding her new relationship. It wasn't because Nina was embarrassed and shy about meeting someone she liked; it was because they didn't want the press finding out. Nina couldn't handle that attention. All that sneaking around; all those mysterious, loved-up smiles when she came back from 'days out with Jimmy' – all lies.

She'd been with him. This whole time *she'd been with him.*

I'd sat on her bed and told her how I felt about Chase. She'd read my fan fiction. She'd comforted me when I got turned away from events that he was at, trying to get him to notice me. I'd told her everything. I thought we were friends. I was so happy to have my sister back, and she was laughing at me all this time, sneaking out and dating the person I was in love with behind my back.

I have been telling everyone that I'm the one Chase is looking for and she just let me! She let me make a complete fool of myself in front of my family, my friends and my entire school. I feel embarrassed and angry, but, more than anything, I feel hurt. So hurt that I feel physically sick. I have to get out.

How could I have been so *stupid*?

I stand up dizzily and hurry towards the door, past the crowd surrounding Nina.

'Nancy!' she cries over the noise, leaping to her feet as I trip over someone's bag. 'Wait! I'm so sorry!'

I don't stop. I can't even look at her. I never want to speak to her ever again. I don't want anything to do with her. I don't know her at all.

I slam the door of the classroom behind me and run down the corridor towards the toilets as quickly as possible.

'There she is! Chase's girlfriend!'

A voice squeals down the corridor as a group of girls from the year below look up excitedly from their phones as I near them.

'No, that's not her,' one of them says, looking back to her screen and pointing at it. 'Chase is going out with *Nina* Palmer. Wrong twin.'

I push open the door to the toilets and shut myself in a cubicle, trying to slow down my breathing while their words echo in my brain.

Wrong twin.

They couldn't be more right. I *am* the wrong twin. I've been wrong about all of it. About Chase. About #FINDTHEGIRL. About Nina. About everything. As I slide down to sit on the cold bathroom floor and hug my knees to my chest, I burst into tears.

The morning of Summer Cowley's ninth birthday party, I climbed into Nina's bed and I told her I was never going to let anyone hurt and humiliate me like that ever again.

I was wrong about that too.

CHAPTER SIXTEEN

NINA

'Nancy! Wait! I'm so sorry!'

My desperate call to stop Nancy is drowned out by everyone else in the classroom shouting above each other, but, even if she does hear me, she doesn't want to listen. She disappears through the door looking as though she's about to cry and I wish I could run after her, but I can't move. I'm completely surrounded.

'Is it true, Nina? Are you really dating Chase Hunter?'

'What's he like?! How did you meet?!'

'Oh my god, Nina, you're dating the hottest boy on the planet!! Does this make you a celebrity too?'

'Have you been dating him all this time? Were you the reason for #FINDTHEGIRL?'

'Nina! Can he come visit the school?'

'Can I have a selfie with you? This is the coolest thing to ever happen!'

I'm bombarded with so many questions at once that no one actually gives me any time to answer any of them, and as they crowd round my desk, jostling each other to get closer, I start to panic. They're so close, it feels as though there's not enough air around me and I'm going to suffocate. And Nancy isn't here to save me this time.

'All right, that's enough!' Mrs Smithson suddenly bellows, parting the crowd and helping me to my feet. 'Come on, Nina – let's go for a time out. Everyone else, back to your desks and you can start getting on with your homework. If I hear any noise coming from this classroom, then you'll all be in detention for a week.'

The class descends into whispers as Mrs Smithson gently escorts me out of the door. The second the door closes we hear an eruption of excitable noise.

'Well, that threat worked.' Mrs Smithson tuts, rolling her eyes. 'Are you all right, Nina? You look very pale. Let's get you some water in the staffroom.'

All I can think about is Nancy's face when she found out what was going on. She looked as though someone had knocked all the wind out of her. I need to find her to explain. I need her to understand.

'Nancy,' I whimper, as Mrs Smithson ushers me to sit down in one of the staffroom chairs.

I feel numb as everything begins to sink in. The perfect shield of secrecy that Chase and I had, protecting us from the world, has been shattered.

'Nancy has popped to the toilet, I think,' Mrs Smithson says. 'I saw her heading that way down the corridor.'

'She's going to hate me.'

'Why would she hate you? I've noticed you've both been a lot better with each other recently. It's been lovely to see. I never really understood why you two were so averse to being friends. You're so lucky to have a sister!'

I look down at my feet.

'You look like you're in shock,' she says, bringing a cup of water and placing it down on the coffee table next to me. 'Do you want to talk about it?'

I shake my head. 'Chase is going to be so angry.'

'Can you tell me what's going on? Just an overview is fine.'

I bite my lip. 'It sounds a bit unbelievable.'

'Judging by the reaction of your classmates that I just witnessed, I'm ready for that,' Mrs Smithson assures me warmly.

'I've been dating the lead singer of a pop band. We've been keeping it a secret.'

Mrs Smithson nods. 'I see. Nothing unbelievable about that. It makes sense that you'd connect with another talented musician. I was so very proud of you at the talent show.'

A tear slides down my cheek. 'Mrs Smithson, I've ruined everything. Everyone is going to hate me. Especially Nancy – she loves Chase. I don't know what to do.'

'It will all be absolutely fine in the end, you'll see. Have some water.'

I pick up the cup of water gratefully, taking a small sip, but my hands are shaking too much and I have to put it back down again. Mrs Smithson notices that I'm shivering and puts the nearest coat she can find around my shoulders.

'Everyone knows about me and Chase.' I sniff, wiping my tears with my sleeve. 'This wasn't supposed to happen. I don't know how they took that photo. We've been so careful . . .'

As I say the words, I know I don't mean them. At first, we were careful when we met up, making sure that we went places as low key as possible so Chase wouldn't be recognized. But that photo was taken the day Jimmy met Chase. We'd left the studio and walked down the street all together. I'd felt so happy about Chase's comments on my performance and that Jimmy and he were getting on so well.

In that moment, we'd completely forgotten to hide how we felt.

'I'd better go and talk to the headmistress about this,' Mrs Smithson says, her voice full of concern as she passes me a tissue. 'Thanks to the joys of social media and Layla's speedy upload this morning, I can't imagine it will be too long until the press finds you.'

'The reporters won't be interested in me, will they?' I squeak, my mouth turning dry. 'They . . . they only care about Chase.'

'Let me get the headmistress. You sit tight and I'll be back in a moment.'

'I have to find Nancy.'

'You can do that once we've talked this through. I think everybody needs to calm down for a moment. Now, deep breaths. I'll be back in a moment.'

She leaves and I sit in silence for a few minutes, but my phone feels heavy in my pocket. I can't stop thinking about it and eventually I give in. I need to see how this happened. I put my mug down again, get my phone out and type 'Chase Hunter' into the search engine.

I wish I hadn't.

The picture of us walking together holding hands is *everywhere*. Already there are hundreds of news pieces listed about it, as well as mentions and comments all over Twitter and Instagram. There's even a new hashtag that has gone viral through Chase's fan club: #FOUNDTHEGIRL.

And then I see one of the latest tweets at the top of the search and I suddenly feel nauseous:

N is for Nancy! Miss Nancy Palmer who lives in Norfolk is Chase's girlfriend! #FOUNDTHEGIRL

Poor Nancy! Whoever tweeted it must have seen her Twitter picture and assumed it's her. People mixing us up is only going to make this worse.

I quickly turn off my phone, shutting my eyes as tightly as possible. I know Chase might try and call but I can't handle talking to him right now. I can't even handle EXISTING right now. I wish I could run home and hide, but then I'd have to face Mum and I can't deal with her asking me a load of questions either.

And the image of Nancy's face when she found out everything just won't go out of my head. I keep reliving the moment. I've never seen her look so hurt. How could I do this to her? I need to explain.

I jump to my feet ready to go and find Nancy just as the headmistress walks in and asks me kindly to sit down again so I can tell her exactly what's going on. I reluctantly do as I'm told and I go through all her questions, all the while desperate to get out and find my sister.

'I think it's best to carry on today as normal,' the headmistress eventually decides, and Mrs Smithson nods in agreement. 'Now that we know all the facts, we can make sure you're protected from any unwanted attention.'

'Can't I go home?' I plead. 'If you could just let me and Nancy go back home then we could –'

'You're safest here,' the headmistress says sternly. 'I've spoken to your mother and she agrees that's the best thing to do. Apparently, she's been fielding some calls from reporters at her shop.'

'Already?' I gasp. 'How can they know how to reach my mum?'

'Oh, they have their ways. And after that picture went up of you in class this morning, you wouldn't have been very difficult to track down. Speaking of which –' the headmistress sighs and gives Mrs Smithson a pointed look – 'could you ask Layla to come to my office at lunch? I'd like to have a word with her about that particular decision of hers.'

'It's because she hates me,' I murmur, burying my head in my hands.

'I doubt it,' Mrs Smithson chuckles. 'I think you'll find you're more of a celebrity in her eyes. Layla loves all that nonsense.'

'You don't understand,' I say as tears roll uncontrollably down my cheeks. 'She's best friends with Nancy and I've been lying to her.'

The headmistress forces me to stay in the staffroom until the end of morning break, so I don't have the chance to find Nancy, and when I build up the courage to go to my next lesson, guided by Mrs Smithson and her cheery encouragement, it's a complete disaster. I stare straight ahead or down at my book, but I can feel everyone's eyes boring into my back the entire time. I already hear whispers and snide comments as I walk down the school corridors.

'Don't you think it's weird?' I hear a boy say to his friend as I swap books from my locker. 'Why *her*?'

'I know,' his friend replies. 'I'd never even really noticed her before she won the talent show.'

At lunch, I seek refuge in the staffroom again and try to ignore all the teachers' sympathetic looks. I don't touch any of my food and I can't even think about turning my phone on again. If that's what people are saying about me within earshot, what might they be saying online?

I hear a commotion at the door and suddenly I feel a glimmer of hope. Nancy. It has to be her. Maybe she understands why I did what I did and she's decided to forgive me. I sit up as Mrs Smithson stands aside to let whoever it is in.

'Cool, I've never been in the staffroom before,' Jimmy says, waving at a disapproving Mr Barber. 'Hey, Mr B, good class today. I think it's the first time I haven't got detention in a while.'

'Jimmy,' I say, standing up and throwing my arms around him.

'Hey, you,' he says, holding me close. 'Are you OK?'

I start crying again and wonder if I'll ever be able to stop crying. Surely there can't be many tears left and I now have a horrible headache. I release him after sobbing into his shoulder and he sits down next to me, his eyebrows furrowed.

'Have you spoken to Chase?'

I shake my head.

'What? Why not? Hasn't he called?'

'I've turned off my phone. I don't think I can face him or anyone else quite yet.' I give Jimmy a small smile. 'I think you might be the only person in the world I *can* face right now.'

'I'm honoured.' He takes a deep breath. 'What about Nancy?'

'I haven't been able to talk to her. She stormed out of class this morning. She wouldn't even look at me.' My face crumples. 'Everything has gone wrong.'

'Nina, it's OK. It's going to be fine,' he says soothingly. 'You knew it was going to happen one day, right? You and Chase were never going to be able to keep this up forever.'

'I know.' I sniff, grabbing another tissue. 'But I just wanted it to be secret a bit longer. Until I knew how to tell Nancy and how to deal with what was going to happen. I don't want any attention.'

'I'm not sure you're going to have much of a say on that one.' He sighs, patting my hand. 'You did decide to fall in love with an internationally famous musician. People tend to notice that kind of thing.'

'What do I do?' I ask quietly, searching his eyes.

'I'm not sure,' he admits, slumping back and running a hand through his hair. 'I think you need to talk to Chase and go from there. He'll be upset too that this has happened and will probably feel guilty for dragging you into the spotlight.'

'It's not his fault.'

'Tell him that.' Jimmy reaches forward and puts a hand on my shoulder. 'Nina, you couldn't keep your secret forever. You have to deal with it. You can't hide away and nor should you.'

'I wish this hadn't happened,' I say, shaking my head as I look down at the floor.

'Can you go home until things cool down?'

'No. I tried but Mum and the teachers think it's better to stay here, so I'm stuck until the end of the day. The press has tracked down Mum at the shop.'

'Whoa, they work fast. Well, look, you don't need to worry. I'm here to protect you – we'll face this together.'

'Thanks, Jimmy,' I say, attempting a weak smile. 'I don't know what I'd do without you.'

Sitting through another afternoon of staring and pointing is torture and I can't concentrate on anything else. I just have to get through the day. I get waves of panic whenever my thoughts drift to the idea of reporters and photographers, so I try to focus on Chase and that warm, tingly feeling I get when I'm with him. But it doesn't work. When I think about him, I'm hit by a wave of guilt about Nancy. Nothing makes me feel better or comforted, not even the thought of Chase. Even the shell in my pocket seems to have lost its magic.

Nina

The bell rings for the end of the day and I start packing up my books, aware that everyone is still watching me. I haven't been pestered by my class since this morning and I guess that Mrs Smithson has told them that they're not allowed. But that hasn't protected me from the hordes of students in the corridor as I leave my classroom asking for selfies and autographs, and asking a million questions about Chase.

I keep my head down and say nothing as they all crowd around me, walking as fast as possible towards my locker and attempting to type in my passcode but my brain is so muddled in my panic that I get the combination wrong twice before I finally get it open.

'Hey, leave her alone!' Jimmy's voice is raised as he shoos people out of his way. 'Unless you want me to start singing an array of songs from musical theatre at the top of my lungs, I suggest you all move along.'

For a moment, those gathered around me are unsure what to do until Jimmy takes a deep breath in and belts out the first verse of 'Listen' from *Dreamgirls*. It sends them all scattering in different directions.

I laugh and it's the first time I've smiled since the news broke about Chase and me this morning.

'I have to admit, I wasn't actually expecting them to literally run away when I started singing, but I guess either way the plan worked.' Jimmy grins, leaning on the locker next to mine. 'So, you made it through the day. The hardest bit is over.'

'Not quite,' I say, any good feeling from Jimmy's singing slipping away back into glumness. 'I still haven't spoken to Nancy. Or Chase. Can you stay with me while I turn on my phone? I'm scared I've got lots of horrible messages.'

'Who would send you horrible messages?'

'Chase's fans for a start. They're hardly going to be happy he's dating someone like me, are they?'

'I'm choosing to ignore the "someone like me" comment, because it's silly. And anyway, Nina, how could they send you horrible messages? You're not on social media. That will have played massively in your favour. How can they find out anything about you?'

'You're right,' I say, staring down at my phone as though it might bite me at any moment. 'I should just get this over with.'

Jimmy waits by my side as I turn my phone on and wait for the screen to light up. I hold my breath. It instantly starts vibrating as the messages and missed calls stream in. Most of them are from Mum and Chase.

'Wow, Chase has tried calling you so many times,' Jimmy says, looking over my shoulder.

'I should call him back now,' I say, reading the last text from him that just says *Call me.*

Jimmy nods. 'I'll go wait for you outside by the school gates, OK?'

'Thanks.'

Nina

I walk down the corridor and push open the door to an empty classroom, pressing Chase's number. He answers on the first ring.

'Hi.'

His voice is short and cold. I know instantly something is wrong.

'Chase, I'm sorry, my phone was off and I had to –'

'I can't believe you did this to me! I trusted you!'

'Chase, I had no idea about the photo and this girl in my class tweeted that picture of me before I had a chance to stop her!'

I'm so shocked by his harsh tone that I sit down on the nearest chair to stop my legs shaking.

'I'm not talking about the picture, Nina!' he snaps. 'Or should I say . . . Nancy!'

'Nancy . . . Chase, what are you talking about?'

'I found your website and all your fan fiction about the band. There're pictures of you all over your Chasing Chords blog, *Nancy*. I'm completely humiliated! I can't believe you lied about your name, just so I wouldn't find your website. Miles told me about running into you when you were camped outside our hotel. Did you follow me to the record shop and make it seem like fate? How have I been so stupid?! And our publicity team has pulled out plenty of tweets from you that you've been sending the band for years. It's so embarrassing!'

'No, Chase, please, you've got it wrong,' I sob, trying to get the words out but he won't let me. He cuts across me again.

'You lied to me about your name. You lied to me about not having social media. You lied to me about absolutely everything!' he shouts. 'And I fell for it like a total idiot! What were you planning on doing? Getting as many secrets out of me as possible and then plastering them all over your website for the whole world to see? I trusted you! I fell for you! And the whole time you were playing a part. Well, congratulations, you won. You truly got me.'

'Chase –'

'Nancy, Nina, whatever your name is, I don't care what you have to say. I thought you were different. But you're nothing but an obsessed fan girl. It's *pathetic*. Never contact me again.'

The line goes dead as he hangs up. I try calling him back but he doesn't pick up and the second time I try he's turned his phone off or blocked me.

How has everything gone so wrong? I should have told him about Nancy but I was terrified of losing him if he found out that my twin sister was completely obsessed with him and his band.

After all that, I've lost him anyway.

I start to breathe too heavily and a cold sweat breaks out across my forehead as I get that panicky feeling. I know that I need to get out of the school but I'm so upset and hurt that I feel too weak to move. Chase is right; I am pathetic. I push myself up from the chair and then rush out of the classroom, running down the corridor to the doors, tears streaming down my face.

I burst out into the cold air, praying that Jimmy is the only one left hanging around school but there're still loads of students standing in clusters, laughing and chatting together, waiting for their parents to pick them up. I quickly wipe my face, hoping no one will see how puffy and red it is, and I rush down the steps with my hair falling forward over my face, desperately searching for Jimmy.

'Hi, Nina!'

Layla steps right in my path so that I almost slam straight into her.

'Sorry, Layla, I can't talk. I have to go.'

'Oh, don't worry. Your mum isn't here yet. Nancy just got off the phone to her and she was delayed because of all the reporters at the shop. So, you and Chase, huh? I never would have guessed.' She hesitates, peering at me. 'Hey, have you been crying?'

'Layla, please! I have to go!' I beg, trying to step past her. She grabs my arm, stopping me.

'Before you go, I wanted to invite you to my birthday party coming up. Obviously Chase is welcome too. I think it's really cool that you're dating him and didn't tell anyone. That's just what I would be like if I dated someone famous. Really classy of you. So you guys should come! If you're worried about all the attention he might get, you don't need to be. I already decided that I won't be inviting anyone immature who would go obsessive crazy over him and embarrass all of us,' she says, rolling her eyes. 'Like Nancy.'

As I pull my arm loose from her grip, I see Nancy standing only a few metres away from us.

She's heard everything.

CHAPTER SEVENTEEN

NANCY

Layla's words hit me so hard it feels like someone has punched me in the stomach.

'Nancy,' Nina croaks, shaking her arm from Layla's grip, 'please, I can explain.'

Nina looks terrible. Her eyes are red and swollen and her pale cheeks are wet from fresh tears. Just looking at her makes my eyes well up again. I don't want to cry in front of anyone, but most of all I don't want to cry in front of *her*.

'Don't bother. Just leave me alone,' I snap, giving her and Layla a disgusted look before turning away and marching towards the school gates.

'Nancy, please!' Nina yells, her voice carrying across the school yard so now everyone is turning to look at us. 'Please, you have to listen to me!'

'No, I don't!' I shout back, as she runs over and blocks my path. 'I don't have to listen to a word you say! You lied to me about everything! Leave me alone, Nina.'

'Please,' she begs, tears streaming down her cheeks. 'I was waiting for the right time and I never meant to hurt you.'

'Well, you *have* hurt me. You've lied to me, you've humiliated me, you've taken Chase from me and now, by the sounds of it, you've taken my friends from me too.'

I glare pointedly at Layla who is watching the drama unfold like everyone else. There are paparazzi EVERYWHERE. They're crowded around the school gates, unable to come into the grounds. Cameras are pointing in our direction, flashbulbs are going off and you can hear the reporters shouting, 'Nancy! Nancy Palmer!' They've got the wrong twin, too.

Parents chatting outside the school gates are craning their heads to see what's going on, and out of the corner of my eye I see phones pointed in our direction. People are filming our big bust-up.

I just want to get out of here and Nina won't let me.

'Nancy, it just happened with Chase. I didn't plan it,' she whines desperately. 'If you could let me explain rather than –'

'Nina, I don't care about what happened with Chase!' I explode, furious that she just doesn't get it. 'I care about what happened with us!'

It had hit me at lunchtime. After reapplying my make-up, I'd returned to the classroom to find that Nina had been escorted to the staffroom by Mrs Smithson. I tried to ignore all the whispering and pointing, and sat down at my desk, pretending to get on with work. While Sophie kept shooting me sympathetic looks and biting her lip, Layla had tried to get me to talk about it, asking if I'd had any idea, wondering aloud whether Nina had been hanging out with any other cool celebrities since the concert.

'Do you think you upset her by telling everyone it was you Chase was looking for?' she asked me at one point, and then when I didn't answer she sighed and said, 'I always thought it would be a bit weird that he would create that #FINDTHEGIRL hashtag for someone he's never even met.'

Thankfully, Layla's loud ponderings were cut short by Mrs Smithson coming back to begin our lesson, and as soon as the lunchtime bell rang I made my excuses and ran to hide in the library, the last place anyone would look for me. I sat in the far back corner and tried to call Mum, desperate to talk to someone, but the line was busy. I thought about skipping school for the rest of the day, but I didn't know where I'd go. It was too cold to wander around all day and I couldn't bear the idea of being home on my own. The paparazzi might have worked out where Nina lived and then there was the question of my room – Chasing Chords is *everywhere*. The pillows, the photo frames, the merchandise. All reminding me of this complete and utter humiliation. And, more importantly, it's Nina's home too.

And that's when it really hit. What was really going on. Why I was *this* hurt. It wasn't because I wanted to be with Chase and she had nabbed him from under my nose. Yeah, that was hurtful but it wasn't that which was causing this ache. It was because I thought Nina and I were friends.

That was the real sting.

'You let me believe we were friends again,' I hiss, pushing past her.

'We *are* friends!' Nina cries in exasperation, grabbing my arm. 'Of course we're friends! You're my sister! I was trying to protect you!'

'What kind of sister does what you have done?' I yell. 'I love Chase and you took him from me! I don't want anything to do with either of you.'

She recoils from me, anger flashing across her eyes. Her expression changes from pleading to fury.

'You know what, Nancy? I'm not going to stand here in front of everyone and let you shout nasty things at me. I've said I'm sorry and I've tried to explain everything to you, but you're too wrapped up in your own self-pity to listen.'

'Chase and I –'

'You don't know Chase, Nancy!' she yells, stepping forward so boldly that I'm taken aback and stumble. 'You've never met him! You made up a fantasy about him in your head and you've convinced yourself that you love him. But I know him. He's nothing like the person you think he is. And now he hates me anyway, and it's all because of you!'

'Me?' I shake my head at her in disbelief. 'How can you possibly blame *me* for anything?'

'Because he found your website and he thinks that I'm an obsessed fan – he thinks I'm *you*!'

'Oh, so you didn't even tell him you had a twin sister? You pretended I didn't exist?'

'I was scared, Nancy!' she cries, throwing her arms up in the air. 'I was terrified of losing him and I was terrified of losing you! Now, I've lost you both anyway.' Her eyes meet mine, and I swallow the lump in my throat. 'So, if you don't want anything to do with me either, Nancy, that's your decision. All I wanted to say is that I never meant for any of this to happen. I'm so sorry I hurt you.'

'Nina! Nancy!'

Suddenly Mum is next to us, pulling Nina into a hug. 'I've been so worried!'

Nina begins to sob into her shoulder.

'Come on, both of you,' Mum cries, gesturing for me to come closer and get under her other arm. She glances at the crowd waiting at the gates. 'We'll have to battle through the reporters together.'

'I'm not going home with *her*,' I say stubbornly, glaring at Nina. 'I'll find my own way back.'

'Don't be ridiculous, Nancy. Come on,' Mum pleads. 'It's total chaos – we have to get out of here.'

'She's a liar and I don't want to be seen with her.'

'Nancy!' Mum shouts so sharply that my eyes start to sting with tears. 'This is not a joke! I will not leave you here.'

'Fine,' I mutter, shocked by her tone.

She puts her arm tightly around me, her other still gripping Nina close, and we barrel our way through the paparazzi, who shout questions so loudly at us and push their lenses so close to my face that I suddenly feel frightened and dizzy from all the camera flashes. I'm grateful for Mum's strong arm, guiding me to wherever the car is.

She stops, opening the car door and ushering me into the back seat, slamming it behind me. As Nina gets into the front and Mum makes her way around to the driver's seat, batting away the reporters, we are both silent, breathing heavily in shock as people bang on the windows and continue to take photos.

'This is all your fault,' I hiss.

'You don't know what you're talking about, Nancy,' Nina replies, turning away from the window and covering her face with her hands.

'If you and Chase had handled the situation a little better, none of this would have happened. Mum and I wouldn't be being harassed right now.'

'Oh please, Nancy,' Nina groans as Mum slams her door, turns the key in the ignition and pulls away into the road. 'Don't pretend that this isn't exactly what you would love.'

'Girls, please,' Mum croaks, blinking through all the flashbulbs. 'I'm trying to concentrate.'

A reporter leans on to the bonnet to try to get a shot of Nina in the front, and Mum beeps the horn loudly.

'What is wrong with you?!' she yells, beeping and beeping until they reluctantly clear the path, camera lenses bouncing off the windows as we edge forward.

'See what you've done, Nina? You're upsetting Mum! She's shaking!' I snap, leaning forward to place a hand on Mum's arm. 'Don't worry, Mum – it'll be OK.'

'This is not my fault, Nancy!'

Mum puts her foot down on the accelerator, changing gear clumsily. 'I've got to get you two out of here.'

'How can you say that? This *is* all your fault, Nina!'

'You just can't bear the fact that you're not the centre of attention for once!' Nina yells, turning round in her seat to look at me, her eyes flashing with anger. 'You don't care about me or my happiness. It's always you, isn't it, Nancy? You can't handle that they don't want your picture. They want mine!'

'Nina, stop!' Mum cries, a tear running down her cheek.

'That is not true!' I scream back at her. 'I was the one who told you to enter the talent show! I was being supportive! You've been the worst sister in the world!'

'Nancy –'

'No, Mum, she needs to hear it!' I yell, hot tears streaming uncontrollably down my face. 'You lied to me!'

'I did it to protect you!' Nina whines.

'Girls! Please stop! Stop right now!'

'You humiliated me when I was nothing but kind to you!' I retort.

'The only reason you were being kind is because you wanted my help! Your friends knew you were being ridiculous about #FINDTHEGIRL but you just had to get your way! I was the only one who bothered listening to you!'

'GIRLS!'

'You were supposed to be my friend, Nina!'

'Nancy, I never meant to –'

'I NEVER want to speak to you EVER AGAIN!' I shout, slumping back in my seat and looking out of the window, wiping my cheeks with my sleeve. Nina looks as though someone has punched her in the stomach.

'GIRLS, PLEASE!' Mum wails, her eyes fixed on the road ahead. 'Please, just sto–'

Suddenly a high-pitched screech pierces my ears. There's a loud bang and everything seems to spin upside down.

Then it all goes black.

Nancy! Nancy!

My eyelids feel heavy as I try to open them. It's all hazy, but I can make out someone's face and their green uniform.

'Nancy? Can you hear me?'

Everything is blurry. My ears are ringing.

'Where am I?' I try to look around but everything aches. I'm lying on something hard and cold. The ground. I'm on the ground. Suddenly I notice the searing pain in my left arm. I cry out. 'My arm! My arm hurts! What's happening?'

All of my senses hurt and my vision keeps going blotchy. There are flashing blue lights and I can see coloured glass scattered about the road.

'It's all right. There's been an accident, but you're OK. We're just going to move you on to this stretcher, OK? Then we're going to get you in the ambulance and fix that arm.'

An accident?

I remember the noise. The loud crashing noise. Oh my god. Mum. *Nina.*

'Where's my mum? Nina! Where's Nina!'

All of a sudden, I feel hands grip me, lifting me on to a stretcher. And that's when I see Mum, covered in scratches and bruises, holding Nina's hand – Nina, who is lying on a stretcher nearby, being wheeled away from me. Nina's eyes are closed.

'Nina!' I croak, trying to reach out but my limbs are too heavy. 'Nina! Wait! I want to go with Nina!'

'Your mum and Nina are going in the other ambulance,' the paramedic explains, as I'm lifted into an ambulance and she shuts the door behind us. 'We've got to get you all to hospital.'

'What happened?' I choke through tears, the pain becoming unbearable as she and another paramedic start saying things I don't understand to each other and fiddling with scary equipment next to me. I hear the muffled sound of the siren come on and the ambulance begins to move. 'I want to go with Mum and Nina!'

I struggle with all the energy I can muster to get up but I can't move. I finally give in. The paramedic gently tells me it's going to be OK, before everything fades back into darkness.

CHAPTER EIGHTEEN

NANCY

The first thing I see when I wake up is Mum. She's sitting on the side of the hospital bed, leaning forward, stroking my hair.

'Hi,' she whispers, her eyes glistening. 'How are you feeling?'

'Uh . . .' My mouth is really dry, I have a horrible headache and every muscle and bone in my body hurts. 'Fine. Mum, what happened? I can't remember what happened. The car. Where's Nina?'

'It's OK, Nancy,' she says soothingly, as I try and fail to sit up. 'We . . . we were in a car accident and your arm is broken.' She chokes back tears as she continues. 'A car went through a red light, straight into the side of our car. The side you and Nina were on . . .'

Her face crumples.

'Mum,' I whisper. 'Is Nina OK?'

She attempts a weak smile. 'She's in a stable condition but they've had to put her in a medically induced coma.'

'*What?* A coma! I have to see her!' I struggle to sit up, but it's too hard to move my arm in the plaster cast and I can't seem to get my body to properly function. It aches so badly. Mum gently presses me back into the pillow.

'You have to rest.'

'Mum, please! I have to see her!' I plead. 'Please, Mum. Take me to Nina.'

She hesitates, pursing her lips and then nods. 'Give me a moment – let me find a nurse.'

After what seems like an eternity, Mum returns with a nurse who has agreed to help me to get to Nina's room. With a wave of motivation to see Nina, I've managed to get myself sitting up on the edge of the bed and they come over to help me into a wheelchair. On the way, the nurse explains that, although I'll have a few nasty bruises, it was my arm that took the brunt of the force; it was broken in the impact.

'And Nina?' I ask him in a panicked voice. The tiniest of movements seems to hurt. 'Mum says she's in an induced coma. Will she be all right?'

He searches for the right words. 'It's hard to say, but we're hopeful. She's lucky it wasn't a lot worse.'

He stops at a door and turns into the room, setting the wheelchair next to Nina's bed.

Nina is lying there as though she's sound asleep, with all these tubes attached to her everywhere. Mum sits on the other side of the bed, gripping Nina's hand.

I can hardly bear to look.

'This is all my fault,' I sniff.

'No, Nancy,' Mum says, horrified. 'This isn't your fault! Someone ran a red light and –'

'If I hadn't argued with her after school, we would have left earlier and then that car wouldn't have hit us.'

'Nancy, you can't think like that.' Mum shakes her head. 'You just can't. This is not your fault.'

'I was so angry at her for something so stupid,' I say quietly. 'And now none of that even matters. All I want is for her to be OK.'

'She will be,' Mum says firmly, turning back to look at Nina as though telling her. 'It's an induced coma, so the doctors will pull her out of it when she's ready. She'll be all right, you'll see.'

The doctors tell us that I can go home, but Mum insists on staying overnight with Nina. I try to argue the same, but they won't let me, so Mum asks her friend Sharon to pick me up from hospital and take me home.

'I'll come back,' I whisper to Nina before I leave, squeezing her fingers using my good hand.

When we pull up to the house, Sharon bustles me into the warmth and tries to get me to eat something, but all I can do is think about Nina and everything I said to her before the accident. Thanks to the cast, I need Sharon to help me change into my pyjamas and get into bed and, even though I'm exhausted, I can't sleep. The image of

Nina lying in that horrible blue hospital gown floats into my mind every time I close my eyes.

'If you get through this, Nina,' I say out loud to my ceiling, 'I'm going to tease you forever about how silly you looked in that hospital gown.' I let out a long sigh. 'I know you're not one to care about fashion, but, trust me, you'd be mortified if Chase saw you in that thing.'

As soon as I say the words, I try to sit bolt upright.

'Chase!' I cry out into the darkness. 'ARGH!' I cry even louder, because I sat up too quickly and everything is so bruised.

Using my good arm, I fumble for my phone on the bedside table, knocking over my glass of water but I don't care.

'Nancy?' Sharon asks, creaking my door open. 'Is everything OK? I heard you shout something. Are you all right?'

'I'm so stupid,' I say, as she switches on the light.

As it has been such a horrible day, I don't care what Sharon is wearing. BUT I couldn't *not* notice that Sharon is wearing a caterpillar onesie, which is luminous green and has two antennae sticking out of the hood. It doesn't come as too much of a surprise, because Mum's friends are always as bonkers as she is, but I promise myself that WHEN Nina comes through this I will be sure to tell her Sharon's nightwear gave hers a run for its money.

'I was reading online earlier that people in medically induced comas can still hear voices and things. A lot of people have reported that they heard conversations when they were in one.'

'Right, of course,' Sharon says, sitting down on the end of my bed and swatting one of the antennas out of her face. 'Careful of your arm.'

'Nina thinks that Chase doesn't want anything to do with her any more. She told me right before . . .' I feel a stab of pain and my sentence fizzles out.

'Before the accident,' Sharon finishes gently.

'Right. Anyway, if Chase comes to see her in the hospital and if he talks to her, maybe it will help!'

'Her coma is medically induced, Nancy. They're controlling it,' Sharon points out. 'They'll bring her out when she's better.'

'I know, but I'm not saying he should come wake her up. I'm saying it will comfort her knowing that he's there for when she wakes up. All I need to do is track him down, tell him about the accident and he'll rush to her bedside, you know, like in the movies.'

'Is this a boy at your school?'

'No. He's a famous pop star.'

'Oh!' Sharon looks surprised. 'Seriously?'

'Yeah, it's a long story. It does make it hard to get to him though. Trust me, I've tried. That's part of the long story.'

I bite my lip, desperately trying to think how I can get to Chase when something catches my eye in the corner of my room: Nina's bag. I brought it back with me from the hospital.

'That's it!' I cry, pointing at the bag. 'Sharon! Can you get Nina's phone? It should be in there somewhere. Please don't be broken, phone, please don't be broken, please don't be broken!'

'It's working!' Sharon declares triumphantly, holding it up from the bag and passing it to me.

This time, I don't hesitate when it comes to the passcode.

'If ever there was a time to need all the powers of that magical key,' I say, typing in 9481, 'it's now.'

Her homescreen appears and I go straight to her messages, knowing that she probably hasn't saved Chase in her phone under his name but I'd definitely find him in her texts. At the top of the list is a conversation with the contact 'CH'.

'Not that original, Nina,' I say, clicking on it. 'You'd think she'd be a little more creative.'

I only mean to check the texts to find the contact, but I can't help but read the last few messages from him, instructing her to call him straight away. I scroll up and the difference in his tone before today is unbelievable. He must have been so angry when he found my website, thinking that Nina was behind it. I get to his messages from the night of the talent show.

Nancy

You're worth the risk . . . And
who cares?! YOU WON! I'm so
proud of you. You were amazing

He was there. Chase was there in the audience that night, cheering on and supporting my sister, just like I was. I close the messages and lower the phone, feeling terrible.

'What's wrong?' Sharon asks, looking concerned.

'I think I may have ruined something really special,' I admit quietly, gesturing to her phone. 'He really loves her. It's obvious from his messages. They had something real. I didn't have anything except fantasy.'

I shake my head at my Chasing Chords pillows. 'I've been so stupid.'

'Who cares?' Sharon cries, with such vigour that her antennae shake about wildly on top of her head. 'Nancy, it doesn't matter what has happened! All that matters is Nina! And in my opinion, your idea to get this boy she likes, whoever he is, to her bedside in her time of need is extremely thoughtful of you. Very mature for a teenager, and I know because I happen to have a teenage son and the most thoughtful thing he's ever done is to occasionally put the toilet seat down, and even that is few and far between.'

She may have antennae on her head but Sharon is right. I have to do this for Nina. It's the least I can do after the chaos I've caused. I pick the phone back up with a new sense of determination.

'OK, Sharon, I'll do this. From his messages, it looks like he won't pick up the phone to Nina but I can try anyway.'

I find CH in her contacts and press call but it beeps and cuts out mid-ring.

'It didn't work. He won't answer.'

'There must be another way of tracking him down,' Sharon says thoughtfully.

'Tracking him down ... Sharon! You're a GENIUS!' I yell.

'I am?' She blinks.

I fumble with Nina's phone to get to her apps, but it falls out of my injured hand.

Sharon chuckles. 'Here, let me.' She places it on the duvet in front of me. 'What's your plan?'

'Tracking him down! Nina has a tracking app! She and Mum use it to check where each other is.' I hold my breath, opening the app and hoping with all my heart that 'CH' is tracked. 'Please, please, please, please ...'

The pin appears in the map.

'Oh my god,' I whisper, 'it worked. IT WORKED! And look where he is!'

I shove the phone into Sharon's face.

'Norwich,' she says, peering at the screen closely. 'But I haven't heard of that road.'

'I have. I know EXACTLY where to go. Sharon, I know this is a lot to ask but please could you —'

'I'll go get my car keys.' She grins, jumping to her feet. 'There's no time to change! Let's get going!'

As she hurtles from the room, I slide my legs out of bed, grab my coat and wriggle my feet into my trainers, thanking myself for being too lazy earlier to undo the laces with one hand. Before we go, I run into Mum's room and grab a photo frame from her bedside table.

In the next few minutes, we're out of the house and flying down the country lanes towards Norwich, Sharon hunched over the steering wheel, still in her caterpillar onesie. When we get to central Norwich, I'm able to direct her and she parks on a side road near the alleyway, asking me twice if I'm sure we're in the right place.

'This is the right place, trust me.' I nod firmly, undoing my seatbelt and opening the door.

I run down the narrow alleyway, ignoring Sharon's comments about the smell from all the bins, and get to the door, banging on it as hard as I can and pressing all the buzzers. The door opens and standing in front of me is Chase Hunter.

Finally.

'Chase,' I say. 'Hi, I'm –'

'I told you never to contact me again,' he says, glaring at me. 'You shouldn't be here. Go home.'

'No, Chase, wait!'

But he shuts the door before I can put my foot in the way to stop it. I look back at Sharon.

'Well, try again!' she orders, nodding encouragingly at me. 'Don't give up. Think of Nina!'

I turn back to the door and knock and kick it until it opens again.

'Chase, I . . . Oh!' I step back, as Miles stands in front of me, his arms crossed.

Anger flares in his eyes as he says, 'So it really was you dating Chase all along? I couldn't believe it when I saw you with Chase in that pap shot. The persistent girl I almost took out with the hotel door. Who would have thought?'

'NO. It wasn't me dating Chase! That's the whole point! *It was my twin!*'

'You have got to be joking,' he says, shaking his head. 'Haven't you done enough? And now you're seriously trying that one?'

'Oh for goodness' sake,' I cry. 'I don't have time for this! Nina's sick!'

And I charge past him, pushing him aside with my good arm and racing up these narrow, old stairs before he can stop me. I burst through the door at the top into a flash studio where the whole Chasing Chords band are sitting with their producers. They all turn to look at me. Chase is at the back of the room and, as I come in, he looks down, his cheeks flaming red.

'Excuse me,' Chase's manager begins, stepping forward with a look of thunder on his face. 'You have to leave. I'm calling security.'

'I don't have time for you either, Mark. I have to talk to Chase Hunter.'

I hold out the photo I took from Mum's bedside table.

'Look!'

I hold it up for all of them to see.

'You see? We're twins! That's Nina, with the terrible hat,' I say, shoving the photo into Mark's hand so I can point at the picture. 'And that's me, Nancy, with the amazing blow-dry. Mum forced us to take this photo together on our birthday a couple of years ago. At the time we weren't exactly seeing eye-to-eye, so that's why we look very bored. But it was actually quite a nice day. We went to . . .' I trail off when I hear Miles cough from behind me. 'Sorry, not important. The point is, we're TWINS! I have never met you before in my life. *NINA has*. How do you not know this yet? It's all over the press. We had a bit of a showdown in the school yard; you can google it if you don't believe me.'

'We've been avoiding the media,' Miles explains as Chase slowly gets to his feet.

'What's going on?' he asks, coming forward to take the picture from me.

'Chase, you have been dating Nina. I'm Nancy, her twin. It's nice to meet you.' I take a deep breath. 'I also happen to have a website of fan fiction dedicated to Chasing Chords and a Twitter and Instagram account, which I use regularly. I can't play the piano but I am a naturally talented dancer.

Nina, the girl you've been seeing, had never heard any Chasing Chords music until I dragged her along to your concert in London a few weeks ago. I believe that's where you met and blah blah blah, you know the story WAY better than I do. I only found out very recently.'

Chase is staring at me wide-eyed. His eyes are so intense.

'Nina isn't on social media,' I continue when he doesn't say anything. 'She's a complete loser when it comes to any of that kind of stuff. She likes books and old conductors called Amos, and she's an incredible pianist who is hoping to go to Guildford someday.'

Chase raises his eyebrows. 'Guildhall?'

'That's the one.'

'Nina . . . has an identical twin?' Chase says, blinking at me. 'She never said she had a sister.'

'You can kind of see why she wouldn't mention it,' Miles says behind me, leaning against the door frame. 'If her sister is obsessed with the band, she probably thought you'd freak out.'

'OK, please can people stop using the word "obsessed"?' I sigh, rolling my eyes. 'I prefer the term "fangirl" and, you know what, you could be a little more grateful. I showed your music video to everyone at school and before then none of them had ever –'

'Nina doesn't have a website dedicated to Chasing Chords,' Chase says, still staring at the photo. 'And she's not a crazed fan.'

'She genuinely thought you were terrible musicians.'

Miles coughs again.

'Before the concert, obviously,' I say hurriedly. 'When she heard your music, she realized how good you all were. I'm the big fan. The biggest fan, some might say. Not in a weird way,' I add, making Miles snigger.

Chase nods, really looking at me now. 'You're not Nina,' he says. 'You're –'

'Nancy, yes. I know, up close you can really tell the difference, right?'

My coat has slipped off my shoulder and my cast is now fully on show. His eyes flicker from the cuts on my face to my arm. 'What happened to you?'

'We were in a car accident. Quite a bad one. A car bulldozed through a red light and . . . well . . . Nina is in a medically induced coma.'

'She's *what*?'

'Look, I don't know what's really been happening with you two, but I can promise you this: Nina is crazy about you. You've changed her for the better. Everyone's noticed. You've made her more confident in herself; it's amazing! So, I'm here to ask you if you'll come to the hospital and talk to her, if only to bring her some comfort. She might be really scared in the coma and I want her to hear your voice and know that you're there. It'll get through to her, I just know it. Taking you to her is the least I can do. She needs you.'

He doesn't hesitate. 'Let's go.'

'Yes! Thank you!' I cry, spinning round to head out of the door – and I almost slam straight into Miles. 'Whoa! Watch my arm!'

He holds up his hands. 'I didn't move. You almost walked into me!'

'Whatever. By the way, well done on all those recent T-shirts, Miles. I was so right about the floral shirt. You can thank me later.'

'I intend to.' He grins, standing aside to let me fly down the stairs, with Chase hot on my heels.

CHAPTER NINETEEN

NINA

My eyes flicker open and everything is way too bright. So bright that I have to close my eyes straight away again. Am I in a spotlight? Am I on stage again at the talent show? My limbs feel heavy; I try to move them but I can't. It feels like I'm trying to move around in a thick sludge. I can just about twitch my fingers. I try opening my eyes again – they're getting used to that blinding white light. I'm not in a spotlight; it's OK, I'm not on stage. The light's coming from strip lights on the ceiling.

I'm in a bed. And there's Nancy, asleep in the chair next to me, with her arm in a cast. What's happened to her arm? And there's a book open next to her. She must have fallen asleep while reading it. It's not just any book either. It's Austin Golding's book. Why is she reading that? I don't remember lending it to her. And why has she fallen asleep in my room? She hates my room. She hates me. We haven't spoken in years.

I try to reach out to her to ask her what's going on, but I have no energy and my muscles are aching too much. Everything is foggy. And there's a song playing in my head.

A familiar, comforting tune. 'If the Rain's Got to Fall'. That's it. The song Nancy and I used to love. I've heard it recently, I think, but I can't think where. I'll just let it play and close my eyes for a moment.

I wake up and there's a fuzzy blue shape next to me. It's a person standing there wearing all blue. Their voice is muffled. They're talking to someone. They might be talking to me but I can't speak. My jaw won't open; my muscles won't work. There's someone else in the room. That's who the person in blue is talking to. It's Nancy, I think, and she's with a boy. But Nancy is wearing different clothes to what she was wearing just a few moments ago when I last opened my eyes. She's still got the cast on that arm, though. They're nodding to the person in blue. The person in blue is leaving the room. Where are they going?

And why is Nancy holding flowers. Nancy hates gardening. Who is that boy? He's speaking and his voice is gentle. He's saying something about shells. Why is there a boy in my room and why is he talking about shells? I'll ask Nancy in a minute because I remember now: I was wrong before. She doesn't hate me any more. We made friends again and we have been speaking to each other. We watched Mary-Kate and Ashley movies together. I want to ask her about the boy and the shells and say how much I like Mary-Kate and Ashley, but my eyes are too heavy to keep them open. I'll ask her later.

*

Things are more in focus when I next wake up. Mum is in the room now and she's holding flowers, too. Another bouquet of flowers. I can just make her out by the window, arranging them in a vase next to a line of other vases, all bursting with colours. And there's something else in a line by the flowers. Sea shells. Loads of them. Why are there sea shells on my windowsill? Hang on, that's not my bedroom windowsill.

Where are we? I don't know that window although it looks a bit like the window of a hotel where we once stayed overnight in Scotland right next to the airport to catch our early flight. I don't remember going to Scotland recently, though. That can't be right.

I try to say something to Mum but it feels strange moving my lips. Like they're not quite sure how to say words. I'll try again in a moment. I'm too tired to try right now.

When I wake up again, I'm more aware of everything. I work out that I'm in a hospital but I can't remember why. My body still feels heavy but my brain isn't so muddled, and, after blinking a few times so that my eyes can focus, I see Mum and Nancy standing at the foot of my bed, talking. My mouth feels dry and my throat is aching so I lie still, listening for a bit. They're disagreeing about something.

No surprise there, then.

'Well, how was I supposed to know?' Nancy says.

'You should have checked!' Mum sighs, pointing at something on the table. It looks like an open box and they're talking about whatever's inside it. 'Didn't you think you should check it online before you placed the order?'

'Why would I check it online when I already knew?'

'Because you didn't know!'

'Yeah, but I didn't know that I didn't know. You know?'

'She talks about it all the time, how could you possibly not know?! What are we going to do now, then?' Mum asks, folding her arms.

'What do you mean? It's fine! She'll love it.'

'But it's all wrong.'

'She'll find it funny. Honestly, I've only noticed it recently, but she's got quite a sarcastic sense of humour. You should have heard what she said about your parrot costume.'

Mum looks confused. 'What parrot costume?'

'Sorry, the dress. The parrot dress.'

'I don't have a parrot dress.'

'Yes, you do, Mum!' Nancy says, exasperated. 'The awful one with all the feathers!'

'You mean my sixth form dance dress? That's a beautiful item of clothing! It's not awful!'

'OK, sorry. It's not awful. It's . . . unique. Like Sharon's caterpillar onesie.'

'I bought her that,' Mum says proudly.

'That does not surprise me at all.' Nancy gestures at the box. 'Are we agreed to leave it then? Chase said he liked it.'

'Chase has seen it?'

'I took a photo and sent it to him when I realized the mistake. He found it hilarious. He said she'd love it.'

Hang on. This can't be real. Nancy and Mum don't know about Chase. Am I in a dream?

'Although,' Nancy continues thoughtfully, 'Chase did also say he liked your neckerchief the other day, so this could be another lie.'

'What?' Mum gasps, all insulted. 'Chase wasn't lying when he said that! He said he thought it looked very retro.'

'Mum, he's a pop star. They're trained to charm people. That's why they have an entire PR team.'

Wait. I remember something. Nancy looking at me across a classroom. Her expression was full of hurt. She does know about Chase. She found out about Chase! That's why she was hurt! It was online. That must have been this morning. I remember now! She was furious at me. Because we were friends again and I had been lying to her. I need to tell her how sorry I am; how guilty I feel about it. I want her to forgive me.

'Nancy,' I try to say, but I can't quite work out how to move my lips right to pronounce the right sounds. I keep trying until I manage her name, or something close to it, but after all that effort they don't hear me anyway.

'Chase was NOT lying about the neckerchief,' Mum protests. 'It was a lovely thing for him to say.'

'Yeah, well, he's dating your daughter. He HAS to be nice.'

It's weird, though, Nancy doesn't *sound* that mad. But I remember her being so angry that she wouldn't even look at me. And she wouldn't talk to me. I'm so confused and my head hurts from trying to make sense of my blurred memories. When did Chase meet Mum? That's impossible.

I've only been asleep for a couple of minutes, haven't I? He can't have met her that fast. Especially when . . .

Chase and I broke up. Yes, I remember now, he was angry too. He was furious, like Nancy. Now my heart is aching as much as my muscles do because, although I can't remember exactly what he said when he was angry, I think about his tone and the way he snapped at me. It was as though he didn't know me at all, and he was the person who knew me the best. Why was he mad at me? What did I do? I wish my mind would think straight. I remember arguing with Nancy. We were at school, arguing. Why can't I remember anything else?

If I could sit up, maybe that might help. I try to push myself up but I'm too heavy and even that small movement feels exhausting. Someone else comes in the room now; someone I don't recognize. A doctor.

'He does not *have* to be nice, Nancy,' Mum points out to her, both of them ignoring the doctor. 'He didn't have to say anything at all about my neckerchief. If he didn't like it, he wouldn't have said anything at all. Why would he go to the trouble of pointing out that he liked it if he didn't?'

'To make conversation? He was stuck in a hospital room with his girlfriend's mum and nothing to do. He had to say something. And your neckerchief was an obvious thing to talk about because it was so . . . out there.'

WHAT? Chase was *here*? In this hospital? With Mum? And what does Nancy mean when she says 'girlfriend'? Is she talking about me? Or does Chase have a new girlfriend already and she's in this hospital too?! None of this makes sense!

I need answers.

'Nancy,' I whisper again, a little more forcefully, but they still don't hear.

The doctor bends over me and smiles.

'Excuse me, but I can tell when someone is lying and when someone is telling the truth, thank you very much, Nancy,' Mum says. 'I've raised you, haven't I?'

'And what's that supposed to mean?' Nancy huffs.

'It means, I know when you're lying, Nancy Palmer. You'd be terrible at poker.'

'Oh, is that so? Go on then, tell me a time you knew I was lying.'

'*Ahem.*' The doctor coughs gently, but she's ignored. Nancy and Mum are in full flow now.

'That time you said you were going over to Layla's and instead you went on a date with that boy to the cinema.'

Nancy gasps. 'HOW DO YOU KNOW ABOUT THAT?'

'I followed you,' Mum says smugly. 'I could tell you were lying when you told me you were off to Layla's so I followed you in the car. I took Nina with me, too. We both saw you.'

Brilliant, thanks, Mum. Drop me in it when I'm unable to defend myself.

'I can't believe you both followed me! You never said anything!'

'Because I didn't want you to think I didn't trust you.'

'Well, clearly you didn't trust me.'

'Well, clearly you were lying to me!'

The doctor is waiting patiently. This is so embarrassing. I would roll my eyes but I can't find the energy.

Nancy narrows her eyes at Mum. 'How often has this happened?'

'A couple of times,' Mum says innocently. 'I'm your mum – it's my duty.'

'What about your duty with Nina, huh? Does she get this kind of treatment, too? Because I don't remember you and me going on an exciting car adventure to spy on her!'

'Nina never gave me any reason not to trust her and she didn't go out on any secret dates.'

'She's literally been going out on secret dates with a famous pop star for weeks!' Nancy practically yells.

'Nancy,' I croak. 'Mum!'

The doctor beams at me and turns back to them, still trying to get their attention.

'Yes, well,' Mum sighs, still unaware that I'm awake, 'that just goes to show that Nina would be very good at poker.'

'Oh, so when Nina lies to you about dating a pop star, you're not mad – you're just impressed by her poker face!

I see how it is. You know what, Mum, you know what this is? Favouritism. That's what is happening right now. I see it VERY clearly. And I won't forget this when I'm rich and famous.'

'Excuse me!' the doctor says, waving at them.

They both turn to look at her and she nods towards my bed.

Nancy and Mum gasp in unison, before rushing forward and throwing themselves on me.

'Nina!! You're awake!' Mum says, instantly bursting into tears and kissing my face all over.

'We missed you!' Nancy squeals, holding my hand and squeezing it so hard I can't feel my fingers. 'Mum, give her some space!'

'What's going on?' I ask, as they both stare down at me. 'I feel terrible. What happened to your arm, Nancy? Did you break it?'

'Yeah, I did. And I'm not surprised you feel terrible.' Nancy grins, her eyes welling with tears. 'You just woke up from a coma.'

'Hi, Nina, I'm Dr Scott. You've been in a medically induced coma, so you're going to feel a bit groggy. That's completely normal.'

'I've been in a coma? No, I was just asleep.'

The words are starting to come more naturally to me now, as though my jaw is slowly but surely loosening up after being shut up tight.

'You were in an accident, Nina,' Mum explains gently through a wide smile. 'But you're OK. We've been so worried about you.'

Nancy nods, as I try to make sense of this new information. 'You were out for a few days, and you've been slowly coming round.'

'But I don't remember an accident,' I say in a panicky voice, my forehead furrowed in concentration which makes my head hurt more.

'That's natural,' Dr Scott says, after checking all the equipment around the bed. 'Try to relax, Nina. It's going to be a while until everything goes back to normal but, as I've told your mum and sister, you're going to make a full recovery.'

'Dr Scott is amazing, by the way,' Nancy says, making her laugh.

'She's been taking good care of you.' Mum smiles through tears. 'Thank you so much.'

'I'll let you have some time to yourselves and I'll be back soon to check in.'

I'm too dazed to process all of this. None of this feels real . . . but it *looks* real. The intensive care unit seems authentic and the hospital gown is scratchy and thin, and the way Nancy and Mum are watching me, their eyes brimming with a mixture of concern, relief and hope . . . well, that seems very real, too.

'I've really been in a coma for a few days?' I swallow hard. 'Are you sure?'

'Yes, very sure.' Mum says, helping me take a sip from a

plastic cup of water. 'But everything is OK, Nina. Like Dr Scott says, you're going to make a full recovery.'

My head is whirling. How can I have been in a coma for a few days?! It feels like I just had a nap. But a really, really deep one.

'What can you last remember?' Nancy asks, reading my expression.

'I don't know.' I hesitate, putting all my energy into trying to remember. And then it hits me and I grip Nancy's hand. 'Nancy, I'm so sorry! Chase! You found out and I –'

'Nina, it's all right,' she says gently, as Mum nods along with her. 'I'm really happy for you and Chase. We all are.'

'No, you were so angry. I lied to you!'

'Shush, Nina, it's OK.' Mum leans forward to stroke my hair. 'Nobody is angry at you.'

'I'm sorry for overreacting,' Nancy says, resting her chin on our entwined hands. 'I said some really horrible things before the accident and I'm so, so sorry, Nina.'

'No, it's not your fault,' I say firmly. 'I can't remember exactly what happened, but I'm sure of that much.'

She smiles warmly. 'I completely understand now why you kept your relationship a secret, Nina. Chase told us everything.'

'You've spoken to him?'

'He was here,' Mum says. 'He's a lovely boy, Nina. And so handsome, too! Those cheekbones are really quite something. Although I do wonder if his jeans are a bit too skinny. But apparently that's the look he's going for with the band. I told him that I was pleased he didn't wear ripped jeans, like *some* people.'

Nancy rolls her eyes. 'I'm never going to stop wearing my ripped jeans, Mum, I love them.'

'I'm just saying, it looks like you can't afford to get them mended.'

'Can we focus, please!' Nancy says, exasperated.

'Chase was *here*?' I ask, baffled.

'And Jimmy, too. He's been worried sick,' Mum assures me. 'He's gone home to get you some books.'

I smile. 'Sounds like Jimmy. But . . . can I just confirm . . . Chase came to the hospital?'

'Don't worry,' Nancy tells me smugly. 'I made him wait outside for a couple of minutes before he saw you so I could brush your hair first and make sure you weren't dribbling and stuff. You're welcome. He brought you a load of shells that he specially collected from your beach or whatever,' she says, gesturing at the windowsill. 'The one you had in your pocket fell out and was lost in the accident. Obviously, some girls might prefer amazing bouquets of flowers when they're stuck in a coma rather than sandy old shells but each to their own.'

'I don't understand,' I whisper, shaking my head. 'I remember he broke up with me.'

'Nah, not really. He only broke up with you because he thought you were me. When I went to the studio to explain everything –'

'Wait. You went to the studio?'

'Yeah, it's really cool in there. I had to fight my way in, even with a broken arm, because grumpy Miles wouldn't believe that we were twins at first, but I showed them that picture of us on our birthday – you know the one where you were wearing that weird hat. They all believed me after seeing the photo.'

'Nancy worked out where Chase was. She was determined to bring him to you,' Mum says proudly. 'She wouldn't take no for an answer. Sharon told me.'

I look back at Nancy and she shrugs.

'I read online that when you're in a coma you can sometimes still hear stuff, and I figured that, if you could hear voices at all, his should be one of them.'

'Wow. Thanks, Nancy.'

'And that's not all,' Mum adds with a mischievous smile. 'Nancy has also been singing to you. I caught her singing that one you love from *Half a Sixpence*.'

'I think I heard that!' I gasp. 'I remember the tune playing in my head!'

'Yeah, well, I didn't sing it very well,' Nancy says hurriedly, her cheeks flushing. 'You're the one who got the musical genes.'

'It really comforted me.' I smile up at her and she beams back at me, her eyes suddenly welling with tears. Mum notices too and clears her throat.

'I'll just leave you two to it and get some water. I'll be back in a moment.' She leans forward and kisses me on the forehead. 'Good to have you back.'

She leaves the room and Nancy pulls up a chair beside the bed.

'Chase is coming here this evening to see you. He feels terrible about what he said on the phone before the accident. He's been here almost every day. The paparazzi have been having a field day. Honestly, you should see what it's like when he arrives. It's mad. He felt so bad about the hospital having all these reporters bothering them that he made a big donation to the intensive care unit and bought all your doctors and nurses flowers.'

'So, he definitely doesn't hate me any more?' I ask hopefully.

'Are you kidding?' Nancy laughs. 'He's crazy about you! He tried to push back the band's tour date in Paris last night, so that he could be with you all day today but we wouldn't let him. He's flying back this evening and he said he'll come straight here to the hospital. I made him promise to drop into Disneyland Paris and buy everything in the gift shop. I told him that would be the only way you might forgive him and take him back.'

Even though everything still feels strange and achey, my heart warms at the idea that things aren't over for me and Chase. But that's not actually what feels most important in this moment.

The most important thing is that Nancy is right here.

'I'm sorry for lying to you,' I say again, just in case she didn't believe me the first time. 'I should have just told you from the start.'

'I'm sorry, too, for being so –' she sighs – 'silly about everything. And I'm also sorry for ruining your cake.'

'What cake?'

She points at the box that Mum and she were arguing over earlier. 'I got you a cake with all your favourite things on it but I may have made a teeny, tiny mistake. I accidentally told the lady to write *Guildford* instead of *Guildhall*.' She grimaces. 'Mum won't stop going on about it.'

'I'm sure it's perfect.' I laugh, giggling away until I notice that Nancy is watching me with this weird expression. 'What? Are you that upset about the cake? I really don't –'

'It's not that,' she says quietly, looking at her hands. 'I just . . . I want to tell you something.'

'OK.' I nod. 'What is it?'

'There was a moment when . . . I wasn't sure if you were going to . . . pull through.'

'Nancy –'

'Wait, just let me say this.' She takes a deep breath. 'I know that we have our differences and I know that . . . well, it hasn't exactly been a smooth ride with us. But I want you to know that when I thought you might not make it I felt completely broken. I can't describe it. As though half of me had just crumbled away.'

She pauses, bringing her eyes up to meet mine. 'Whatever happens, you're my other half. You always have been.'

I smile as a tear rolls down my cheek, reaching for her hand and linking our fingers together. 'Always will be.'

CHAPTER TWENTY

NANCY

Nina is going to kill me.

But it's too far down the line now and I can't go back on my word. I promised Chase I would make it happen. When he suggested this whole thing, I told him that firstly we don't have enough time to organize it and secondly there was no way Nina was going to go along with it.

'Nancy Palmer,' he'd said with a mischievous smile. 'Can you not handle a challenge?'

Which of course was the best thing he could have said in the situation because, HELLO, I can handle anything. So I told him I was in.

Nina obviously has no idea what's going on. She just thinks we're heading to Norwich to go shopping, which actually I now realize isn't one of my best ideas because it takes some work to get her out of the house and into the car.

'Shopping?' she says, lowering her book. 'Didn't you get enough presents at Christmas?'

'Why do you assume I'm shopping for me?' I say innocently. 'I might be shopping for other people.'

She raises an eyebrow. '*Are* you shopping for other people?'

'That's not the point. And excuse me, but I deserve presents. I have a very sore, horrifically broken arm.'

'Didn't the doctor say the cast can come off soon?'

'Stop chattering, Nina. Come on, get your coat on. Mum's going to drive us in.'

'Yes!' Mum says, jumping out from behind me and giving Nina a thumbs up. 'We're going shopping! How exciting! Shopping!'

I roll my eyes. I had told Mum very, *very* clearly to be SUBTLE.

'Why would you want to go shopping on New Year's Eve?' Nina says. 'Norwich will be packed. I thought we were just going to have a nice cosy day at home. You guys go – I'm happy here with my book.'

This was NOT going to plan. I have to do better than this.

'Nina,' I say, perching on the edge of the sofa so she has to move her feet, 'you remember a few days after you got home from hospital, your feet were cold and I lent you a pair of my favourite Mickey Mouse slipper socks?'

She looks at me blankly. 'No.'

'OK, I'll forgive you for forgetting my kind gesture because you were still in recovery from the accident and it was a few weeks ago now, so maybe your memory is hazy, but you were sat on this very sofa telling me how cold your feet were while we were watching series one of *One Tree Hill* and, instead of just sitting around letting your feet be cold, I ran upstairs and brought down my favourite pair of Mickey Mouse slipper socks.'

'I guess I do remember you lending me some socks. But what has this got to do with anything?'

'You don't remember what you said when I handed you the socks?'

'Was it something along the lines of "thanks for the socks"?'

'No!' I sigh. 'You said "I owe you".'

She stares at me as I nod solemnly.

'Yes, Nina,' I continue. 'Those were your very words: *I owe you.*'

'Let me get this straight,' she says, closing her book. 'Because you lent me a pair of slipper socks a few weeks ago, I now have to go shopping with you?'

'That's exactly correct. I really need to get some things and PLEASE don't make me shop alone with Mum. You know what she's like.' I swivel to face Mum. 'No offence.'

'None taken,' she assures me, holding up her hands. 'I am a *complete* nightmare. I can't resist trying everything on. Plus, Norwich is so beautiful at Christmastime. All the twinkling lights up everywhere . . .'

'People drinking cosy hot drinks and wearing bobble hats . . .' I add.

'Crisp, fresh air, happy music, plenty of cheer,' Mum says.

'It really is magical.' I grin.

Nina giggles. 'All right then. I guess it might be fun if we're all together.'

While she goes to find her shoes and coat, I wait by the door and send Chase a quick message.

THUNDERBIRDS ARE GO!!

What?!

We're on our way

Oh, right, great!

I roll my eyes. Further proof that Chase and I are not compatible.

'Don't forget your gloves,' I say to Nina as she comes round the corner, wrapped up in her scarf. 'It's very cold out.'

'Got them,' she says, patting her pocket, before rolling her eyes. 'Thanks, *Mum*.'

It would be fair to say that for the past month since the accident I've been potentially a little bit overprotective. But it's not my fault. The first time she left the hospital to walk to the car, there were paparazzi swarming the car park and when they saw Nina emerge through the doors the reporters went crazy. Luckily Chase had foreseen that this might happen and had arranged for some security men to escort us to the door, but I don't think any of us were prepared for the chaos that greeted us.

'Nina, Nina, are you and Chase officially an item?'

'Nina, how are you feeling?'

'Are you going to join Chasing Chords on their American tour?'

'How does it feel to know that you were #FINDTHE-GIRL?'

'Can you tell us about the accident, Nina?'

'Nina, is it love with Chase?'

I noticed that not ONE of them asked about how I was feeling, even though the cast on my arm was right there, on show for everyone to see.

Anyway, I always thought it would be quite cool to be a celebrity, but now I'm not so sure. You can't see where you're going with all those flashbulbs going off in your face. I knew instantly that Nina must be HATING every moment, especially as she doesn't like crowds, so I held her close, guiding her to the car with Mum, all of us grateful to be protected by the security men.

After that experience, I decided it would be a good idea to never let Nina out of my sight. She was too fragile physically and emotionally for any of that, and the best thing for her would be to stick with me. I still had to go to school during her recovery, but I spent every evening and weekend and then all of the Christmas holiday with her.

And now, before I know it, we're inseparable.

I can't seem to do anything without checking her opinion first. I don't know exactly when hers became the one that matters most, but it does. We may be different but she makes me laugh all the time until I cry. We seem to know exactly how the other one thinks.

'You've got this look,' Mum tells us proudly, one dinner. 'You used to have that look when you were younger. I'd forgotten it.'

'What look?' Nina asks, as I give her a second helping of cheese-and-potato pie.

'You give each other a look and you have exactly the same smile on your face, as though you know what the other one is thinking and you're in on the same joke. It's like a twin thing.'

I glance at Nina.

'You're doing it now!' Mum points out, waving her fork at us. 'See?'

Nina sighs. 'How can we know what the other one is thinking? I think you're imagining it, Mum.'

'You've lost it, Mum,' I add.

And then, while Mum insists she's right, we smile into our food, knowing EXACTLY what the other one is thinking.

Getting close to Nina has meant getting close to the people she loves, too. Chase comes round to the house as often as possible and now that Nina is fully recovered they go out on dates in the village or in town. The first time Chase came to ours, Mum went crazy, flapping and fussing about everything because a famous pop star was coming over. She put up so many lights and decorations that it looked like we were living in Santa's grotto. She tidied the house five times that morning and then when he arrived she said in a very flustered manner that he must excuse the mess.

It's been amazing getting to know Chase. Not because he's the lead singer of my favourite band but because he makes my twin sister so happy. They're so relaxed around each other, as though they've known each other for years. Jimmy and I are now firm friends, too, and, when Chase is here at the same time, Jimmy and I are sure to give them their space but we also do some stealthy spying.

'We can hear you outside the door!' Nina yelled, when Jimmy and I were listening in on their conversation about how cute otters are and we got the giggles.

I never thought in a million years I'd have more fun hanging out with Jimmy and Nina than I would hanging out with my friends, but I do. After the way Layla acted around Nina when she found out she was dating Chase, I decided that maybe she wasn't such a good friend after all. We didn't fall out or anything – she came to the hospital with Sophie and they brought Nina a beautiful bouquet of flowers when she was still in a coma. Layla apologized for everything she'd said and we hugged. I still hang out with Sophie at school when I can, and Layla and I are still friends, but it's not the same.

'You've got us now, anyway,' Jimmy said one evening over a bowl of ice cream. 'Welcome to the nerd crew.'

'Please don't use the phrase "nerd crew",' I plead. 'That's incredibly . . . nerdy.'

'Get used to it. You're now part of the crew.'

'I'm not in the crew.'

'Welcome to the crew, my friend.'

'There is no crew.'

'Ooooh,' Mum had said, coming in to get something from the fridge, 'can I be in the crew?'

And then Jimmy, Nina and I had laughed until my stomach ached.

So it wasn't any problem to get Jimmy on his own and explain what's going on on New Year's Eve, swearing him to secrecy. I've arranged for him to meet us in Norwich and, when he 'coincidentally' bumps into us when we're parking, Nina gives me a strange look.

'Jimmy!' I say, patting him on the back. 'How weird to see *you* here! What are the chances! I can't believe this! What a surprise!'

'Yeah, weird.' He smiles, before leaning in to whisper, 'Maybe tone it down a bit, Meryl Streep.'

'Anyway,' I say, linking my arm through Nina's and dragging her away from the car, 'let's all go shopping.'

The Forum is this massive glass building with loads of cafes and a huge library, but at Christmas and New Year it's way better than usual. There is a beautiful tall Christmas tree outside in the main square, twinkling with hundreds of lights, right at the bottom of the steps leading to the building. A Christmas market is just inside the main doors with plenty of festive food and craft stalls, so crowds of people are bustling about or sitting on the steps outside, wrapped up in their scarves and hats, enjoying hot steaming drinks.

'What's that?' Nina says, as we get closer, noticing a small crowd of people beginning to gather round outside the Forum and near to the Christmas tree.

'I wonder,' I say thoughtfully, winking at Jimmy behind her back. 'Let's go and check it out!'

'Good idea, Nancy,' Mum says, clapping her hands before making sure her hat is on properly. It's the one Sharon gave her for Christmas: a bumble-bee hat with antennae sticking out of the top.

I lead Nina over and edge our way to the front of the crowd.

'Is that a piano?' Nina asks in confusion. 'That's so cool! What is it doing outside?'

'I think it has something to do with him,' Jimmy says, nodding towards a guy who has his back to us with his hood up, checking some speakers on the ground, which are attached to the microphone set up on the piano.

'Wait,' Nina says, narrowing her eyes at the boy with his back to us, 'that's –'

As Chase turns round, Nina gasps in surprise. He sees us and grins, waving for me to come over.

'What's going on?' Nina asks, baffled. 'I thought Chase had a concert on New Year's Eve!'

'He does.' I nod, as Mum gives her a squeeze. 'You, Nina Palmer, have front-row seats to Chase Hunter's first ever solo acoustic concert. Now, I have to go introduce him. See you in a bit.'

I walk over to the piano, my jaw aching from grinning so widely at her reaction. Chase says he got the idea to do this crazy event from Nina, when she showed him the photo she'd taken of him at the piano playing his song 'Ghosts' the night of the London concert. Apparently, she'd told him that he'd been most himself on stage when he was playing it.

About a week after she came home from the hospital, Chase pitched me the challenge: organize an acoustic concert for him without his management knowing.

My first reaction was actually to throw the pen I was holding right at his head because I thought he was telling me that he was leaving Chasing Chords. But then, once I'd calmed down and stopped raging at him for being a traitor, he explained that he didn't want to quit Chasing Chords, he was still in the band. But, he said, he'd like to give the acoustic set a try – with the band's blessing.

'And what does Mark think about this?' I'd asked warily. 'I can't imagine he'd approve, considering his three-year plan for the band.'

'That's why I . . . hang on, what three-year plan?'

'You don't know about the three-year plan for Chasing Chords?'

He'd looked at me like I was mad. 'And you do?'

'Of course!' I'd said, shaking my head. 'You know, you should really take some time to check out my website. I think you'd learn a lot about yourself.'

He'd laughed and said, 'Thanks for the tip, but Uncle Mark can't know anything about it until it's over. He wouldn't let me do it but I want to show him that I can. So, what do you say? Can you organize it for me under the radar here in Norwich?'

I'd narrowed my eyes at him. 'Why me? You're Chase Hunter. You could pick any event planner that you wanted.'

'I don't want any other event planner. I want you to do it. I have a feeling that you'd be a natural when it comes to taking charge. Besides, you know the city, you know the music and –' he'd paused – 'you know me, now. The real me.'

After that I couldn't exactly say no. Plus he was right, I was totally a natural leader. Organizing an open-air concert which involved getting a world-famous pop star to perform in the middle of Norwich, in the square right outside the Forum, without anyone finding out what was going on, was difficult but it had all come together perfectly thanks to my colour-coordinated strict schedules and to-do lists.

Hiding it from Nina had been the difficult part, especially with my terrible poker face but somehow I'd managed it.

'Are you ready?' I ask Chase, joining him at the piano.

'I'm nervous,' he says, eyeing up the crowd. 'But, yeah, I'm ready.'

'Good luck. Not that you need it,' I tell him, before turning to face the growing audience and clearing my throat and announcing, 'Chase Hunter, everyone!'

Chase pulls down his hood and gives an awkward wave as he sits down at the piano. There is a collective gasp before the audience erupts into cheers and applause, quickly getting out their phones, unable to believe their luck. I hurry back to stand next to Nina.

'How did you know about this and I didn't?' Nina whispers to me, joining in with the applause.

'It's called a surprise, Nina,' I say with a laugh.

'Thank you,' Chase says shyly into the microphone. 'Before I start, I need to tell you all that none of this would have been possible without Nancy Palmer. She made this happen and, Nancy, I am truly grateful.'

He nods towards me and I blush as camera phones are pointed in my direction. I feel so proud to be a part of it all, grinning from ear to ear.

'You're amazing!' Nina squeals, squeezing my hand.

'I'm not sure you'll think that for long,' I reply under my breath as Chase begins to play.

He starts off with two new songs that he's written recently and, even though they may not be Chasing Chords'-style, they're really good and I know that he is on to something. The reaction from the crowd is amazing. When the second song comes to an end, he catches my eye and gives me a nod. Time for the next surprise.

'There's someone very special and very talented in the crowd that I would like to introduce to you,' Chase says to the now-packed crowd surrounding the piano. Thank goodness I decided on such a large space. 'Please can you put your hands together for Nina Palmer!'

Nina's jaw drops to the ground as everyone applauds around her.

Yes, she is definitely going to kill me.

'What?' she hisses, looking at me in panic. 'What's he doing?'

'Nina,' I say quickly, knowing we can't keep everyone waiting for long, 'you're a born performer. You won that school talent show for a reason and it is time to show everyone else what you can do.'

'You want me to go up there and play?' she squeaks, her voice quivering. 'With all these people watching?'

'Yeah, I do,' I say, linking my arm through hers and pulling her out of the crowd. I lead her to the piano where

Chase is now standing, getting the piano ready for her. 'Because I really think this is where you belong. At a piano, playing music like it deserves to be played. It's just like Chase says. All it takes is practice.'

I plonk her down on to the piano stool.

'Chase –' she begins, staring at the piano keys as though they're going to bite her.

'Nancy and I know you better than anyone,' he says firmly, picking up the microphone. 'Trust us, Nina. You can do this. You just needed a little leg-up on to the stage, that's all.'

He looks out to his audience. 'Nina is going to accompany me on the piano. The first song we're going to play for you all is one called "Ghosts".' He beams at Nina. 'You could do this one in your sleep. You ready?'

She takes a deep breath, lifts her hands to the keys and looks up at me. 'OK,' she says with a hint of a smile. 'I guess I'm ready.'

I hurry back to stand with Jimmy and Mum, and, as soon as Nina starts to play, Mum bursts into tears. Jimmy passes her a tissue as he films Nina and Chase's performance on his phone.

'I'm so proud of my girls,' she sniffs, dabbing her eyes.

When she plays the piano, Nina is mesmerizing, and she's never played like this before. Chase up there with her injects more confidence and she plays as though she's done this sort of thing a thousand times. I watch her, bursting with pride, before taking a sneak peek at social media. Chase's secret concert is being talked about everywhere, and the feedback to the videos is incredible. There are calls for him and Nina to release an album together and I have to fight back tears of pride when I spot Nina's name trending on Twitter.

'Nancy, you should go into talent management or something,' Jimmy says as the crowd erupts into applause when their second song together comes to an end. 'I can't believe you made all this happen. It's incredible.'

'Thanks, Jimmy,' I say, nudging him. 'I'll consider it.'

'You should,' Mum encourages excitedly. 'Why don't you ask Chase if you can get some work experience with his management team?'

I nod, coming round to the idea. 'Yeah, maybe I will.'

When Nina and Chase launch into the next song, I recognize someone across the way at the front of the crowd. Miles is grinning at me and I get this weird sort of fluttery feeling in my stomach. He gives me a small wave. I wave back.

Now that I really think about it, Miles has always had a much more mysterious, attractive air to him than anyone else in the band. And his arms *are* nice from all that drumming. Just a thought.

The song ends and Chase holds his hand out to take Nina's. He pulls her up to stand next to him in front of the piano and they bow cutely together. The crowd's reaction is so overwhelming and wonderful that Nina looks like she's about to be knocked backwards at any second. She clutches Chase's hand at the huge roar of cheering and enthusiastic applause. I've never felt so proud in my life. She stands there in disbelief as the applause refuses to die down and continues to get louder. Everyone is calling out for an encore.

Sweeping her gaze across the crowd, she catches my eye.

'You see?' Mum laughs over the noise. 'You're doing it! There's that twin look! I very much hope it never disappears again.'

'It's funny,' I say, as Nina and I share a smile. 'We were just thinking the same thing.'

ACKNOWLEDGEMENTS

We firstly want to thank everyone at Penguin Random House Children's for the opportunity to bring out our first book! This has been so exciting every step of the way and it's a dream come true to see the finished book! A big thank-you to our 'dream team' gleamies, Lauren Sherry and Jessica Joseph at Gleam Futures, for always being our biggest supporters, helping us with this project but also all the other amazing work we have been lucky enough to do.

We would like to thank Abigail Bergstrom for starting us off on this project and Katy Birchall for helping us bring the girls and our #FindThe Girl story to life! From the first moment we met Katy and saw the way she worked, we knew we wanted her to be a part of our #FindTheGirl dream team! We could not believe how close her vision for this story was to ours – it felt as though the three of us had known each other for years!

We really want to thank our mum and dad for being so encouraging and for always believing in us, particularly

Acknowledgements

when we handed in our notices at work to enable us to do incredible things like bringing out our first book. We especially want to thank our sister Courtney who has been with us on this book journey and who we've been able to turn to for guidance every step of the way.

Lastly but not least, our favourite people in the world: our supporters. We wouldn't be able to do any of this without you and your support in all that we do means the absolute world to us! We are so proud of this novel and hope that after reading the pages, and meeting Nina and Nancy, you will love the story as much as we do!

The lovable twin duo **Lucy and Lydia** are well known for their eponymous YouTube channel and are steaming ahead in the digital world. Their uplifting platform features all things beauty, fashion and music related, and they're known for their infectious enthusiasm. They regularly upload their hugely popular 'Get the Look' videos, which cover some of their favourite music artist looks. As a result of this successful content thread, the girls filmed an exclusive series for MTV, *Lucy & Lydia: Style Sisters*, which amassed an incredible 6 million views. Following this, the girls went on to do a Snapchat takeover for growing channel PopSugar, which resulted in over 1.4 million views. With a highly engaged and fast-growing audience across all their platforms, Lucy and Lydia are certainly the ones to watch. They have excellent relationships and have worked closely with brands such as Disney, Misguided and Soap & Glory.